Loving
the
White Bear

TERRY SPEAR

DEDICATION

To Denise Thomas McWethy, whose life was cut short. My best wishes to her family who will keep her memory alive.

ACKNOWLEDGMENTS

Thanks so much to Donna Fournier, who always helps me with edits and brainstorming! I couldn't do it without you! And to Dottie Jones, who, despite the tragic loss of her daughter, helped to edit the book and make it so much better. Hugs and prayers to Dottie and the rest of her family during this period of mourning.

And thanks to all my shifter fans who encourage me to keep on keeping on with the shifters!

CHAPTER 1

As soon as Alicia Raycroft walked into the White Bear Lodge's indoor swimming pool room in White Bear, Alaska, she saw Rob MacMathan doing a breast stroke across the aqua water, his well-sculpted back muscles glistening under the fluorescent lights. When she'd seen Rob dressed in his white parka, heavy knit sweater, pants, and boots, she hadn't been able to tell that his body was this hot. He was one of their tour guides for tomorrow's journey into the Alaskan frontier—a trip to see the northern lights and polar bears, and cross over into the Arctic Circle. She'd heard that he and his brother, Edward, another of the tour guides, had a home nearby. Which meant they didn't have accommodations here, so she hadn't expected Rob to be swimming at the lodge's pool.

As similar as the brothers looked, she wondered if

they were twins. Both men had dark brown hair, tanned skin, and brown eyes, but Rob's eyes were darker and his hair had streaks of gold from the sun. How was he able to tan in the winter here? His face, maybe, from the reflection of the sun off the snow or water. But his whole delectable body? She wasn't a fan of tanning beds since it wasn't healthy for the skin, no matter how good it looked, and she doubted he wore the fake tan from an airbrush spray can. He sure did look healthy and mouthwatering.

Rob came up for air on the opposite end of the pool and went under again. He stayed under so long, she thought he was like a seal that could hold its breath for nearly half an hour to over an hour, depending on the type of seal. When she timed him, he'd only been under for three minutes. Much longer than she could swim under the water, but still, that was remarkable for anyone.

She wondered how he managed to get into the hotel guests-only facility. Had one of the tour group members let him in? Then again, if this was where he regularly booked the lodging for his tour groups, management might give him free access as compensation for the business.

She set her phone on the table next to a group of chaise lounges. She slipped out of her flip-flops and pulled off her ankle-length, semi-sheer zebra bathing suit cover up. She'd bought it for when she'd vacationed at a resort in the Amazon rainforest, where they had a swimming pool for guests too. It didn't really suit the Alaskan trip, but it was the only one she had. She draped it over one of the blue chairs. In her zebra bikini, her hair pulled back, she turned to get into the pool when she saw Rob watching her. Afraid the pool would be packed with guests, she was glad they were the only two here. As a photojournalist, she wished she had brought her camera to take pictures of him swimming laps. He was seriously fit.

"You're Alicia Raycroft and going on the tour tomorrow?" Rob treaded the water as he watched her.

"Yeah, and you're one of our tour guides, Rob MacMathan?" She was impressed that he remembered who she was since only his brother had spoken to the group briefly to welcome them. Since she had read up on the three men when she booked the tour, the two brothers and one other man, Casey MacIntosh, also one of the guides, it had been easy for her to keep their names straight.

"I am," Rob said.

She loved etymology, researching the original, literal meaning of names. It was just a hobby of hers, but sometimes she could strike up some fun conversations over names. Mathan was so unusual, she had wondered if it meant anything. When she did a search, she found that it meant bear in Gaelic. Mac referred to son, so Rob and his brother's name meant son of bear. As unique as the name was, she suspected the MacMathans, who owned the tavern in town, were related to Rob. Did the family ever wear kilts? In the summer, of course. The guys were all brawny, tall, carved from granite, and she thought they'd look great in kilts. Shirtless. Muscled. Tan. She could see Rob lifting a long-tapered pole, and tossing it so that it turned end over end for the perfect Scottish caber toss, while wearing a kilt. She loved taking pictures of them and writing stories on the Scottish Highland games in Texas.

Her own name of Raycroft referred to a farm dweller who grew crops of rye. She didn't think it was as interesting as the meaning of Rob's name.

She had only taken a few steps toward the pool when her phone rang. She sighed, suspecting it was her roommate, Judi, calling to tell her she was delayed for one reason or another. She always seemed to be.

When Alicia saw the caller was her ex-boyfriend, she couldn't believe it. They'd broken up before she'd left on this trip, but it had been a long time in coming. Bill Hollinger was so controlling.

She answered the call, just to make sure it wasn't something important, or else she wouldn't have. "What do you want?"

"I don't want to end it this way between us." Which

meant, if he had his way, never. "Your neighbor said she was picking up your newspaper while you were away for the next ten days. You didn't tell me you were going to Alaska."

Alicia hadn't thought she needed to tell her neighbor she'd broken up with Bill too and not to tell him anything about what was going on with her.

"We broke up, Bill. It's over between us." Even though Alicia was trying to speak low to Bill over the phone, she felt her words echoed across the swimming pool room. She really hadn't wanted anyone to overhear her private conversation. Even if Rob was the only one here at the time. Bill had to have gone to her apartment if he had talked to her neighbor about where Alicia had gone. That irritated her more.

"I'm going to join you. In Alaska. I can handle the cold."

"No way. You're too late to join the tour in any event, and I don't want to see you any further. It's over between us. And it has been for months." Alicia had been afraid this might happen. Every time she'd tried to end things with Bill, he'd tried to change her mind. He'd grown so controlling with her, showering her with gifts, making dinner dates and luncheon dates, just any way he could think of to spend more time with her, and giving her no room to breathe. Which was exactly what the problem was in their relationship. Even so, she was a little surprised he wanted to come here. He had given her a million reasons why he couldn't go to Alaska—the biggest: he couldn't handle the cold. Which was why he lived in San Antonio near her. He didn't have warm enough weather gear. He'd never been that far north and it was way too wild for him. But she knew it had to do with the avalanche he'd witnessed at some point in his life. Not that he'd told her about it, but the first time they'd touched, she'd envisioned it—in his past.

"Which tour group are you going with? Where are you staying now?" Bill's tone was insistent.

Bill spoke as if she hadn't just told him she wasn't seeing him anymore. She was so looking forward to this trip and already he was making her feel tense and stressed. She knew she couldn't talk to him about this any further. He wouldn't change. And she wasn't having any part of it.

She hung up on him. Then she let out her breath, muted her phone, and set it on the table again.

"Where are you from?" Rob asked.

"San Antonio, Texas. This is the furthest north I've ever been." She slipped into the water, noticing Rob was taking in her appearance as much as she'd been gawking at his muscled physique. Now *he* was seriously beautiful, which helped to put Bill out of her thoughts for the moment. "Are you from here, or have you lived elsewhere?"

"I'm from here. Born and raised."

She waded into the deeper part of the pool, then swam toward him. A polite distance away from him, she treaded water. "So you are an expert on the area. Is Edward your twin? The two of you sure look similar, but even so, your hair is longer and has a few more highlights. Your eyes are a darker brown than his."

He smiled a little, and she felt her body temperature rise. She didn't want him to think she'd been ogling him because she was looking to hook up with him or anything. Despite how hot he appeared. Long distance relationships didn't work out, not that he was interested in one. But she wasn't interested in one-night stands either. Besides, she was just getting over a stormy relationship with Bill.

"I thought you might be twins. That's why I was studying the two of you so much. My grandmother and great aunt were twins," she quickly added. "My great aunt had darker hair and she was always thinner than my grandmother over the years. My grandmother had green eyes; my great aunt had more hazel eyes. So they weren't identical."

"Yes, Edward and I are twins. Not identical either."

"And the MacMathans that own the tavern, are they kinfolk?"

Rob's smile grew, and yet, there was a darkness to his expression. Guarded, maybe, as if he didn't want to give her the impression that he was into hooking up with women in his tour group for a one-night stand either. Which she appreciated. Though maybe he had a girlfriend, fiancée, or wife. She hadn't seen any pictures of him with a woman on their site, just tour group photos. She always did some research—par for the course because of the job she did—so she'd searched about the tavern too, but other than business-related photos, menus and décor, she hadn't seen any pictures of the people who ran the place. She'd even searched Facebook to see if either of the brothers or Casey had pages. Just to learn more about them before she came. Nothing. She would have thought they'd share on social networking sites to help sell their tours.

"I just thought the name was so unusual that if any others living here had the same last name, they were possibly related to you," she finally said, when Rob didn't answer her right off, probably thinking she was too nosy.

"My aunt and uncle own it. My three male cousins help there sometimes. One works there all the time."

"That's neat. You doubtless know that your name means son of the bear in Gaelic, right?"

"It does." He appeared amused that she had looked it up.

She was thinking how gorgeous he'd be wearing a kilt and boots. Nothing else. "Do you ever wear a kilt?"

He laughed. She liked his hearty laugh.

"Well the name *is* Scottish." She shrugged. "So, you *could* wear a kilt. In the summer. Or in the winter, lounging fireside with your Irish wolfhound."

Smiling, Rob shook his head.

"Your clan may not have a recognized tartan pattern though. I've taken pictures on some Highland games and talked to several people from different clans. What do you do when you're not guiding tour groups in the dead of winter?" she asked.

"Are...you a reporter?"

She smiled this time. She couldn't help her inquisitive nature. It was part of her job. She enjoyed it too, and she'd found people usually liked to talk about themselves, so it worked well for her job. "Sorry. I'm a photojournalist. What I love doing most of all is taking pictures and sharing them in magazines or newspapers, but in addition to my work, I do some interviews to go along with the photos."

"That means good press for us?" Rob arched a brow.

She laughed. "Well, I take great photos, if I do say so myself. And yeah, if someone is looking for a tour excursion in Alaska, my pictures can interest potential customers to purchase the tour too, if they like what they see."

"Does that mean bribery can help?"

She laughed. She wasn't sure what he meant by bribery, but she was willing to play with him a bit. "Depends on what you mean by bribery."

He cast her the most devilish grin. "Thanks. We appreciate it."

The door to the pool room opened, and she turned to see who it was. Judi Hall, her roommate. She was a vivacious redhead and lots more outgoing than Alicia. She was also Alicia's assistant and had been thrilled to have the chance to go to Alaska with her.

"Are you getting a guided tour of the swimming pool too?" Judi asked Alicia, teasing.

"See you ladies tomorrow." Rob climbed out of the pool at the deep end. His board shorts clung to his glorious gluteus maximus. When he turned, Alicia saw the way the board shorts clung to his thighs and his crotch, molding to a swell of an erection. As hot as her cheeks were, she swore they were on fire.

Grabbing a towel off a chair, he smiled a little at Alicia, as if to say he was amused to see her reaction, dried himself off, then wrapped the towel around his trunks and left the pool room. Only then did Alicia glance at Judi, who had been watching Rob too.

"Omigod, he is so hot!" Judi pulled off her lace cover up, revealing her green bikini. Then she jumped into the water. When she resurfaced, she said, "I guess I scared him off."

"You probably did. One woman, he could handle. Two? Time to take off."

"If the way he was aroused was any indication, I'd say that you must have inspired it."

Alicia just smiled.

"Did you ask him if he was going to the tavern later?"

"His aunt and uncle own it, so maybe. But no, I didn't ask him that. Just a million other questions, so maybe *I* was the reason he vamoosed." In a way, Alicia was glad he had left because she was afraid they would have run out of things to say to each other, and then the "moment" would have been lost.

Judi laughed. "I'm sure he would have left for that reason *if* he hadn't been interested in visiting with you. All the guides are seriously buff. Edward and Casey were entering the lodge's workout room. They were wearing gym shorts, sneakers, and no shirts. Do you think they get a discount to use the facilities for booking us in here as part of the tour package?"

"Or it's complimentary and they don't pay a cent for the privilege to use the facilities. Were they as tan as Rob?" Alicia swam across the pool.

"Yeah. I was wondering how they managed that. A tanning machine?"

"I can't imagine how they get so tanned all over otherwise. Unless they went to a tropical island resort recently."

"I agree. Hey, I tried calling you, but I guess you were already in the pool. I was going to tell you I was running late. You know, Calvin called and he wanted to know how the flight out was, if you were watching out for me, that sort of thing. I'm glad we're doing this without the guys tagging along, but I have to say once I saw my bed in the room, I started thinking of how much more fun sleeping here tonight would be if Calvin and I were sharing a room."

Alicia shook her head. "You and he both needed a break and when you get home, it will even be better. Bill called and so that I didn't have to put up with his calling me further, I put the phone on mute."

"Wow, he doesn't give up, does he."

"Nope, which is just why I called it quits. It just shows how he is when he doesn't get his way. He said he was coming here even!"

"After all the crap he gave you for coming here and not going to someplace warmer so he could join you? He's not really coming, is he?"

"I doubt it. Even if he flew out today, he wouldn't make it before we left tomorrow morning. I think when he realized that, he decided not to come. He's just not going to let it go while I'm here. When I get out of the pool, I'll just block his calls. I should have done it before, but I've never had to before, and so, didn't even think of it."

"Sounds good to me." Judi swam across the length of the pool. "Once we start our adventure tomorrow, I sure hope I can do all right in the cold. I have a ton of clothes to layer for the excursion, but the temperature was still in the nineties when we left San Antonio. We had no time to acclimate."

"Same here. I had to run the air conditioner on high at my apartment, just so I could try on all those layers. I'm going to swim, then return to the room, take a shower, and get ready for dinner. Unless you want to eat here at the lodge's restaurant."

"Nah. Because of the hefty discounts we received to encourage us to eat at the tavern, everyone in the tour group will be there. I'm so excited about starting the tour tomorrow," Judi said. "You pick the greatest places to take trips."

"You didn't like the bugs in the Amazon rain forest." Not that Alicia had either, but that was part of the jungle experience. Looking for ticks and leeches around their ankles every night was just part of the tour. The cold weather was part of this one. Alicia got out of the water "At least there are no bugs here."

Judi laughed. "They're frozen solid. Though I understand they just lie dormant until it warms up. Are you going to need me to help you with any equipment for the dinner tonight?"

"I was going to say we'd just enjoy ourselves, but you know me."

"You always take your camera along."

"Right. But I'll just take a camera; no need for you to do anything." Alicia wrung out her ponytail and grabbed a towel sitting on a shelf for guests. "You just enjoy yourself. I'll take a few shots of our food, the atmosphere—"

"Rob?"

Alicia smiled at Judi.

"You were really close to him in the pool. Maybe that's why he was so aroused. Did you touch him? Did you see anything about his past?"

"No. I didn't touch him. You know it doesn't work that way. Exactly." Well, it did sometimes, but not always and oftentimes Alicia didn't want to see what had happened in people's lives—disturbing or not. Not unless she was working a case for the police.

Judi sighed. "You should have taken some photos of him in those wet trunks."

Alicia laughed. "I don't think so."

The door opened just as Alicia was slipping into her flip flops. Edward and Casey walked in wearing board shorts. Both men had light beards like Rob. Most of the men they'd seen wore them in the winter up here. Casey was fairer than the MacMathan brothers, his blue eyes catching her attention. He smiled at her.

"Judi said the two of you were just in the workout room." Alicia was surprised to see them in the swimming pool area now.

"We take some laps after we work out in the exercise room. We have to be prepared for anything tomorrow, and we always like to get some workouts in before we go on a trip," Edward said. "Are you going to the tavern for dinner?" He sounded hopeful that they were.

"Yeah. Are you?" Alicia asked, pulling her cover-up on over her wet bathing suit.

"We sure are. If we didn't, my aunt and uncle would give us grief. They like to always see us before we take a tour group out."

Alicia smiled, thinking how nice it was that they were close to their family. "Great. We'll see you over there." She glanced at Judi, who was smiling at the guys. She looked like she was planning on hanging around.

"See you in a bit, Judi." Then Alicia wrapped the towel around her hair and left the pool room.

By the time Alicia had dressed in the hotel room and was ready to go to dinner, all she could think of was touching Rob, and seeing what she could learn about him. Normally, she couldn't sense a lot unless the person had experienced terror or panic, something that had happened to them in the past that had imprinted on them forever. Making physical contact with someone didn't always result in visions. Even so, she never did it just for curiosity's sake to see if she could learn anything about the person. Yet there was something about that mysterious smile Rob had given her, the dimples in his cheeks, the lights highlighting his dark eyes that made her want to do what she never allowed herself to do—to learn more about him. In a deviously paranormal way.

***

For a good forty-five minutes in the exercise room at the lodge, Rob used the treadmill and weight-lifting machines, the whole time thinking of Alicia— remembering her smile, her bright eyes, her sexy bikini. He'd enjoyed the easy banter with her and her inquisitiveness. If her roommate hadn't shown up, he would have stayed in the pool longer and talked with her further. Smiling, he was still thinking of the question of bribery. It wasn't like him to be interested in a single woman taking one of his tours—for several reasons, the biggest one of all—he was a polar bear shifter.

He left the lodge and headed back to the house that he and his brother, Edward, owned. But as soon as Rob parked in the garage, a vision struck him cold.

Out of the white cloak of snow, a grizzly bear swung its massive paws at him, the claws tearing at Rob's flesh, his teeth biting. Rob pounced at him with his massive polar bear weight, knocking the bear down, realizing at the same time just who the bear was. Gary Spitzer? What the hell. The shifter was a troublemaker for certain, but why in the world would Gary attack him?

Rob bit him back, his teeth just as wicked, and clawed at him, but Rob's polar bear weight gave him the advantage. Yet Gary was in a real rage, and a grizzly's claws were even wickeder. Rob had to give it all he could to keep the bear from killing him.

Screaming and yelling filled the air some distance away. Were they the members of his tour group? Hell, Rob hoped no one had witnessed him shifting to take Gary on.

Something jingled, pulling Rob out of the vision and for a moment he stared out his windshield, not sure what had startled him, and what he'd seen. Then he recalled the vision, wondering where the hell he was going to be when he had to fight the grizzly. Hopefully, he wouldn't be in the fight while he was with the group on their tour. Yet all the screaming and yelling made him think that he was. Any visions he'd had always had occurred within a week or so. This tour started tomorrow and lasted ten days.

Then his phone rang again. He grabbed his cell and looked at the caller ID. The call was from his brother. "Yeah, Edward?"

"Casey and I are at the pool now. I'll meet you at the house in half an hour. All right?"

"Yeah, sure." His heart still racing, Rob hadn't meant to sound so growly, but he felt as though he'd just come off an adrenaline high from fighting the bear.

"Are...you okay?" Edward could probably hear Rob's heart beating faster than normal, as if he'd been in his polar bear form chasing a seal for dinner, not that he ever did such a thing.

"Yeah, I'm fine." Rob got out of the full-size van and headed into the house.

"Okay, then I'll see you shortly." Edward sounded like he didn't believe everything was fine with Rob.

Not that Rob was surprised.

They ended the call and Rob went inside and took a hot shower in his bathroom. Once he had finished his shower and dressed, he called his Aunt Genevieve. "Hi. This is Rob. Have you or anyone else seen Gary Spitzer around lately?" Rob had to know if the grizzly bear intended to attack him while he was still here. Or if he was going to attack him while they were on the tour. Maybe Gary planned to fight him after Rob had dinner at the tavern. Though Rob hadn't intended to wear his polar bear suit anytime soon. He never did when he was about to take a guided tour group out, never in town, and never on the tour.

"No, dear. The last time I saw him in here was about a month ago. After the last time that Gary caused a brawl, your uncle told him he couldn't buy drinks at the tavern, and he couldn't come in drunk either. The damages were around two-thousand! If he hadn't paid the cost of repairs, he would never have been allowed back. If he can't drink here though, I doubt he'll bother showing up. Why?"

"I just thought of him and wondered." Rob had never told his aunt or uncle about his ability to see future visions. He thought they'd view him as a freak. Not even his brother knew what he could see, though he'd told him of some of his earlier nightmares. Rob hadn't believed they were anything more than that, just like Edward hadn't.

The frustrating part was that Rob would envision a situation like the one he had seen this time: a bear, a fight, and a snowstorm, but not a place or a time or—wait. A snowstorm? A virtual blizzard. He didn't recall seeing any snow in the forecast for the ten days they'd be on the tour. The swirling snow had concealed the bear until it was almost too late, so that was key to when what he had envisioned would occur. He tried to think of any other details he might have seen. The woods, a water source, the proximity of glaciers, just anything, but all he could recall was the grizzly's small eyes, his big teeth, and super-sized claws. All of them being in Rob's face.

"You and your brother and Casey are coming to the tavern for dinner before you leave, correct?" his aunt asked.

"Of course. We'll be over and everyone from the tour group will be there too, if we were able to convince them the tavern is the best place to eat."

"Oh, you will. You always do. We always worry about you boys, so we want to see you before you go. And, Rob, when are you or your brother going to find mates and have babies? I swear my own sons are never going to get married. So maybe I'll have to rely on the two of you instead."

Rob laughed. "Well, Ben keeps trying to match Edward and me up with women, but it's not working." Not only did Rob have to find a woman who was a polar bear shifter like him, he'd have to share the secret about his visions with her too. He was afraid not too many women would be open-minded enough to accept that he could have them. "We'll be over in about half an hour."

After speaking with his aunt, Rob checked the weather report on his phone, but no winter storms were headed their way. Maybe the vision revealed a timeframe that was after he took the tour group out and returned home with them. But usually the visions occurred within a few days of when he witnessed them, maybe as late as a week.

Usually something triggered them, but Rob could never be sure what really caused the visions to suddenly occur. Oftentimes they were tied to emotional, even passionate, or traumatic events. What had happened before he had the vision? He'd spoken to Alicia and then Judi had arrived at the swimming pool. Was one of the women responsible for Gary going off the deep end and tearing into Rob? Why was Rob wearing his fur coat though? He couldn't be anywhere near where the tour group was. That would be a disaster. But he definitely had been outside. Rob tried to recall if he'd heard anything during the vision—the wind, Gary growling, and Rob growling just as viciously. Rob had been concentrating so hard on the fight, he couldn't remember any other details, except for the aggressive smell of the bear and his own aggressive scent that told the other bear to back off. And blood, his and Gary's. Instead of dissuading Gary from escalating the fight, Rob seemed to have enraged him further.

Rob walked out of the bedroom when Edward entered the house. "Hey, are you going to jump into the shower first before we run over to the tavern?" he asked Edward.

"Yeah, be just a sec. I can't stand the smell of chlorine in my hair and on my skin. I was thinking—why don't you go over to the tavern instead of hanging around here? Get us a table. I'll just meet you over there. Hey, did you know that Alicia is a photojournalist and her friend Judi is her assistant? Could be good publicity if we play our cards right," Edward said, pulling off his gloves, hat, and parka.

"Yeah, she told me." Rob gave him a look that said no fooling around with the tourists just to promote the business, even if he'd asked Alicia about bribing her to get some good promo.

"Just saying. You never know. We could have some fun and get some good promotion out of it." Edward frowned at him. "What's wrong? I know from your concerned look and the way you reacted on the phone earlier when I called that something's not right."

Rob considered telling Edward about the vision he had, worried the fight between Rob and Gary might be during the time they were on the tour, and Edward should know about it. That was if Edward even believed what Rob had to tell him.

Looking his brother straight in the eye, Rob told him flat out, "I had a vision. Gary is trying to kill me. I'm attempting to stop him. And we're both fighting as bears."

CHAPTER 2

Just as Alicia was ready to go to the tavern, she got a text from her ex-boyfriend. Annoyed with herself for not learning how to block a call, she finally did it. No matter how much she was adamant about not getting back together with him, Bill Hollinger wouldn't take no for an answer. He wasn't willing to change. And she wasn't willing to constantly give in on important issues.

He was way too domineering. She supposed he reminded her of her mother, and Alicia never wanted to be in a situation like that again.

"Don't tell me," Judi said, curling her hair. "That loser of an ex-boyfriend is still trying to talk you into changing your mind about dating him again. See? Even when you said no and stopped seeing him, he can't take no for an answer. I told you so. While you were dating him, he always attempted to decide everything for you.

Everything from where you'd go, what you'd eat, and what you'd do when you weren't working. *Un*real. I couldn't even believe he'd insisted you skip out on assignments that you'd finally managed to snag just because he had time off from his job. He wanted you with him right then and there. What if you didn't work at all? Would he have been happy then? I doubt it."

Alicia humpfed. "I doubt it either. He'd complained that his former girlfriend mooched off him all the time, and he really liked that I earned an income, though he always insisted on paying for meals and entertainment." He was witty, fun, well-educated, and a hard worker—like she was. The play time was the part she had difficulty with—the lack of having a say in what she did with her free hours. Like when she wanted to chill out at home or hang out with a girlfriend, he'd nix that and try to plan her whole weekend for her.

She worked long hours, always chasing after the perfect photos to sell her stories, always perfecting what she did, and creating visuals that would make her work stand out in a crowded field. She enjoyed her work, but if she was going to continue to make an income at it, she had to continue to take pictures at different times of the day, and any day of the week. Sometimes that meant visiting unusual locations. Like coming here.

Which, of course, he hadn't approved of. He didn't

want her going anywhere he wasn't interested in going. In retrospect, she thought she'd made the plans just because he was so against coming. A way to see what he'd say and if he wasn't agreeable—which he hadn't been—she would call it quits for good. Which she did.

Sometimes, she just needed a weekend to de-stress. Bill didn't see it that way. If she was off, she was off to do what he wanted them to do.

"Yes, but we're not getting back together," she assured Judi.

"At least—except for text messages, emails, and phone calls—he can't tell you what to do here." Judi tugged a jade green sweater over her head. "But he's been constantly texting ever since we arrived. You just need to turn off your phone."

"Can't, in case I get a good assignment before I return. But I finally blocked his calls. That's a nice sweater. Is it new?" Alicia thought it was. She didn't remember seeing Judi wearing it before.

"Yeah, just for the trip. Just in case. You know. Some of these guys are seriously hot. Though some aren't. And some are married, so not going there."

"You have a boyfriend. We're only going to be here for ten days."

"Oh, I know. But what if one if these guys is even a better match for me than with him? Who knows what might happen. What if I met Mr. Right? My dad always said that no matter where you go, you always need to look your best. Just in case. I mean, the first time I went to the grocery store when I was wearing a raggedy old pair of sweats I only wore at home, I ran into two guys who were hotter than sin. Except they were only interested in a woman who was dressed to kill. That taught me a lesson."

Alicia smiled at her. "If they're only interested in what you wear, I wouldn't worry about it."

"Which is why you were wearing that hot zebra bikini. Did you know it makes you look like you're the prey among a pack of wolves?"

Alicia laughed. "Only you would see the bathing suit in that way." She pulled a soft blue sweater over her head.

Judi eyed the sweater and pointed at it. "Okay, so you are wearing a new ice blue sweater that I've never seen on you before. It looks great on you. Are you wearing it for Rob?"

"No. I'm wearing it because we're eating at a nice tavern, and not roughing it like we'll be doing for several days. It's my dress-up-when-we're-in-civilization sweater. When we return, I'll wear it again."

Judi laughed. "All right. You know you could tell Bill you met some other guy up here. Not one of the tour guides because they live here, but one of the people in the tour group. Just for pretend."

"And? Then I return home and I'm not dating any guy? No, I'm not going to make up stories to get him to back off. I'll just be as persistent as he is as far as not going out with him again if he bugs me when I return home."

"Good luck with that. Are you ready to go?"

"Yeah, but I'm not looking to hook up with Rob or anyone else, despite what you think. So don't push it."

Judi just smiled.

Alicia was determined not to get too close to Rob, as much as she was dying to see what she could about him. What appealed to her about him was that he was friendly, yet not overtly so. Nice, but not overbearing, which was the problem with her ex-boyfriend. Rob did his thing, she was doing her thing, and that was all there was to it.

She reminded herself what a disaster it could be if she touched Rob and learned something bad about his past. She'd feel uncomfortable the whole time she was around him on the group tour. Then again, she might not envision anything.

So why was she trying to think of ways to just…bump into him…accidentally, no premeditation on her part, so if she learned something it was purely by mistake?

***

Drinking honeyed mead from his beer stein, Rob

MacMathan studied the new tour group gathering at the tables in the White Bear Tavern in the small Alaskan town of White Bear—concentrating on Alicia, like she was studying him back. He'd been glad when he'd arrived there that she was already sitting with several of the tour group participants and there hadn't been any available seats for him. Before they took off tomorrow, he preferred some quiet time where he could sit away from the group and observe them, if he wanted to, soak up the cheerful atmosphere, and relax. No need to be anything he wasn't. No need to be the perfect host, because here, he didn't need to be. The actual tour started tomorrow.

He still couldn't believe how his body had reacted so intensely interested in Alicia though, due to her proximity to him in the pool, the way he couldn't quit breathing in her sweet scent—human scent, he repeatedly reminded himself—and the appealing, soft sound of her voice.

Trying to get his thoughts off her, he let out his breath. He knew when he told Edward what had happened in his vision, his brother hadn't believed him about having them, though Edward had been in a rush to take his shower and get over here. That might have been the reason for his not saying any more about the issue than, "really," before he disappeared into the bathroom.

Rob glanced back at Alicia and saw her taking pictures of the tavern's décor. The place was decorated in old world charm—the distressed wood paneling on the walls and ceilings, the wood floors, the scarred wood tables and chairs and long bar. It reminded Rob of a time when his parents were here still, and how they'd always visit with his aunt and uncle too. The family gatherings. The game nights. They still had them when Edward and Rob weren't off guiding a tour, but it wasn't the same.

Smoky mirrors behind the long bar made the large tavern seem even bigger. It was the local gathering spot for tourists and locals alike. Like Edward, Rob loved being a tour guide who took groups into the wilderness, seeing the excitement on everyone's faces, the joy they felt in witnessing all the new sights, and loving all the new experiences they had. He couldn't imagine any job he'd love more.

He studied Alicia again, thinking about the way she had looked in the zebra bikini. And the thought occurred to him that a polar bear with a zebra made a strange pairing. Not that she was a zebra shifter, or that they really existed, but he did give it a passing thought. She was a sporty brunette, her hair nearly black, straight and long, pulled into a tail that rested over her shoulder now, a tease enticing him to want to unbind the tail, to drape the soft strands about her shoulders, setting it free. Her eyes were crystal blue like a clear lake, her skin alabaster, except for the tip of her nose and her cheeks that were a pretty blush from coming in from the cold. Her lips were a pale pink, unsmiling as she switched her attention from the redhead, and studied him as if challenging him to look away first. In the wild animal kingdom, that was a taunt, a fighting gaze. In humans—intrigue, interest.

A white parka hung on the back of her chair, and he thought how she'd be lost against a snowy backdrop if she wore such a coat in the Alaskan wilderness during a snowstorm. Though his own was just as white.

He preferred blending in with the snow just like his polar bear half did. Bears that were all polar bear and not shifters lived in the northern reaches, but the shifters lived in the more hospitable areas of the state, loving the forests—both the coastal rain forests and the boreal forests. They were just careful not to run through the wilderness as polar bears during the day—if they could help it. Which, normally they could, since all were born shifters from long generations of shifters, so no problem controlling when and where they shifted.

When they went up north, they usually didn't shift into their polar bear fur. Polar bears were territorial, and none of the shifters wanted to get into a fight over territory up there.

Ben, one of Rob's cousins who worked for his aunt

and uncle at the tavern, came over with a refill for Rob's mug. "Do you want me to give the woman a drink and say it's from you?" Smiling, Ben turned to take his eyes off Alicia. His blue eyes were alight with humor. He was the fairest haired of any of them in the MacMathan family, and he was always giving Rob and his brother a hard time about trekking through the wilderness with humans. "She's not with anyone." Ben set a bowl of chips and dip on Rob's table. "I asked." Then he gave him another big smile. "On your behalf."

"I'm not interested in getting to know a tourist better."

"Who said anything about getting to know them better? Just have a drink with her. Hey, I put my whole reputation on the line for making short-term get-togethers happen. Like one drink, dude. One drink. And hell, it's on the house anyway, being as you're like my brother." Ben slapped him on the back. "Got to get back to work before Dad fires me."

"Uncle Ned wouldn't. Not when you're so good at making short-term matches, which means more sold drinks." Rob and Edward and their partner, Casey MacIntosh, always brought all their tour groups here for drinks and food. Family helped family. His uncle and aunt made sure that the tour groups had a wonderful time while they were here. It was part of their special tour package. Plus, the tour group received a lot of discounts while they were here too.

"Well, suit yourself, but the way she's eyeing you, I'd say it was a sure deal." Ben shook his head and left to drop off drinks at another table.

The tavern was run by Rob's aunt and uncle, their great grandparents having established it in the days gone by when the gold rush was in full swing, and the town was ten times its current size. Only one of Rob's male cousins still worked in the tavern, a purely family venture. Craig flew a seaplane now and took people on sightseeing tours, dropped supplies off in wilderness areas, and helped with rescue missions. And Rob's cousin Andy, was a trooper. Sometimes Rob felt guilty that he didn't become one too, like his parents. But Rob much preferred sharing the joy and beauty that was Alaska rather than tracking down criminals.

Rob and his brother had lived with their aunt and uncle for a time, and worked here too until they were old enough to begin taking tour groups into the wilderness. The tour groups loved the antiquated gold rush feel of the place and gave it great reviews, telling everyone just how much they enjoyed this part of the tour package. The tavern was the only one run by polar bear shifters in the area. Bear shifters came from all around just to drink the honeyed mead, much preferred over any other alcoholic drink. Some loved the honeyed margaritas and berry wine.

White wolf shifters came in from time to time and scoffed at them for not drinking beer instead. So did the triplet snow leopards, all male, who visited on a more regular basis. He was surprised one of the big cats wasn't here tonight. Usually one, if not all three of them, would show up on a Friday night. The bear shifters all took the ribbing in good humor. The pastry and sandwich shop down the street was also polar bear run. White Bear Deli's claim to fame was the berry pies they made especially for hungry bear shifters. Though Rob's brother was one bear who preferred chocolate to everything else, making him an oddity in their world. Rob was always telling him he'd turn into a Kodiak bear if he kept eating so much chocolate.

Then four male Arctic wolves entered the tavern and headed for a table. They glanced at the tourists, the women in particular, smiled their wolfish smiles, then saw Rob watching them. Their smiles broadened. Four quadruplet brothers. In the wolf world, as it was in the shifter world, they mated for life. That only applied if they mated with wolf shifters though. Dating humans was just something they could do at will. Once they settled down with a wolf shifter mate, they were set for life, no divorce, and no fooling around with a human or a different wolf shifter.

Bears and the snow leopards didn't mate for life in the wild world, but as shifters, they generally did. Some divorced though.

Then Rob saw Gary Spitzer enter the tavern and Rob's Uncle Ned hurrying to intercept him. Wary, Rob watched Gary, ready to come to his uncle's aid if he needed him. The grizzly bear could be a decent sort on a good day, but one hell of a fighter on a bad day. He was tall, like Rob and his brother and cousins, with dark brown hair and beard, and bushy eyebrows. His small brown eyes widened a little, and he motioned to a table. Uncle Ned nodded, but spoke to him again. Then Gary took his seat, and Ben quickly went to his table to take his order.

Rob wondered what in the world would cause him to get into a big fight with Gary. He turned his attention back to the tour group seated at one of the long tables. Eleven men and four women, more women than usual, who had signed up to trek through the wilderness to see the northern lights and polar bears. They would probably see moose and grizzlies too, so everyone had to be careful. Which again made Rob think of Gary and the trouble the grizzly was bound to cause him soon.

Three bearded men at a table kitty corner to Rob's were drinking whiskey, and Rob overheard their liquored-up conversation. "Gonna hunt me a big grizzly and this time I'm bringing home the bear claws."

"Hell, Hanson, every time you've gone out to hunt that 'grizzly' you can't find him to shoot him."

Rob frowned at the men, knowing he shouldn't get involved. He hated men who hunted off-season just to kill something. He rose from his table and walked over to theirs. They all looked up at him, frowning at him, not sociable in the least. He could tell from their belligerent expressions they would just as likely fight him if he said what he intended to.

"What is your problem? Don't like where you're sitting? Just get the hell out of here then," Hanson said. The other men laughed.

"Hunting season is over. Don't even think of hunting grizzly or anything else, or you'll regret it," Rob said, keeping his voice level, despite how growly he felt about this issue.

"You the law?" Hanson asked, his steely gaze trained on Rob.

Rob suspected the man had run-ins with the law before. Men like him usually did.

"Let's just say I have connections. You've been forewarned."

Hanson gave a rough laugh. "Yeah, got me real scared."

The other men weren't laughing. They looked like they'd be happy just to pummel Rob for telling them what to do.

Rob gave them each a look, silently willing them to just try and take him on.

"Yeah. We hear you," one of the other men finally said as if trying to appease him.

But Rob knew the type. They'd be out there anyway, killing to their heart's content.

The tavern door opened and a tourist walked in. Edward followed right behind him and saw Rob right away. Rob returned to his table and waved at him as Edward brought in a blast of cold air because the tourist was being polite and holding the inner door open for him. Edward was always way more cheerful than Rob. Which had a lot to do with the way Rob's world had tilted on end when their parents died in the avalanche, and Edward had saved Rob, who had been buried alive also.

It wasn't just because of losing their parents at fifteen, or nearly losing his own life, if his brother hadn't rescued him, that had changed Rob's life so drastically either. After being rescued, the visions of future happenings—clairvoyance—had come to Rob, and could be the stuff of nightmares. He had no control over the visions. How could he be cheerful when he saw a sudden snowstorm that would obliterate everything in its path, and out of the heavy mist of snow, a grizzly would appear, teeth bared, wicked claws slashing at him?

Edward slapped a couple of men on the back in greeting, waved to the tour group, then headed for

Rob's table, casting a wary glance in Gary Spitzer's direction.

Edward reached Rob's table and took a seat. "In this vision of yours, are you sure you didn't see any distinguishing features to let us know where it was exactly that would help us define when it happens?"

Rob considered his brother, unsure if he was making a joke about what Rob said he'd seen, or Edward really believed him.

Casey came into the tavern, spied them, and headed their way.

"Are you feeling superstitious that so many women are in the tour group this time?" Edward turned to study Rob, his gaze worried.

"No, that has nothing to do with anything."

"I've always known you could see things. Things no one else can see. You could pretend you didn't, but you couldn't hide it from me."

Rob nearly choked on his mead. "I thought you didn't believe me."

"Of course I believe you. I mean, not in the beginning when you first had the visions and you told me about them. I thought you were just having nightmares. Hell, that's what you thought too. I guess that's why you didn't want to tell me about them any longer. I just thought you never saw another one. Like it was some fluke. The time the fishing boat sank and you tried to warn the captain not to take the boat out, of course I was like him, until they were lost at sea. Well, even then, I thought it was just coincidence. It happened from time to time and anyone could predict that a fishing boat would be lost at sea.

"When you mentioned Ben was going to break his arm when he was playing with me—we were roughhousing a bit too much—I started to wonder if there was something more to it. Then, for years, you didn't say anything about having these premonitions. I figured it went away. Why didn't you tell me you were still having them?"

"I didn't think you believed me."

"Well, I do. So how should we handle this? I think we need to tell Casey."

"What if he doesn't believe me?"

"Then he'll be a believer when it happens. At least we can be more prepared for it, right?"

Rob shook his head. "Not once in my fourteen years of dealing with this have I been able to stop a catastrophe from happening. When I knew a fishing boat would sink and all lives would be lost on another occasion, I warned the owner and he told me it was their way of life. They had to fish for a living. Fishing boats were lost at sea on occasion. What can I do about it? Nothing.

"No one ever believes that I know what I'm talking

about. That what I see will come to pass. If the others heed my warning, will it change events? Is their time up anyway? I mean, what if they didn't go out in the boat? Would they die in some other catastrophe? I don't know. If I tell you that we should delay the trip because we'll end up in a snowstorm and a grizzly is going to attack, what would you do?" Rob asked.

Edward pulled out his cell phone and looked up the weather. "We're not supposed to have a major storm for the next ten days or so."

Rob shrugged. "I told you what I'm concerned about. Out there is the wilderness. Those who come here seeking adventure are city-folk for the most part. They aren't prepared for the dangers that could befall them. It's not a theme park. This is the real thing. And Gary is the bear that I have to fight."

"Gary Spitzer? Right. The guy is a catastrophe waiting to happen. Okay, so who's going to get in trouble? The wild redhead? One of the cute blonds? Or the dark-haired woman?"

Rob sighed. "All of them will be scrambling for their lives. Maybe. Or it's while we're on another tour at a later date or maybe not even on a tour. I can't ever be completely certain until something happens."

"Which is exactly why we can't just cancel the tour for no really good reason. What if we did and nothing happened? Already the Jamison brothers are trying their damnedest to get our business. All we'd have to do is say we can't go, and they'd take them. Then what if nothing happened? But the next group we took out ended up in trouble instead?" Edward drummed his fingers on the table in a tell-tale sign that he was feeling aggravated. "Okay, do you see *me* getting into trouble?"

Rob took his eyes off the tour group and looked at his brother. "I can't see anything about family members or friends any longer. I don't know why, but after the incident with Ben's broken arm, I just can't."

"What's going to happen exactly?"

"I told you: blinding snow, the bear, screaming, hollering, everyone running for their lives, snarling and growling. Chaos."

"And us?"

"I don't see you. I can't see you. Like I said, it might not even be while were out with this group of tourists."

"Do you recognize any of them?"

Rob shook his head. "I'm concentrating on the bear in front of me. His teeth and claws. I don't know. Maybe I got a glimpse of people running, but my focus is mostly on the enraged grizzly."

"Can you close your eyes and conjure it up?" Edward asked. "Just so you can get more details?"

Sometimes Rob could. He closed his eyes and tried to envision the fight. Rob could see the grizzly's snarling face, his nose wrinkled, his lips pulled back to expose his long, wicked teeth. He heard someone screaming for help. But he couldn't look away from the bear in front of him. The bear could kill him, if Rob turned his head to see what else was happening.

He opened his eyes. "I can't look away from the bear. That's all I can focus on. Hell, he's trying to kill me."

"That makes sense. Can you recall what anyone's wearing before or afterwards? Alicia is wearing a white parka. Is she in the middle of this?"

"You know what a whiteout is like. Everything is white. If she's wearing that parka, I won't be seeing her. Everyone would be bundled up, their faces covered. Most could be wearing ski goggles."

Edward snapped his fingers. "Smells. Do you smell scents in your visions?"

"Snow, cold, Gary's halitosis, the smell of vodka—"

"Hell, he's drunk."

"Most likely. Let me assure you, that doesn't slow him down as far as scrapping with me."

"Okay, okay. So you're trying to keep him from killing you. Do any of us survive?" Edward sounded worried now, like maybe they shouldn't be going on this trip.

"Really, I just don't know. We could lose some of them in the whiteout; the bear could kill them. I don't see anything beyond the bear and the snow. No blood or anything, well, just mine and Gary's, and then you interrupted the vision when you called me. When I try to recall what I see, I don't envision anything further."

"Do you often see more the closer we get to the event?"

"Occasionally. Other times the period is too close to the event. Like with Ben's arm breaking. I think he was in so much pain, it made me envision it happening before it did. I only saw it the one time, and only about four hours before it happened."

Edward let out a long-suffering breath. "Do you see polar bears? Have the rest of us shifted to try and protect the tourists?"

"I only see the grizzly and he's damn big. You know what Gary is like even when he's not wearing his fur coat."

"Yeah, damn big. Wait, if you see him and the snowstorm, it means you're there, right? You don't see things that don't involve you, do you? I mean, you're not seeing something through someone else's eyes." Then Edward frowned. "It means you're going to shift? And fight him? To protect everyone? And then you're going to make mincemeat of the grizzly?"

"Yeah, it's me, not me seeing this through someone else's eyes. I hope no one sees me shift either. Let's just say, I am doing the best I can and hoping it will work."

Rob had played around with his brother and

cousins and friends as a polar bear when he was growing up—typical bear behavior—both in and out of the water. And even today, they would horse around as grown bears. Fighting a raging grizzly bear shifter wasn't the same as play fighting with shifter friends. But yeah, to protect the people on the tour and his brother and friend, Rob would do anything.

CHAPTER 3

Alicia was almost disappointed when Edward and Casey had taken seats at the table where Rob was seated. She had thought that her group could move some more chairs over to their table to accommodate their guides. Maybe the men liked to distance themselves from the tour group for the last day of freedom they had. The next ten days meant babysitting the tourists so she understood their need to do their own thing tonight.

Still, Ben, cousin to Rob—he had been sure to tell her his relationship to Rob—had served her free drinks, twice, both times saying they were from a secret admirer. Only he gave Rob's full name, his occupation, tour guide like his brother, Edward, and that he lived in a log cabin a short walk from the tavern. When Rob and Edward ordered shrimp and lobster tails, Ben had brought her a serving also, saying it was from Rob. She knew it hadn't been though. Sure, he acted a bit interested in her, but she thought if he was really intrigued, he would have asked her to join him. Or he would have joined her.

The other women in their tour group smiled at her.

Judi Hall leaned across the table. "What did you do to get all the attention? Did something happen in the pool between the two of you that you're not telling me?"

Alicia shrugged. "I think Rob's cousin is into matchmaking."

"Well, he can match me up with Rob's brother," Judi said. "But Ben only seems to be interested in hooking Rob up with you."

"Maybe Ben knows Rob likes brunettes," Lizzy Howard said, the darker haired blond of the two. "Too bad Ben couldn't go with us. He's just as cute as the brothers."

The other ladies all ordered what Alicia had to eat.

Dipping her breaded shrimp in cocktail sauce, Alicia smiled. She wasn't used to guys showing her this much attention. Except for Bill, but she didn't want his attention.

She really wasn't surprised that Rob didn't have anything to do with ordering drinks and dinner for her. She glanced back at him and caught his eye. She smiled and mouthed a thank you anyway.

**

Rob guessed his cousin had told Alicia that he had ordered the meal and drinks for her. Rob was glad Ben didn't do that every time a pretty brunette was in the place when he dropped in to have something to eat or drink.

"She looks interested in you," Edward said about Alicia.

Casey grabbed a mug of mead at the bar, then headed in their direction, his hair fairer, his expression jovial.

"Are you going to tell Casey about what you see?" Edward asked Rob.

"I will, but I doubt he'll believe me."

Casey reached their table and set his drink down before he pulled out his chair and took his seat. "You both look like you're having a serious discussion. Anything wrong with going on our tour group adventure tomorrow?"

Ben joined them and said, "Your usual? Shrimp and lobster tail?"

"Yeah, thanks, Ben," Casey said.

"Hey," Rob said to Ben, "what's the deal with Gary being in here? I thought he'd been banned from the place."

They all looked in Gary's direction.

"Meals only. Water, sodas, no alcoholic beverages. Dad doesn't want to hurt our business with the grizzlies, so he wants to keep it as agreeable as he can. Even though Gary can be a real ass, he has a lot of influence over the others in the area."

Rob shook his head. He understood Uncle Ned's reasoning, but the guy was too volatile for Rob's taste. Especially when Rob knew he'd be dealing with Gary as a bear sometime soon. Did the confrontation begin here then?

Ben took a tray of drinks to another table.

"Okay, Rob has something to tell you that he's already shared with me," Edward said, low for their ears only. "It's something he never shares with anyone because so many people just don't believe him."

"He's psychic and sees stuff that is going to happen way before it occurs," Casey said, as if everyone knew that. "From your glum expressions, I'd say it's something that's going to happen while we're on tour and it's not a good thing."

Casey's family had come during the gold rush too. They knew that supplying goods to the miners was a sure-fire way to get rich. They owned both the grocery store and the hardware store. Casey's blue eyes sparkled with devilment, his mouth curving up a hint. He raised his brows a smidgeon. "Okay, so I'm right, correct?"

Rob let out his breath. "Hell, yeah. I…just didn't think you'd believe me. I figured you'd think I was joking."

"After you predicted a couple of ships being lost at sea and Ben's arm breaking? I became a firm believer in the paranormal. Not to mention we're kind of paranormal ourselves. So why couldn't you have a psychic connection? What's going to happen that has you so concerned that you're willing to tell us about it?" Casey asked.

Rob was relieved that Casey and his brother believed him. He explained the situation and Casey whistled.

"Are you sure we don't shift to come to your aid?" Casey asked. "I can't imagine letting you deal with Gary on your own. That guy is one big, mean, son-of-a-gun."

"You would need to get our group to safety. I don't think you'd shift to help me, rather, you'd gather our tour group and get them safely in the vans so that we don't lose any of them. In any event, I don't envision any other bears in the picture. Certainly, two more bears added into the fight would create even more havoc for our group."

"True," Edward said. "Are you sure you're fighting Gary and it isn't one of us?"

All of them looked in Gary's direction. He was eating a grizzly bear-sized steak, mashed potatoes, gravy, and pile of mixed vegetables.

"Yeah, because I taste his blood and feel his teeth and claws tearing at my flesh. I don't see this as a spectator, but more as a gladiator in the middle of the battle."

"Okay, I'm taking a tranquilizer gun just in case," Edward said.

"Just don't shoot me." Rob hoped that when he shifted, the snowstorm and the panic filling the people would help cover up the fact he was a shifter.

Ben served Casey his order of fried shrimp, lobster tails, and a fresh mug of frosty mead, then carried an order of crabs and clam chowder to another table.

Neither his brother nor Casey were the kind to spread rumors, and Rob had kept this bottled up for so long that he felt It was time he told someone. Especially when this would probably affect all of them.

Music and conversation filled the noisy tavern, Rob leaned into the table and said low for their enhanced hearing. "From what I can tell from Googling it, I'm clairvoyant."

Immediately, Casey got on his phone and Rob worried he'd misjudged him. But then Casey showed him the page he'd pulled up on a search to find the description of what being clairvoyant meant: the supernatural ability to perceive events in the future. Also known as telepathic, psychic, visionary, or second-sighted. "Hell, you're an oracle." Then Casey handed his phone to Edward.

"Yeah, that's it," Rob agreed.

"Well, hell, so you thought you've been keeping this secret all these years?" Casey asked. "I already knew that you were gifted."

Rob still couldn't believe they knew and had believed in him. "This isn't for public consumption. Just the two of you can know."

Then the two blond-haired women from their tour group headed for their table. "Here they come. Both in graduate school, final year. Both biology majors, cousins Lizzy and Jessica Howard," Casey said.

Rob stood. "Night all. Have fun." He didn't feel like socializing. He glanced over at the hunters. Hanson raised his glass to Rob in salute, as if to taunt him that the best hunter would win.

"No hunting until spring," Rob warned again.

The other men just looked surly at him. Rob knew the bastards had every intention of hunting as soon as they could and they had no intention of waiting until spring to legally hunt.

Edward and Casey greeted the women and ordered new drinks.

Rob headed past the table where Alicia and her friend, Judi, and the men in the tour group sat. They waved at him and he said, "See you in the morning." He hoped it wouldn't turn out to be a disastrous trip.

***

Edward and Casey seemed much more happy-go-lucky, whereas Rob appeared darker, brooding, moodier this evening at the tavern. Alicia was curious as to what he was all about. Yet she noticed the little bit of a smile he cast in her direction, maybe amused she'd think the free drinks and food were from him. She wanted to tell him that she knew better.

And she wanted to touch him.

Once, Alicia had shaken a bank loan officer's hand and learned he was having sex with a bank teller who happened to be a friend's daughter and the loan officer already had a family of his own. So sometimes it made for an awkward situation, but somehow, she had to reveal the truth without letting on the way in which she knew what was going on. When she'd been younger, friends had distanced themselves from her because of her gift. They had been afraid she'd see things about them that were better left alone. Bill hadn't known about what she could do. He was too busy concentrating on his own needs and wants and had no clue about hers.

Sometimes Alicia could cloak her thoughts in a shroud of fog so she could get through a day without having to deal with all the extra sensory information, but sometimes the visions slipped through anyway. Like the time the woman bumped into her, and that contact revealed her husband was abusing her. After pretending to know her, Alicia convinced her to seek help. She'd always hoped the woman had left her abusive husband and was well on the road to recovery.

After Alicia finished her drink and meal, Edward and Casey and the two women joined their table.

"Seeing the polar bears is guaranteed on this trip, right?" Alicia had come here mostly to get pictures of the polar bears, and to get photos of the northern lights. Everyone would love the light displays, but especially photos of the polar bears—animals or people always helped to sell her stories better.

"Of course. The whalers leave carcasses for the polar bears in one location and the bears eat the remains. We'll see a lot of them," Edward said. "All the tour groups go there to see them. But we'll be the only group there at the time. We try to coordinate our tours so that we don't have several in an area at the same time, less impact on the environment, and it gives our tour groups the feel of what it's really like out there— the quiet, the beauty, the wildlife."

"That sounds good," Lizzy said, cozying up more to Casey.

"Have you ever had trouble on a guided tour before?" Alicia asked. She always asked the same question on any of the tours she took, whether they were in a city or the Amazon rain forest, or just anywhere. Trouble could happen at any time, and she just wanted to be prepared.

"No. That's not to say we can't have." Edward finished his drink. "Just that we haven't so far."

"Hell, Edward, you're getting to sound like your brother. We've never had trouble before." Casey cast Edward an annoyed look.

"Do you live here?" Lizzy asked.

"We do," Edward said, smiling.

"Does Rob live near the two of you?" Alicia asked.

Edward and Casey exchanged looks and smiled at her.

"What?" she asked, just curious if the men all roomed together or they had separate places. Not that she wanted to know for any reason other than curiosity's sake.

"Yeah, Rob and I have a home near here," Edward said.

Casey raised his mug to Edward. "What did I tell you? All the women like that dark, brooding type."

"What makes him that way? Certainly, neither of you seem to be like that," Alicia said.

"When we were fifteen, our parents died in an avalanche. Once I freed myself, I went to Rob's rescue. He was closer to me location-wise. Mom and Dad were farther down the slope. We couldn't save our parents in time," Edward said, frowning.

"Omigod, I'm so sorry," Alicia said. All the women agreed.

Casey nodded. "He was just like us back then. Enjoying life. No cares in the world. Now he's much more circumspect. Serious. He rarely lets his hair down."

"I'm so sorry." Alicia said again. She thought maybe a girlfriend had dumped him, or something like that. Nothing so life-altering that time wouldn't heal it. "Is he usually one of the tour guides for these trips?"

"Yeah." Edward sat taller on his chair. "Always. We love what we do."

"The brothers own a home at the edge of town. Hey, why don't we have a nightcap there?" Casey asked.

"I'm game." Alicia wanted to read Rob and learn what she could about him before they journeyed on their way first thing in the morning, to see if maybe his parents' deaths still disturbed him. Or if there was something else in his past that was causing his concern.

The other women were agreeable, but she thought Edward looked like this might get him into a bit of trouble with his brother. He wasn't super enthusiastic. She wondered why Casey wouldn't offer to have them over to his house instead. Maybe he roomed with someone else who wouldn't be happy about them all barging in.

"I'll just give Rob a heads up so we don't catch him running around the house naked or something." Edward pulled out his phone and winked at Alicia.

She felt her body warm in embarrassment.

"Oh, don't bother calling him on our account," Judi said, chuckling.

Everyone laughed.

"Hey, Rob," Edward said on the phone, "Casey and I are coming to the house with a couple of women who are going on the tour tomorrow, and I wanted to just let you know. All right. See you soon."

"He's agreeable?" Alicia asked, surprised. She'd expected him to object.

"No. But the house is half mine. I bring over whomever I want. If he doesn't want to be around, he'll be in his office playing video games or something. If he wants to join us, he will."

So, Rob did object. Maybe this was what he needed. Alicia smiled. "I'm ready." There was something about Rob that just made her want to make a connection. If she could see if his parents' deaths still tortured him, maybe she could reach out to him. Help him to feel the joy in the world. She'd done it before with others who were dealing with a horrific loss.

When they reached the two-story, log cabin-style home, a nice large upper deck and lower deck great for summer-time activities, and a steep metal roof to help deal with heavy snows, she thought how nice it was. Lights were on inside and out making it appear warm and welcome, despite what Edward had said concerning Rob not being agreeable about them coming over. Maybe Rob hadn't minded, or had changed his mind.

Wisps of smoke curled out of the chimney, and she thought how nice it would be to sit before a warm fireplace and have a drink before they called it a night.

Now she was waffling about touching him too. She would have to play it by ear. See how he reacted to her coming to his place also. Maybe he would initiate the contact between them. She really felt it was better that way.

Then again, if he didn't, she figured she wouldn't sleep, wishing she'd touched him instead. Yet, if she saw something she wished she hadn't, that would be a whole other story.

CHAPTER 4

Rob wasn't surprised when Edward and Casey brought the two blonds with them to the house. Bringing the intriguing brunette, yes—that surprised him. Mostly because he hadn't believed she'd want to come over here. Maybe she thought that Ben had told her the truth. That Rob had paid for her drinks and meal. He had figured she knew Ben was teasing. He was also surprised Alicia's roommate hadn't come, since they seemed to be together a lot.

Casey and Rob's brother were friendly, but also super professional on the hikes, watchful of danger, and so before the tour began, they'd often enjoy the company of the tourists. This time, with so many single women who seemed interested in them, he knew enjoying their company further was bound to happen.

Casey's place was too far out of town to take the

women there. Edward and Rob's place was always the logical spot to bring folks if they were going to have guests.

Rob had considered going out on a run, or locking himself away in his office to play video games, but he decided to chaperone his brother and Casey tonight so they'd be ready to go in the morning.

Rob served as the bartender. "One drink, and then it's time to call it a night."

The women looked a little surprised. The blonds anyway. Alicia didn't. She studied him like a wolf would. Edward and Casey hurried to take everyone's parkas, gloves, and hats. For a second, Rob wondered if she *was* a wolf. Then he shook his head at himself over the thought. She didn't smell like a wolf, and if she was a shifter, she'd know he was a bear. The species didn't mix in the wild and they didn't as shifters. They just weren't drawn to each other, which probably had to do with their drive to procreate more of their shifter kind. If they mated some other species, then what? No kids? A mix of wolves and bear shifter babies? A shifter that had bear and wolf features like dog breeds that were mixed? It just wasn't in their nature to mix the different species.

"A martini, if that's all right," Lizzy said, settling on one of the leather couches.

Both Alicia and Jessica asked for the same thing.

"Tell me about the polar bears." Alicia sat on one of

the bar stools while Rob made up martinis for the women.

Jessica and his brother and Casey joined Lizzy in the living room and Edward began talking about the northern lights.

"Polar bears are white." Rob poured the martinis for the ladies. Then he began making the drinks the guys liked the best—blueberry sangria for Edward, honey grapefruit spritzer for Casey, and a wild honey margarita for himself.

Alicia was smiling at him, her expression saying he was being a smart-ass.

"Truly? Our hair…" Rob said, then stopped himself.

Edward quit speaking and both he and Casey glanced at Rob, brows raised.

Rob quickly said, "The polar bears have transparent strands of hair. The white of the snow is reflected off their fur." He never made the mistake of talking about himself as if he were a polar bear. Not that she'd ever guess he was a shifter, but the woman unsettled him.

"Wow, I didn't know that. But sometimes their fur is kind of yellow," Alicia said. "I wondered about that."

That was some of the fun of taking people out on tours. They often didn't know a whole lot about Alaska or about animals that lived there. That meant Rob and the others provided an educational service and he liked that. He appreciated that she was interested too.

"In the summer, the polar bears' fur looks kind of yellow, sure. Depending on the season and the amount of sunlight, it can even look like it's brown or gray. If you take pictures of them at different times of the day, you can see what I mean. Did you know that their skin is black?"

"No, I didn't. I thought they were white like their coat to hide from predators."

"Nope. It's black to absorb the sun's rays and warm them."

"That makes sense."

He handed her a martini and when he reached out with the glass, she touched his fingers. It wasn't a conscious effort on his part to touch her or for her to brush her fingers against his, but the shock of the contact jolted him.

Their gazes collided, her eyes saucer size. He felt something cataclysmic explode between them, but at first, he couldn't tell what had happened. Until he had a vision of her, terrified, in the frigid water, fighting for her life. His heart racing, Rob couldn't believe what he had seen. Was Gary responsible for Alicia being in the water? Was that why Rob had shifted into a polar bear to fight him off? To save Alicia? Rob knew when he was fighting Gary, but he hadn't seen anything about Alicia at the time. Now she'd be fighting for her life in the water? In the frigid temperature, she wouldn't live long.

Why would she appear so concerned also? Like she had witnessed the very same thing as he had.

Shocked beyond words, Rob quickly reached for the two remaining martini glasses, and carried them into the living room to give to the other women, unable to distance himself from the horror—at least as far as what would happen to Alicia—that would befall them. As to the business with the grizzly, the confrontation still might occur at some other time and not coincide with this event. He just couldn't believe what a disaster the journey would be for them, or how he could prevent any of it from happening.

Edward came into the kitchen to help, getting cheese dip and a bag of chips while Casey grabbed his and Edward's drinks. "Are you joining us?" Edward asked, but his brow furrowed. "Is something wrong?"

"I'll join you." Rob couldn't quiet his concern over Alicia, but he would have to tell Edward what he'd seen after the women left.

Alicia hadn't moved from the bar stool, her back to them when he returned to get his own drink. He looked at her pale face and saw her eyes filled with tears. A sickening feeling filled the pit of his stomach as he just stared at her, wondering again what the hell happened between them. Could she see what he saw? He'd never known anyone who could, and he found the notion more than disconcerting.

"Are you going to join us?" Rob asked her. The gentlemanly thing to do would be to take her arm and help her down from the bar stool, especially since she seemed so upset, yet he really didn't want to touch her again and cause the same or worse reaction. Especially if she could see what he could and he didn't want to distress her further.

She avoided his touch as much as he avoided touching her, and climbed down, seized her drink, and hurried over to the couches. Only one was left for the two of them to sit on, so he set his drink on the coffee table, and then brought over a chair from the dining room. Everyone was looking at him with surprised expressions—as if Rob and Alicia had a falling out, and they didn't want to sit near each other.

"Rob, you were talking about what the polar bears are like?" Lizzy asked, sounding like she was trying to smooth things over.

"Many say they're bigger than most other bears out there." Rob glanced at Alicia, but she was just staring at him, not drinking her martini, her face still pale.

"Even bigger than a grizzly? I thought they were the biggest," Lizzy said.

"Well, the biggest Kodiak bear they've found was fourteen feet tall and weighed 2500 pounds. But most are about 800 to 1500 pounds and stand five to ten feet tall. Whereas the polar bears generally are eight and a half feet tall and weigh between 900 and 1500 pounds. On average, polar bears are larger. Though a few grizzlies will be as big as that or bigger." Gary was as big as the bigger male polar bears. "They love to hunt seals, their favorite food, and they're considered carnivores. They can actually smell a seal twenty miles away."

The women's jaws all dropped. Even Alicia's.

"They'll eat about anything, if they can't get enough seals. Only about two percent of the time can they catch them. They hunt in 'still' mode so they don't burn up their food stores. In comparison, a predator like the big cats—jaguars and cougars—often stalk or chase their prey. Polar bears sit and wait at seal breathing holes in the ice. If they can't eat seals, they'll opt for fishing, stealing eggs, and hunting reindeer even. In some parts of the world, they go after birds, berries, and as you'll see on your trip, whale remains. The blubber from seals helps them to stay warm and helps them build up fat reserves to use up between feedings. They overheat if they chase things down, and they burn up too much of their stores also. They need the fat to keep them warm and buoyant in the water."

"How often do they attack humans?" Alicia finally asked.

She couldn't have seen what Rob had about Gary attacking him and her being in the water, could she? If she did see him fighting Gary, Rob was a polar bear, not human. "Bear attacks are extremely rare, but they can attack." He wasn't about to pretend they wouldn't, but when he saw Edward and Casey's shocked expressions, Rob thought maybe he should have been a little less straightforward.

"Like many wild predators, they strike out at humans if provoked or while protecting their offspring. And they're territorial. You don't want to get near their food. The same can be said of any wild animal." He assumed none of the members of the tour group would get into trouble in that way. "They're predatory too, and black and brown bears have been known to kill and eat some of their victims."

Edward shook his head and finished his drink.

Rob figured he needed to finish what he had to say despite how his brother and his friend viewed his explanation. The women seemed interested. "There have been cases where hunters kill a moose or deer and a bear attacks the hunter to secure the kill. Again, territorial. Their territory, their food. Sometimes people feed the bears, despite rangers telling them not to. One man had been doing it for ten years. Until a bear killed him. Sure, it had always been more standoffish than any of the other bears, but they're not a social project. It's not like with a dog that might be coaxed to friendship over the years. You have to be careful about any bears in the region."

"That's grizzlies or brown bears. What about polar bears?" Alicia asked.

Okay, so, Alicia was the one who had started this line of inquiry, not Rob. He wasn't going to make stuff up. "We know only of a couple of wild polar bears killing humans. The others don't count as zoo guests climbed into captive polar bear enclosures and died from their injuries. Again, an enclosure confines the bears and that enclosure becomes their territory. It's only natural for them to protect what's theirs. But then wild polar bears are in more remote areas also so they don't have as many encounters with humans either. If a number of humans begin invading their territory? Very likely, more encounters between humans and the bears, and more attacks could occur."

He waited for her to ask what she needed to. She seemed on the edge of her seat now, concerned.

"Then if a woman is in the water, a polar bear would think she was a seal, and dinner, right?" Alicia asked.

A sudden chill slithered up Rob's spine. Why would Alicia even think of such a scenario? The image revisited him as if it was happening right now, in front of him, the light snow falling, her stricken look, her blue lips, and her gloved fingers clinging to the ice-covered bank until she couldn't hold on any longer. She was wearing the white parka and a white wool hat, no goggles, her blue eyes fixed on his eyes. Only he wasn't human. He was a polar bear. And she appeared terrified.

Casey finished his drink. "Hey, I think it's time to call it a night after that cheerful talk of killer bears and what everyone has to look forward to on our journey tomorrow." He gave Rob an annoyed look.

Rob wasn't going to sugarcoat the truth. Everyone needed to know when they were out in the wilderness, though the guides would try to protect them the best they could, everyone still had to watch out for themselves. He couldn't shake loose of the image that Alicia would be in real peril on this trip though.

"We'll drive you ladies back to the lodge," Edward said, frowning at Rob.

He knew when his brother returned, Edward would have something to say to him about scaring the women.

Alicia didn't make a move to leave. "I want to talk to Rob further." Her gaze remained steady on his.

"It's bound to be more gloom and doom," Edward warned.

"I'm a photojournalist. I try to keep an open mind." But Alicia sounded concerned.

Rob was surprised she'd want to stay. He really hoped she would go with the others so when Edward returned, he could have a private talk about what had happened. *If* Rob could even figure out what had happened between him and Alicia.

As soon as everyone said goodnight and left, Rob

took a seat across from Alicia, not sure what she wanted to talk about, but he didn't think it would be about the weather.

* * *

Alicia couldn't believe what she'd seen when she'd touched Rob. Icy cold chills still raced across her skin. The vision of her being in the ice-cold water, freezing to death as a polar bear tried to bite her still was vivid in her thoughts. She couldn't shake loose of the images, no matter how much she tried. The best defense was knowledge though, right?

"The weather shows it's clear," Alicia said to Rob, trying to resolve what she'd seen—the snow, the bear, the woman. Though she felt it was her, it couldn't be. It had to be a scene Rob had witnessed in the past. So, of course, the weather was clear for them. She'd been so rattled by the vision, she kept feeling that it was her in the water and not some other poor soul.

Raising his brows, Rob looked surprised to hear her mention the weather. "A freak snowstorm is coming."

Her lips parted in surprise. Wait, no, what she'd seen had to have happened in the past. How would he know a snowstorm was coming? "If it's a 'freak' snowstorm, how do you know about it? I checked the weather. There's no mention of any storm."

"They come up suddenly sometimes." He frowned. "Why were you so spooked when we touched?"

Because in that terrifying moment, she had seen herself in the water, freezing to death and a polar bear was trying to grab her with his teeth. She knew he had been trying to eat her. Well, it had to have been some other woman.

She only observed what others had been through. Was she witnessing some woman's death that Rob had seen? As a tour guide? A friend? Or had he had something to do with her being in the water? Alicia didn't believe so though. Not when a polar bear was trying to reach the woman.

Softly, sinking against the cushions, Alicia carefully watched Rob's guarded expression. "Did you feel a strange sensation between us when we touched?" She'd felt a shock and heat spread through her veins, something she'd never felt before when she'd touched an object or person and had a vision.

He drank up the rest of his margarita, then nodded. "Probably static electricity buildup."

She knew it was much more than that. Because as soon as she felt his touch, and the shock, and the heat, she saw the snow and the woman and the bear.

"Did someone you know fall into a frigid source of water and a polar bear attacked her?"

Rob's eyes widened fractionally, and she knew then he'd witnessed the horror, which was why she could see what had happened in his past. "What do you mean?"

he asked.

She rose from the couch and he quickly stood. She closed the gap between them and put her hand on his arm to see if she could envision any more details, to prove to him that she could see past events. She couldn't see anything further this time, but she couldn't help feeling the warmth of his arm under her touch, or breathe in his fresh, clean, very appealing scent. "A polar bear is trying to eat me if I don't freeze to death first. Well, not me. In the past, you must have seen someone fall into the water and a polar bear attempted to get to her. It must be someone you know or an event you've witnessed." A vision suddenly popped into her thoughts of Rob making love to her, and her lips parted in surprise. She quickly pulled her hand away from his arm.

Hot, passionate, under the sheets, kissing, naked, writhing against each other, desperate to have each other in the throes of lovemaking.

Rob's jaw hung slack. "Hell."

Now *that* had never happened to her. Seeing someone make love to someone. But Rob's reaction confused her too. Was the woman he'd lost in the water the one he'd made love to? A beloved girlfriend or wife?

"Do you believe in people having paranormal abilities?" Before Rob responded, Alicia said, "I can sense things that have happened to an individual if I touch them or something of theirs. Especially if it's something to do with emotion, passion, terror, or angst. I see the snowstorm, me falling into the ice-cold water, and a polar bear trying to grab for me and eat me and that's it. Except, it's not me. I only see past events. Sometimes I see them through someone else's eyes, and sometimes through the eyes of the person who is in trouble. In this case, through the eyes of the woman in the water. You had to witness it or you wouldn't be tied to the vision."

"And you envision us making love?" Rob was frowning down at her as if the notion perturbed him.

Unable to fathom how he could know, she just stared at him. "How...how would you know that? I mean, no, not *us* making love, someone in your past. And it came to mind. Into your thoughts. After you thought of the woman in the water. Though I've never seen anything like that before. Maybe the woman you were making love to was in the water? I only see what has happened. I can't see future events. Like when locating a missing child. I can't see where he's going, but only where he's been."

"Hell. I have future visions. I'm clairvoyant. I see things that will occur, not that have occurred."

She collapsed on the couch. "Oh...my...god." Then she frowned up at him. "But I divine facts from touching an object or a person who has something to do with the object. It's called psychometry. It doesn't always happen. I'd be a basket case if it did. If...if what you say is true, then you haven't had this...this experience before? If not, I don't understand how I could be seeing what you witness in the future. I've never done that before."

"Believe me, the woman in the water? I've never seen that happen to anyone before. It's something that happens later. During the snowstorm. I don't know when exactly. Whether it's while we're with our tour group or at some other time."

"Omigod," Alicia said under her breath, the chills whipping across her skin. "Who is the woman?" Alicia was afraid of what Rob would say because she was certain, at least as his vison appeared to her, who the woman was.

"You, Alicia. It's you." Rob ran his hands through his hair, looking frustrated. "Making love to you? That hasn't happened yet either. But, I don't mix pleasure with business. I don't get involved intimately with tourists. I'm not sure when or why that happens."

"Maybe you...you pull me from the water and warm me up and things get...a little out of hand?"

He smiled a smidgeon at that. Probably because from the vision, their actions got *way* out of hand.

She hoped he made love to her *after* the polar bear incident, which meant she survived the bear attack. She couldn't believe all this. No matter how many visions she'd seen over the years, this was something completely new to her, shocking and unbelievable. Future visions? Would it only happen when she touched Rob? "Does everyone know about your gift?"

"No. Just Edward and Casey."

"I understand how you feel. I kept my abilities secret for years, though I've helped with a couple of police mysteries recently. I was more concerned about being wrong in the cases than anything else."

"Were you? Wrong?"

"No. In both cases, I was much more right than wrong and helped the police find the murderer and the weapon he used and where he'd dumped the woman's body. In another, I knew just where a little boy had wandered off while camping with his family. I still don't advertise what I do, but I feel good about helping others when I can. What about you?"

"No one believes me. Like about the weather? I don't see past events. I see what's coming up."

She let out her breath, wondering how they could deal with this. "Are you going to tell Edward and Casey what you see this time?"

"Yeah. I have to."

"Can you change the course of things that you see occur in some future vision?" She again rose from the sofa and was ready to return to the lodge. She needed to digest all this news. She realized she was shaking a bit too. She thought witnessing past events could be terrifying at times. Future events? Maybe because she wasn't used to it, but that, to her, was even more terrifying. Well, not the making love part. That's all she wanted to think of—Rob's hot, sexy, naked body grinding against hers.

"I can't convince anyone the storm's coming. Because of that, I can't stop my brother and Casey from escorting the group on the tour. Everyone's taken the time off to be here. Everyone's paid their money. If a terrible blizzard was a sure thing, then yes, the guides could cancel. We can't otherwise."

"Are you ever wrong?" She was praying he was this time.

"I'm never positive about exact times or places. All I see is you in the water. I can't tell anything about the exact location to give me an idea of where we'll be at that point in time." He paused, frowning at her. "If you see what I see…"

"The accident has to do with me for certain, which means it will have to be during this excursion, don't you think?" She lifted her parka off a peg.

"I would think so." Rob helped her on with it, and she pulled on her gloves.

"You'll make love to me, proving to me that somehow I survived the terrifying experience," she finally said, hopeful that would be the case. That they didn't do it before she fell in the water.

"I told you that I don't have intimate relations with tour guests."

"Sure, not normally, but maybe there's another reason why you do. Because we had this...psychic connection and you did it to save my life."

He smiled a little, but then his expression turned to concern. "Maybe you should stay behind. I'll refund your money. The full amount. Your assistant can take all the pictures you need for your story."

She shook her head. "I doubt it would make any difference."

***

Rob pulled Alicia in for a kiss. No way was he going to make love to her right this minute, but hell, if he was going to go that far with her, there wasn't any reason not to kiss her. She was trembling a little, probably from the upset of learning what was bound to happen to her. As soon as she gave into the kiss, she was all heat and passion. Her need fueled his, her tongue sliding across his in a sexy way.

"You are so hot," she said, running her hands over his chest and in that instant, he wanted to slip her hands under his sweater and shirt, to allow them to slide against his bare skin. Just as he wanted to run his hands over her chest, to mold his fingers around her breasts, and feel her taut nipples beneath his thumbs.

They kissed again, their bodies rubbing against each other, stirring his more primal need to have her, his cock already fully aroused. He growled a little.

She smiled a little against his mouth, unaware of the way her pheromones tantalized his own, not when she was human and couldn't smell that intriguing part of their animal nature. As much as he really didn't want to pull away and end this between them now, he was about to when the front door opened.

Looking a little red-faced and like he wished he hadn't interrupted them, Edward smiled at them.

Rob couldn't believe he'd been so focused on Alicia, he hadn't even heard Edward pull into the garage. Rob was in the middle of the whole mess of dealing with the grizzly and now Alicia falling into the water. And Rob was making love to her. Now he had to warn his brother about his new visions and try to sort out how to deal with this. Though he wasn't mentioning the part about having sex with her.

"Don't tell me now you're ready to leave," Edward said, looking like he wondered if Alicia might just stay the night.

"I am. I can walk back to the lodge," Alicia said, as if she didn't want to make Rob or Edward have to drive her back.

"I wouldn't think of letting you walk back there. I'll

drive you." Edward looked at Rob as if to see if he wanted to do the honors.

"I'll clean up while you're gone. Besides, you're already dressed for the cold," Rob said, but it was more than that. He needed to pack more supplies than he'd planned to, so that he could take care of Alicia when they needed to.

"Night, Rob. I'll see you on the tour tomorrow," Alicia said. "We'll get through this. We have to."

Edward frowned at him. "See you in a few."

When Edward returned, Rob was finishing up packing another medical bag and extra emergency blankets, another pair of heavy sweats and thermal underwear, a tranquilizer gun, anything he could take with him to ensure Alicia survived the trip and to take care of Gary, if Rob could without just killing the SOB.

"What's going on between you and the lady?" Edward eyed the tranquilizer gun. "I take it that's for Gary."

"Yeah." Rob zipped up the bag and set it on the floor. "Alicia could see what I envisioned would happen."

"Hell, you can't be serious. She verified the storm and the grizzly?"

"No, not that part."

"Ah hell," Edward said. "There's another part?"

"She saw the snowstorm and a polar bear trying to

eat her."

Edward closed his gaping mouth. "The storm is going to hit us where we see the polar bears at the whale grave? What happened to the grizzly?"

"That's the vision I have. She saw the storm I envisioned, and somehow, she's fallen into the water. The polar bear that is attempting to rescue her—is me. She doesn't see the grizzly, and I sure as hell wasn't about to bring it up."

"But she sees the scenario as the polar bear is trying to eat her. *Hell.* Which makes perfect sense from a human's perspective." Edward's eyes rounded. "That's why she asked about bears killing humans? Why would you be wearing your fur coat to rescue her?"

"Because of the grizzly attack? And then I came to rescue her after fighting off Gary? That's all I can think of."

"You saw this too?"

"I saw her in the water and me coming for her, and she saw what I had envisioned. At least that's what I believe happened."

Edward paced. "The weather report still shows it's going to be clear. I'd cancel if there was even a hint of a storm coming in. But you're going to be with us the whole time? You don't plan to join us later, to come to the rescue as a bear so no one sees you shifting?"

"I'm there. I've always been there with the tour

group."

"Does she survive?" Edward was frowning at him now, worried.

"I don't know." Rob still had no intention of mentioning the part about making love to her. That could be before, not after the incident.

"Wait, you said she can actually see *your* visions? Is she clairvoyant like you?"

"No, Edward. Not normally. Well, from what she said, never. She perceives things that have already happened, unlike me who sees things before they happen. For some reason, she envisioned what I'd witnessed too."

"I can't believe she can do what you are able to do. Hell, you've finally met your match."

"I don't know if she'll always be able to see what I envision. But yeah, we both have abilities." That didn't change the other half of the equation. "She's still not one of us."

"Okay, so I say we don't worry about the impending disaster between you and Gary and Alicia and the water at this point," Edward said. "Each day we'll check the weather, and if it changes drastically, we'll sit tight. How's that sound to you?"

"That's just what I was thinking. Maybe, for once, after knowing ahead of time what's bound to happen, we can actually take some measures to prepare for it better."

"Right. If we see the storm coming, we'll stay at the lodge or cabins until it blows over. Did you see us near the cabins or any other recognizable landmarks?" Edward removed his parka and cap and hung them on a peg on the wall.

"It's a whiteout. Except for a grizzly bear's teeth and claws, I didn't see much else. I just heard people yelling and screaming and running in every direction. In Alicia's case, I didn't see the grizzly, or anyone, just saw her in the water, and she's about ready to slip underneath its surface, she's so cold."

"Are you in the water or out of it?"

"From the angle that I'm at when I see her, I have to be in it."

"So you dove in after her."

"I have to have. All right. We've got emergency medical equipment. And I'm packing extra clothes to dress her in. I put that in the medical pack that has the two emergency blankets. The rest will be under the first bench seat in my van. If she needs rescuing, you grab this bag and rush to where we are." Rob pointed to the red and white bag. "We'd better get some sleep."

"Yeah, sure. I'll call and tell Casey the news. Night."

"Night, Edward." Rob went to his bedroom, stripped, and got into bed. He'd left his laptop on by accident, and a message dinged its arrival. He growled a little, then got out of bed and was about to turn off the laptop, but what if the message was important?

He checked and it was from Ben. "Don't have too much fun on the trip this time. Did she email you yet? She asked for your email."

Alicia? Had she asked Ben for it, or had he just offered it to her? Rob suspected Ben had given her the information. He checked his email and sure enough there was one from Alicia: Look forward to seeing you tomorrow. Don't worry. Your secret is safe with me. We'll get through this somehow. Night.

He turned off his laptop and climbed into bed. He thought of what an odd pairing that would make. A clairvoyant and someone who dealt in psychometry. Would it create lots more problems between them? Or would it be nice to share visions with someone who understood what he was going through, just like he could understand more of what she was dealing with?

Yet, the point really was moot. She was human and he was a shifter. That was the end of speculating any further about hooking up with someone else who had a gift similar to his.

All Rob could focus on now was how he could keep Alicia from falling into the frigid water in the first place.

CHAPTER 5

Early that morning, Rob and the others packed up the three vans with people, bags, and supplies after having a group breakfast of omelets, sausages, and pancakes. Rob and Alicia had been quiet while Edward and Casey had talked about Alaska and where they were going first.

Then they were on their way for the first part of their journey. He had every intention of ensuring Alicia was riding in his van before they took off on the road that morning. She looked like she had the same idea, sticking close to him. Where she went, so did her friend Judi. He planned to stay near Alicia always during this trip and wondered if her friend knew about Alicia's ability and if so, had she told her what she had witnessed?

"Weather looks good still," Alicia said to him. "I

thought we might check on your weather predictions somewhere on the way to see if anything has changed."

"I'll keep checking my phone, if we have enough of a signal. If I have a vision, I'll share it with you." So far, Rob hadn't seen any more visions.

"Okay, but if we can't get any reception, we might have to use...the other method," Alicia warned. "You know...touching."

He smiled at her. He wasn't used to a human woman who was so plucky. "That's the only reason, right?"

She chuckled.

The tour guides drove the three vans and began their journey. Rob told his group, "Alaska is bigger than Texas, and is nearly 590,000 square miles. That means about a fifth of the size of the contiguous United States. We have 44,000 miles of coastland. You can see the Alaska Peninsula, Kodiak, and the Aleutians in the far south. Southwestern Alaska, Northern Alaska, and Interior Alaska are some of the major areas. The black bears are mostly in the forested areas of the state. The grizzlies, or brown bears, mostly live along the southern coast where they feed on salmon and are bigger. They also live in the northern and interior parts of Alaska. The grizzlies are found throughout Alaska, except for a few islands. The black bears avoid the area the grizzlies make home. You'll see caribou in the northern forests, arctic tundra and mountain tundra.

"What about moose?" Judi asked.

"They wander into neighborhoods sometimes. They live in the spruce forests, river valleys, freshwater marshes, stands of willows in South Central and Interior Alaska and Southeast Alaska. Mountain goat and Dall sheep are also seen in the mountains, but in winter, they seek the high forests for protection and food such as mountain hemlock and blueberry bushes. Muskox are on Seward Peninsula, and a couple of other islands. Some Greenland muskox had been transplanted to Alaska for fear they'd become extinct. And we have wolves. They can be found from the rain forests of the Southeast panhandle to the Arctic tundra."

They traveled to the Tongass National Forest and to Ketchikan.

"Here we have black bears and wolves. Mountain goats and Sitka black-tailed deer are prevalent. We often see bald eagles and over 100 species of migrating birds. Orca and humpback whales, sea lions, seals, sea otters, river otters, and porpoises all swim in the waters here," Rob told the group as they stopped to take a break and see the spruce grouse in one of the trees.

Black spruce, white spruce, quaking birch, larch, balsam popular, and willow filled the boreal forest.

"Most birds migrate," Rob explained as they got out of the vans and took pictures. The guides often took turns talking about the flora and fauna and history of the various regions they were visiting. "They're here in the spring to nest, and then hang around to feed in the summer, and then migrate to warmer climates."

"But the grouse hangs around?" Judi asked.

"Yeah and the ptarmigan. Now some animals hibernate—brown bears, black bears, marmots, and even jumping mice. You'll see wolves, foxes, lynx, caribou, moose, all sorts of animals out foraging for food or hunting for it. The wolves, lynxes, and foxes have thick coats to protect them from the cold. Voles and ermine use the snow to insulate them from the cold. Some of the predators can capture their prey easier when everything is covered in snow. Some of the animals change colors to camouflage them in the changing colors of the boreal forest from greens, browns, yellows, reds to whites and grays. Many of the animals that live in the snow have adapted to be able to move more easily on top of the snow. The polar bear has fur on its paw pads and so does the Arctic wolf."

"Omigod," Judi suddenly said, pointing into the shadowy woods. "There's a wolf!"

Rob smiled at the mated, gray wolf pair.

Everyone began snapping pictures and Rob folded his arms and shook his head at the gray wolf, Roger Wolff, and his mate, Bethany, hiding a little off to his left behind a spruce. Some of the local wolf shifters would appear here to show off their fur coats to the tourists, knowing the MacMathan tour group always stopped to take pictures here. The wolves weren't just having fun either. Edward made sure that if any of the wolf shifters showed up to give their tour group a thrill and a photo opportunity, he or she got a free meal at the tavern for adding to the fun for the tourists.

Then the wolves' twins showed up, around five years of age in human years, so as wolves, they were small, just wolf pups, but they really added to the stop and made everyone's day.

"Oh, oh, baby wolves," Judi said, and that meant tons more picture taking. "How cute."

Even Alicia was quiet as she continued to snap her pictures, looking just as thrilled. He was glad the wolves had taken her mind off a hungry polar bear and ice cold water.

A few months back, a pack of thirty of the wolf shifters had showed up, scaring the tourists to pieces, and so Rob and his brother had to tell them that if they came, limit it to a couple of wolves, or a family like the one that appeared for them today. He suspected the wolves checked with their aunt or uncle to learn their schedule each time. Delays would occur while the group toured so the wolves would never know exactly when they would arrive at certain spots on the tour.

The snow leopards had joked that they were going

to join the wolves sometime to give the tourists a photo op of them. All Rob would say was that they'd better not. It was one thing to see the wolves; snow leopards out in this part of the world, never.

Then the wolves moved off and disappeared into the woods. Rob figured he and his partners would never have moved the tour group back in the vans otherwise.

"Have you seen them here often? The same ones? They almost seem tame," Alicia said to Rob.

"These wolves, yes. They're curious. Still wild. Still unpredictable. Thankfully, we haven't had anyone shooting at them so they've been safe enough."

"They are beautiful. But they're gray wolves. Where are the Arctic wolves? Farther north?" she asked.

"In truth, Arctic wolves are gray wolves, but yeah, they live farther north. Sometimes you can see them, and Arctic foxes too. We'll be seeing muskoxen on part of the journey." Sometimes one of the Arctic wolf shifters came out to see them. But that was rarer.

"Keep watching. You can observe deer here, bears, moose."

"Can't wait to see them," Judi said.

They stopped to eat at a seafood restaurant and everyone ordered their salmon steaks and other seafood choices, then began to discuss the fun they'd had so far. Rob saw Alicia looking at her phone again, checking the weather, he suspected.

In just a few days, they would see the place where the Arctic Circle started. It was an imaginary line that defined the southernmost part of the Arctic region, but everyone who arrived there would take pictures of themselves standing next to the sign marking the Arctic Circle, just to say they'd been there, done that.

"That is the Land of the Midnight Sun," Edward said, the two blonds clinging to his every word as if he was a movie star and not just a tour guide, amusing Rob as he dipped his shrimp into cocktail sauce.

Seated next to Alicia, Rob finished his shrimp and placed his hand on her shoulder and rubbed it. She looked up at him, waiting to see what he had to say.

He'd been trying to see any future visions on his own, but nothing had come to him. He finally decided to see if he could make a connection with Alicia to see anything further, not really wanting her to have to see the vision again as terrifying as it was. But if they could get more details to pinpoint the location, maybe they could be better prepared.

She smiled up at him, looking appreciative that he was trying to make the connection, but he saw nothing of the future, and she shook her head, indicating that she hadn't seen anything either.

After they left the restaurant, they headed to the dock where they'd take a boat trip to another location to go kayaking. They were outfitted with paddle jackets, rain pants, rubber boots, and dry-bags for cameras or other valuables. Then they took the boat ride to the area where they picked up the kayaks and were given an orientation and safety briefing.

This was one of the activities Rob had worried about concerning Alicia. Anytime she was near the water, he grew more concerned. He kayaked with her, while Casey teamed up with Judi.

The guide pointed out pictographs on some of the rock formations along the way as they saw the mountains rising three-thousand feet above, the numerous islands, and the forests.

They saw a black wolf in the woods and Alicia quickly pulled out her camera to take some pictures. The wolf wasn't any they knew, so probably a wolf that was all wolf, not a shifter.

They finally pulled their kayaks above the tide zone where they would get out and begin their hike up a trail through the forest. The shoreline was slippery and rocky as they climbed five-hundred feet. They had a snack of sandwiches and chips at a stopping point, before heading up the trail to learn about the temperate forest—hemlocks, spruce, cedar, and pine trees.

Alicia was taking pictures along the way, sticking close to Rob, as if their connection meant he would protect her or warn her if something bad was going to happen. He *would* protect her, and everyone else he could, if it came to that. Edward stayed behind them, ensuring neither Rob nor Alicia were ever out of his sight.

"I've loved everything so far," Alicia told Rob and gasped when she saw a mink disappear into the woods.

"Did you capture a shot of it?" Rob asked.

"No. He moved way too quickly."

They finally headed back to the kayaks and paddled to where they could pick up the boat to take the twenty-minute ride to the dock, and they'd drive to the lodging where they'd stay the night.

At the dock, they got into their vans, drove to a travel stop, and picked up gas. Most everyone was still inside shopping and taking a bathroom break when Casey and Edward joined Rob.

"Have you seen anything more about the storm?" Casey asked.

"No. Nothing. So far," Rob said, still filling his gas tank.

Edward glanced at the travel stop as the tour group picked up post cards and other gift items to take home with them. "Maybe on the return trip then?"

"Maybe."

"If you have to deal with Gary, one of us will protect Alicia," Casey said.

Rob hoped it would be enough, but he feared it wouldn't be, not if he was rescuing her in the water as a polar bear.

***

That night, the tour group was staying at three separate cabins, though they always shared meals at the one that Rob and Edward roomed in, taking turns to make the meals. Alicia and Judi were staying in the same cabin as them.

In the morning, they had the day to hike to view glaciers and take photos. They could hike at their own pace or stay with the tour guides, so everyone had decided which group they'd go with—slow-paced, medium, and fast-paced hikers. Though that could change in the morning, depending on how fit everyone felt. The five and a half hour kayaking and hiking adventure had been strenuous for today's activity.

Rob had been watching Alicia as she helped Judi and two of the men on the tour prepare a dinner of smoked salmon chowder, green beans, berry cobbler, and chocolate bread —their turn to make the meal.

The others were visiting fireside, drinking wine, but she noted Rob's concerned expression while he observed her. While everyone else was relaxed, he was tense. Worried. She was sure she knew the reason why. Every day that passed brought them closer to the time when the vision would become reality. She'd been trying to focus on sightseeing, picture taking, and tonight, preparing the best dinner ever, anything else but the inevitable. She still couldn't believe she could witness a future vision that Rob would have. She kept wondering if they might share any more visions like that, hopefully that weren't life-threatening.

They finally served up dinner, and Rob sat next to Alicia, as he always did. They appeared to be a couple already, though she had told Judi there was nothing to it. Judi knew they were returning to San Antonio and that would be the end of any blossoming romance Alicia might have had with Rob. If he'd been one of the tourists and lived in San Antonio, that would have been different.

Or not. She wasn't sure if seeing his visions and her own was a good thing.

Throughout dinner, Rob was quieter than usual. She didn't try to draw him into conversation. Nobody did. It was like they knew he was brooding or moody about something. But his brother, Casey, and she knew the turmoil he was feeling.

Edward and Casey were anxious too, but they covered up their concerns better. Or maybe Rob just didn't feel the need to try and hide how he was feeling. She did worry that he might have seen more and didn't want to tell her—that she had succumbed to the cold and hadn't made it.

After another group of four people cleaned up the dishes, everyone but Alicia and Rob went outside to photograph the northern lights as the sky was perfectly clear this evening and the magical lights were in full display tonight.

"All right, I don't think this will work this time either, but the longer we travel, the more it's been on my mind. Let's see if we can learn anything more about this situation, if you wouldn't mind," Rob said.

"Yeah. Absolutely." The whole day Alicia had hoped Rob would try again to see if their psychic connection would reveal anything further.

What she hadn't expected was for him to pull her into a body hug, and then to begin to kiss her like they were a couple. Like she wasn't leaving in a short while to return to San Antonio. Omigod, had he seen her die? And he felt horrible about it?

Before she could ask him what was wrong, he was kissing her deeply, and she wanted him to make love to her, yet she didn't. What if they made love like they had envisioned, and then she surrendered to the cold death, and that was the end of her?

His tongue caressed hers, and he continued to kiss her and hug on her, even though her mind was sifting through a million different scenarios. Rather than question him further, and not seeing any visions of his or her own, she was starting to believe what she'd seen was just a nightmare, only it couldn't be. Not when she'd been perfectly awake when she'd touched Rob and seen the vision. And he'd witnessed it too.

She threw herself into the kiss. Not in a million years would she have guessed she'd rather be with someone else with paranormal abilities, and kissing him, than taking pictures of a phenomenon she'd never see again when she was back home in Texas. If she managed to survive and return there.

Her arms wrapped around Rob's neck, she rubbed her body against his, wishing they were wearing lots less clothes, though even now she could feel his hard arousal pressing against her. "Do you see the end for me?"

"No," Rob said, shaking his head. "Come on." Rob smiled at her, handing her parka to her, and pulled on his own. "Grab your camera. You don't want to miss this. We'll even be in a better position in a couple of days, but you might as well get all the shots you can. Just in case. You never know."

"You can read minds." She didn't believe he could, but she figured he'd smile and he did. "You're worried about what's going to happen, aren't you?"

He shoved on his hat. "Hell, yeah, but I don't see your death."

"Close to it?"

"I don't see the end."

"What do you see?"

He let out his breath. "I see your gloved fingers lose

hold of the icy bank where you're clinging for dear life."

That didn't sound reassuring. She finished zipping up her parka and pulled on her hat and gloves, then grabbed her camera. "All right. I want to share the room with you, but I don't. I want to make love to you, but I don't."

"I feel the same way."

"Okay, then put that thought on hold. If I survive..."

He nodded and wrapped her scarf around her neck, then kissed her mouth again. It was like sealing a bargain with a kiss. She'd hold him to it, if she survived. But she thought she wouldn't need to insist if she did make it.

The two of them went outside then. The sky was filled with wide ribbons of green, pink, and purple lights that looked like a wizard had cast about his magical wand and painted the sky. Enraptured, she quickly pulled away from Rob, lost in the beauty of the lights as she began taking photos.

"Did you see anything when we touched this time?" he asked, leaning close, in her space, his warm breath, frosty in the cold air.

"You're going to kiss me," she said. Not that she would see that in anything he envisioned or that she had seen in her own. But she knew it was inevitable again. Despite his reluctance to get close to someone in his tour group, he wasn't immune to her. And they did have an unusual connection.

"I'd say that was a good bet."

She smiled and continued to take pictures, moving around to get different shots.

He stayed with her, keeping her company, but also helping to block some of the frigid breeze.

"We probably shouldn't keep doing it." He sounded like he really believed it.

"Just a kiss?" She snorted.

"What if our abilities create some kind of cataclysmic reaction one of these times? No telling how dangerous it could be."

She laughed, then grew serious. "The whiteout and the problem with the polar bear are the only real danger to me."

"You don't see the grizzly bear attacking?"

"What? A grizzly attacks me too? Great. Just great. But...they're hibernating by now, aren't they?"

"They can come out. Just like when someone is sleeping, his sleep is disturbed, he gets up, then settles back down to go back to sleep. They can be unsettled. Particularly this early in the fall."

"You really see problems with a grizzly bear? But I didn't see any vison of it. Just a polar bear. Are you sure you're not mistaken? Do you see a polar bear too?"

"A grizzly. I know one when I see one. Dark brown, not white."

"So…" She frowned at him. "You don't see me in the water?"

"I do. I just don't see a polar bear trying to eat you."

"Well, believe me, it is."

Confused about what Rob had seen, Alicia continued to take a ton of pictures, then she slipped her camera into her bag and slung the bag over her shoulder. "I checked the weather report. No snow in the forecast, but maybe some rain tomorrow."

"Rain?" Rob pulled out his phone and checked the weather. "No rain. Sunny, cold, and clear."

She pulled out her own phone and saw the same thing on a different weather site. "Okay, then I must have envisioned I'd seen the new weather report saying it was going to rain. Or maybe it's a past event, because that's what I normally see. I didn't see the date."

"Did you see anything else? The ten-day forecast? Rain turning to snow?"

"No. I just saw the little icon of a cloud with rain falling, but nothing to say how high the chance was for rainfall. Nothing to indicate it was going to switch to snow showers either. Or the actual temperature. I just saw the raincloud. You really see a grizzly? What's he doing?"

"Attacking me."

Alicia's jaw hung agape. "No."

"I survive. I chase him off."

"Before or after I have to fend off a hungry polar bear?"

"I don't know. I'm surprised you didn't see what I'd envisioned."

"Maybe I can only see what happens to me in your visions and in that case, the grizzly bear didn't touch me. And...and that's why I see you making"—she glanced around to make sure no one was close enough to hear—"love to me."

"I hadn't thought of that. So for me, I can't see family or friends that are close to me now. But for you, you can see my visions if they have to do with you."

"Sounds like it." She shivered, partly from the cold, partly from the new vision about the grizzly Rob had shared with her.

"Ready to go back inside?"

"Sure. The lights are fading. They sure are beautiful."

Everyone was beginning to go to their assigned cabins for the night.

Rob and Alicia went inside the cabin, and she pulled her scarf off. He took off his parka and helped her out of hers. And then he pulled her into his arms for another kiss, she thought. She'd hoped he wouldn't really be put off with the notion that they might have some earth-shattering reaction because of their abilities if they kissed. She wrapped her arms around his waist and kissed him back, felt the heat of his mouth warming hers, his body heating hers up. Then their tongues tasted and caressed before they had to come up for air.

The door shut and Casey smiled. "Night, folks."

"Night," Edward said. "Oh, did you want me to bunk with Casey tonight?" Casey was staying in one of the other cabins tonight with the other guests.

"No." Rob gave his brother a look to cool it, while he pulled away from Alicia and then said to her, "We didn't combust."

Three more people moved off to their rooms, including Alicia's redheaded roommate.

"Speak for yourself," Alicia said, smiling, patted his chest, and headed for her room.

"Didn't see anything this time?" Rob asked, walking right behind her to his own room.

"Oh, I saw plenty. Only it was a lot steamier."

He smiled and shook his head. "I didn't see anything except—just felt a whole hell of a lot."

"Good. Maybe we're both wrong about what we think will happen. Night, Rob. I've had a lovely time this whole trip so far."

"We aim to please and keep our guests safe."

"You sure do." Then she entered her room before she kissed him again and tried to change his mind about Edward rooming with Casey so she could join Rob instead. She closed the door and saw Judi already lying on her bed, smiling at her.

"He's so hot. The other tour guides and a couple of the guys on the tour are too. I really thought when Edward offered to bunk with Casey, Rob would have jumped at the chance to be with you."

"He has strong principles. No mixing business with pleasure. I'm a client, not a local. What if we really hit it off and then in a few days, I left, never to return?" Alicia pulled off her clothes and slipped into warm, flannel pajamas.

"Well, that kiss you shared says otherwise. What do you think of living here permanently?"

"It would take some getting used to. I mean, I love it. It's so different from home, and I can't wait to see more. But days with no nights and nights without days? And all the months of the cold and snow? I was reading that in January in Fairbanks they had eighteen to twenty feet of snow. Not eighteen to twenty inches, but feet! My fence in San Antonio is six feet tall. Can you imagine the snow being three times taller? I'm used to gardening most of the year. Early spring flowers, late fall flowers. Even winter flowers surviving the whole year because of the mild winters. No snow. The heat can be tiresome, but I can't even imagine getting used to that much snow."

"Me either. Still, Rob seems to be genuinely interested in having some alone time with you. Maybe it still will happen."

It would, because Alicia had seen that it would...but not tonight.

***

"What was it like? Any news flashes?" Edward asked Rob as they settled into their beds.

"Nope. Just the normal, girl-kisses-guy scenario."

"Looked like a hell of a lot more than that to me. I've seen you kiss other women before and there's something more going on between the two of you. Though I knew it would never work out, being as you're a badass polar bear and she's not. Besides, she's from San Antonio, if you didn't know. Even if you weren't what you are, I doubt she'd be comfortable relocating up here."

"No sense in speculating about it." Rob turned out his lamp.

"I was thinking about the grizzly attack. Have you had a run-in with Gary that I don't know about it?"

"Not me."

"You haven't seen anything else since the first time you envisioned it?"

"No. But Alicia saw a rainstorm. It might not be coming up, or it might be some past event. When we both looked at different weather sites on our phone, there's nothing in the forecast but clear skies and cold."

"She envisioned it then?"

"I guess so. She didn't see the location or the day of the week. I'm not completely sure how it works for her."

"Okay." Edward turned off his lamp. "Maybe we'll still have more warning."

Rob pulled his covers over his shoulder.

"She's a live one," Edward said.

She sure was. And Rob sure as hell hoped she stayed that way.

CHAPTER 6

The next morning it began raining. Just a light rain, but Alicia shared a worried look with Rob. Even Edward and Casey appeared to know something about their concern. They seemed just as worried, so she suspected Rob had told them about what she'd seen regarding the weather report.

Despite the light rain, everyone headed out on the hiking trip, their gear keeping them dry.

"Do you have something to protect us if the polar bear attacks?" Alicia asked Rob.

Rain began to mix with large snowflakes and bits of ice.

"Yeah. Noisemakers."

"Even though we said to hike at your own pace," Edward told some of the younger men, "we don't want you to get lost. If the weather turns bad, we'll need to head straight back to the cabins."

"I'm going with them," Casey said. "No worries. Just watch out for moose, bears—"

"And wolves?" one of the men asked, as they headed out.

"No. They really aren't much of a problem. Muskox can be dangerous too."

Edward took the next group of hikers who were walking a bit faster while Rob stayed with the slower group. One of the blonds was with Casey's group, the other with Edward's.

Rob explained the typography and where they were headed. He hoped they could reach the glacier where they could get some great pictures.

"This is so great," Judi said. "Real snow. I can't wait to show everyone back home in south Texas."

As long as it didn't turn into a whiteout. Rob tried to get them to pick up their pace. He put his arm around Alicia's shoulders and leaned down to speak to her privately. "I want you to stay away from any water sources."

"It's happening now. I can feel you're worried."

"I don't know, but the fact that it's starting to snow, and that we're going to be near the water, that concerns me."

"We'll be near other water sources on this trip."

"Yeah, so we may have nothing to worry about

today."

Everyone but Alicia was taking pictures and it was so unlike her, Rob said, "You might as well take some photos of the snowcapped mountains and like Judi said, it's fun having snowy photos to show to your family and friends back home."

"My camera," Alicia suddenly said, eyeing it. "It's waterproof but do you think it would survive the frigid waters here, if I fall into it?"

"I think you need to just worry about you, if that happens."

Then she brightened. "The chance that a polar bear would show up around here would probably be slim, right?"

He smiled. She was right if the polar bear was all bear and not a shifter.

Then she frowned. "But grizzlies can be anywhere."

"That's right, on both accounts."

The snow began falling at a faster rate and everyone picked up their pace then, afraid to miss seeing the glacier if the weather got too bad. And Rob *did* have a bad feeling about this. Ominous. He just knew that somewhere along the way, he was going to run into Gary, one pissed-off grizzly bear.

When they finally reached the glacier where everyone was switching off to get their pictures taken in front of the ice floes and even where they could climb between caverns of blue ice, snow flurries slowed to a dusting. The sun even peeked through the clouds. They were able to get some great shots and the stress Rob was feeling began to ease up.

Everyone was thrilled, chattering about the beauty of the region.

Alicia asked Rob, "Can you take some pictures of me? I usually avoid getting in the shots, but if I don't, no one will believe I actually was standing between the fissure in the massive glacier."

"Yeah, sure."

She climbed in between the shards of immense ice where the frozen water glistened. Where she was standing, the ridges of ice on either side of her towered to five feet above her. She looked so diminutive compared to the massive ridges of cold ice, her cheeks red, her lips smiling. He snapped several pictures of her as she gave him different poses. Cute, energetic, humorous, and sexy. And then her roommate climbed down to join her for a couple of shots for posterity's sake.

He helped the ladies out of the crevice after that so another couple of guys could get some shots. Then Rob and Alicia stood overlooking the bank of the blue-green lake, a slight breeze rippling the water's surface, snow-coated mountains off in the distance.

"It stopped snowing," he said and was glad for it.

She looked skyward. "Still looks like we could get more snow."

Only about an inch of snow had fallen, but she was right. Nimbostratus clouds were beginning to form. They were thick, low clouds and were beginning to create a dense bank over the water and mountains that could produce a steady snow.

After everyone took as many pictures of the glaciers as they wanted, they started to hike back. Again, the fastest group headed out with Casey.

"We'll start the meal," Casey said, which was the way they always worked it. Whoever was stuck with the slowest group of tourists, when they were on a hike like this, ended up coming in just in time to warm up and eat. But then they cleaned up after the meal too.

The tourists didn't have to cook or clean, but the group had never had anyone on the tour who didn't want to pitch in and help. Sharing brought everyone in the tour group closer. Rob believed that he and his brother and their friend had one of the best jobs in the world.

"Looks like we'll be at the tail end again," Alicia said privately to Rob.

"You're welcome to go with one of the faster groups if you'd like." Rob didn't want her feeling like she had to walk back with the slower group, though he really didn't want her out of his sight either.

Two of the men in the slowest group were older, having more difficulty with the cold. One had stopped to light up a cigarette a few times, which had slowed him down. Rob wasn't sure why Judi was staying with this group. She kept walking faster, then slowing down, waiting for the others to catch up, sometimes taking pictures of the scenery to give her something to do.

Alicia looped her arm through Rob's, not as a sign she wanted to cozy up to him, he didn't think. He believed she thought she might see something more that he envisioned. Maybe about the grizzly bear that she hadn't seen any sign of. He hadn't had any visions since the first ones though.

"Omigod." Her heartbeat rapid, she suddenly pulled away from him and stared at nothing in the distance.

"What do you see?" he asked, concerned.

She took a steadying breath. "I see the grizzly bear, or at least its teeth and claws and nose. That's what you saw?" She shuddered, her eyes wide with terror. She took hold of his arm and began walking again. "God, he's even scarier than the polar bear. How can you know you survive his attack?"

"I'm bigger than him." Rob frowned at himself for making the dumb statement. As a polar bear, he was bigger than the grizzly. Not as a man. But the fact that Alicia could see what he saw, made him forget she wasn't a shifter like them.

***

Alicia took a steadying breath. "You must be standing on top of something. You're right. You're taller than him when he attacks. But, Rob, the way he comes after you, he's bound to...to hurt you really bad. Aren't you concerned about it?"

"I'll do what I have to do. Yeah, I'm concerned. But I can't stop it from happening. I just have to do whatever I can to get him to leave."

The clouds began to gather again and the snow began to fall in larger flakes all at once.

"It's snowing again," Alicia said, as if she needed to tell him that. She checked her phone for the weather forecast, but she had no bars, indicating she didn't have any signal this time.

Rob pulled out his phone and didn't have any either.

"We should pick up the pace," she said, really worried about coming face to face with two huge bears now. In both cases, she saw it was snowing. If it wasn't snowing, they should be safe. But now that wasn't the case.

"We are moving faster." Rob had instantly begun to walk faster, to hurry his group along.

They had a two-and-a-half-mile hike and the other two groups were well out of sight. The snow fell heavier now and the wind began to blow. Everyone put on googles and moved closer together to keep in sight of each other.

Then they saw something moving toward them in the mist of snow ahead.

"My brother," Rob said to his small group with relief filling his voice. "Where's your group?" Rob shouted to his brother.

"Casey and his group waited up for us, and he's taking them all in. I returned to ensure the rest of you make it back safely." Edward waved his phone. "I tried texting and calling you to let you know I was headed to your location, but there's no signal."

Alicia suspected that Edward worried this group was going to run into trouble in the snow and that's why he had returned to help them. She was glad he had. She hoped that she and Rob were wrong about the visions. Because she and he had now had the same one, she was afraid it would come to pass.

Then Edward surprised her. "Keep heading in that direction. I need to talk to Rob for a second."

She couldn't believe they'd send them into the blinding snow alone. Before she could even speculate about what was going on between the brothers as she and the rest of the group continued to trek on, hoping they didn't deviate from their course accidentally, Edward was running to catch up to them.

Alicia glanced back to see where Rob was. Shocked, she saw that he had vanished in the thick curtain of snow.

***

As soon as Edward told Rob he'd spied Gary Spitzer in the blizzard headed their way, Rob knew there'd be trouble. It wasn't just the fact the grizzly bear shifter was in the area, but the whole setup was too similar to what he'd envisioned. Grizzly attacks him, whiteout conditions. The grizzly shifter was big, cantankerous, and always itching for a fight, even on a good day. All Edward said was he'd received word on his phone from Ben back at the tavern, right before Edward lost the connection, to watch out for the bear. Gary's girlfriend had just birthed mixed white and brown bear cubs, which meant she'd been with a polar bear and Gary was pissed. Any polar bear that came into his territory was fair game and he was ready to put them six feet under, even though Rob and his brother and Casey were not from here, but from White Bear. They didn't think any of the polar bears from there were responsible.

The only way to deal with the grizzly was fighting him bear to bear and hoping Gary would break off the attack and give it up. And that neither of them were badly injured in the fight. Far enough out of sight of the tour group, Rob speedily stripped, called on the need to shift, and felt his muscles warming as he took on the shape of his much larger bear form. Standing like a man in a thick, white fur coat, he listened, smelled the air for any sign of the grizzly, before Rob heard screaming and yelling in terror up ahead. Damn it. He hated how his visions always came true.

Rob lunged forward at a run, heading for the grizzly, hoping to stop him before he hurt anyone. Some bear shifters would go into such a rage, they didn't care who they hurt and would lash out at anyone. Even if Gary only concentrated on polar bear shifters, Rob's brother was at risk in his human form. The grizzly could easily kill any of them.

What Rob witnessed next made his blood boil with rage. He saw red as the bear took a swipe at Edward, knocking him down into the accumulating snow. Edward lay still, his head bleeding as Rob raced to join the bear, tearing into the grizzly before Gary could take another swipe at Rob's brother.

Rob managed to knock Gary back, forcing him away from his brother. He was in just as much of a rage, ready to kill the grizzly.

Gary snarled at Rob, his lips pulled back from his teeth, showing off his sharp canines. Claws slashed at Rob as he tackled the bear with his bigger body and knocked the grizzly onto his back. Gary roared. Rob attacked him, biting at his neck and ear, thrashing with his powerful forearms, relentlessly, growling, and pursuing. The grizzly got on all four paws and backed up. Rob lunged at him, knowing in the back of his mind that he needed to shift, dress, and see to his brother's injuries and find his scattered tour group before they lost their way in the snow and wilderness.

Rob hadn't wanted to permanently take Gary down until he attacked Edward and could have killed him. If the grizzly didn't back off, he'd leave Rob no choice. Time was running out. Rob had to ensure Edward and the others were safe.

Gary attacked again, swiping at Rob, but it was more of a half-hearted attempt to show just how angry he was at polar bear shifters in general. Roaring in anger, Rob tore into him again, telling him in no uncertain terms to back the hell off and leave them alone or he would kill him.

This time, Gary moved off slowly, turned his head and growled, then ran off into the blinding snow.

Hell, Rob feared Alicia was freezing to death in frigid water and was about ready to slip underneath its surface. He'd never seen any indication that his own brother was going to be injured though. Then again, he never could see visons of happenings that occurred to family members or close friends after Ben broke his arm.

Rob tore off then, searching for where he'd left his damn clothes, finally locating them half buried in the snow. He quickly shifted into his human form and then dressed as fast as he could. He hated shifting in the cold like this. He zipped up his parka, pulled on his hat, then he ran as fast as he could back to where Edward was. He saw Alicia sitting in the snow with her arms wrapped around Edward, using her body to warm his, the wound on his forehead already bandaged and his face covered with his scarf to keep him warm.

Rob thought the world of her for going to Edward's aid and not abandoning him like the others did.

Rob now suspected her vision of him coming for her as a polar bear wasn't supposed to happen this trip. One near catastrophe was enough. At least he hoped she wouldn't suddenly fall into the water.

When she saw him, she looked relieved, though he assumed she'd drill him about where he'd gone to and why he'd disappeared. Rob had already worked out a half plausible story.

"Alicia, Edward," he called out, running to join them. "Where are the others?"

"I don't know. They ran off. Your brother's badly injured. Where's the grizzly?"

"I chased him off. But it doesn't mean he won't come back if he still is irritated about us being here." Hopefully not, but if Gary was angry enough, he could come back and try to take Rob out as a human, just like he'd injured Edward.

"What about the others?" Alicia asked.

Rob helped bring his brother to consciousness, joking with him. "Bear's gone. You can get moving now."

Edward gave him a lopsided smile. Edward groaned as Rob got him to his feet. "The others?" he asked, his voice shaky.

"I've got to get you and Alicia back to the cabin. Casey and I will go looking for them after that, if we don't find them along the way."

They'd never lost anyone on their adventure tours before. Then again, they'd never had a grizzly attack them on a tour before either.

"She doesn't mind that you're a polar bear?" Edward asked, his words still unsteady.

Rob didn't like hearing the way Edward's voice sounded, and he didn't want him giving away their secrets either. Not that she'd believe Edward. She probably thought he was delirious, just talking nonsense, or trying to make a joke.

"You mean as in jovial and huggable? They are beautiful to look at, but not for one moment would I believe they're anything but wild and wholly unpredictable," Alicia said, her arm under Edward's for support while Rob held him around the waist, and they began the trek back to the cabin again.

Rob and she called out for the other two men and her roommate over the blowing wind and snow. Then they heard the two men calling far off in the distance. Both had gone the wrong way.

"Stay here with Edward, and keep calling for Judi," Rob told Alicia. "I'll run and get the men and bring them to you. Edward is moving much too slowly for us to drag him way out of the way to reach the other men. Will you do that for me?"

"Yes, of course."

"I don't want you to get lost, so just stay here, and I'll bring them to the two of you. I don't think Edward's in any shape to guide you back on his own or I'd just have him take you to the cabins."

"I agree. We'll wait."

"All right. Edward, stay awake and keep Alicia company. I'll be right back." Rob hated leaving his brother and Alicia out in the snowy cold, but it was the best plan he could come up with. He felt like he'd walked forever, calling to the men, careful not to make a misstep and end up in a watery grave himself. They continued to call back to him until he finally saw them trudging through the snow toward him.

"Where's everyone else?" Hamilton asked. He was a bank loan officer, also from San Antonio, mid-forties, and had always been active, from what he'd told everyone when they were sharing about themselves. But he smoked a lot, which contributed to his shortness of breath.

"My brother and Alicia are waiting for us. We still need to locate Judi. We need to hurry."

"Why didn't they come with you?" Hamilton asked.

"Edward is injured. Not badly. Just enough that I didn't want him having to walk all the way out here to join you. Alicia stayed with him." Rob didn't want to mention that the men were way out of their way when it wasn't their fault they'd run away from the snarling bears. Well, particularly when they might have seen the grizzly attack Edward firsthand.

"The grizzly got him?" Doug asked, quickening his step.

"Yeah, not badly though." Rob didn't want to let on Edward was badly injured and then tomorrow, he was healed up just fine. Though it could take a few days to heal up adequately, depending on the severity of the injuries. Rob hoped Edward would be fine by tomorrow morning. Their enhanced healing abilities would shorten the length of time a human normally would take to heal. Not to mention Rob was feeling some burning where he'd suffered claw marks and bites also.

He called out for Judi and heard Alicia calling for her too.

When Rob and the others finally reached Alicia and Edward, Alicia hugged the two men, then Rob. "I'm so glad you're good at locating missing—" She hesitated as if she suddenly knew why.

Rob assumed she figured his visions helped to find the men. His enhanced sight, sound, and smell were what clued him in. Now he was trying to locate Judi by scent.

"Missing persons," Alicia finished.

Rob hollered for Judi, but only the wind howled back.

"Have you ever had that happen before?" Doug asked. He flipped houses in Houston and made good money at it, but had decided he needed to take a break from civilization and this was it. "A grizzly attack, I mean?"

"No, we've been doing this for ten years and we've never had any kind of bear attacks before," Rob said, his arm firmly around Edward's waist again. He seemed to be walking half-time, sluggish, beat.

"Not polar bears either?" Alicia asked, helping with Edward still.

"No bears."

"Something to definitely write home about. If it hadn't scared the crap out of me, and it hadn't hurt Edward, I would have loved to have taken a picture of it," Doug said.

"Me too," Hamilton said.

"Not me. I was just glad..." Alicia paused.

Everyone looked at her expectantly.

"Uhm, that it took off in another direction and that

Rob came back all right." Alicia sounded winded, but also like she had changed her mind about telling exactly what she'd seen.

A polar bear? Fighting the grizzly? Rob had tried to get Gary away from Edward as quickly as he could, but he imagined now that everyone else might have seen a polar bear too, though they'd run for their lives. Now he suspected only Alicia had because she'd been close enough to go to Edward's aid when everyone else had completely scattered and disappeared.

"I've got Edward," Rob told her, wanting her to save her breath.

"Hey!" Casey called out in the blanket of snow ahead of them. "I've got Judi with me. Is everyone else all right?"

"Edward's hurt, but he should be good by tomorrow morning." Rob hoped. He was damn glad the redhead was with Casey.

"Do we need a sled?" Casey asked, running toward them with Judi in tow.

"No. We should be okay." Rob didn't want Casey to leave the group. The more of them that stayed together now, the better.

"Are we almost there?" Doug asked. "Seems like we walked twice as many miles on the return trip."

"As far out of the way as the two of you had run, you added another half a mile for certain." Rob felt

Edward stumble, and he tightened his grip on his brother. "Not that I blame you. I'm glad you got away from the bear."

"We would have come back, but we were afraid we were lost and might end up in the lake as difficult as it is to see," Doug said.

Rob didn't want anyone to believe that he felt anyone had let them down. He was glad they'd saved themselves. "You did right. Everyone's fine now. We'll have a hot meal and lots of stories to tell." Minus a polar bear fighting a grizzly tale.

Casey said, "Do you want to get the rest of them into the cabin, and I'll stay with Edward?"

***

Alicia was thoroughly confused about what she'd seen. She was certain a polar bear had begun to fight the grizzly and had made it back off and fight elsewhere. She'd been terrified, thinking Edward was going to die, that the blood on his forehead would attract the bears and more. That the polar bear would be successful in the fight over territory, and she'd be faced with a hungry polar bear like she'd had in her vision.

Alicia immediately answered Casey's question to Rob about leaving Casey with Edward alone in the wilderness. "No. We stick together." Alicia wished Casey had brought a sled for poor Edward. He did help Rob half carry Edward back to the cabins though. She wondered if Casey had been afraid he wouldn't have been able to call out for the survivors and hear them, if he had been riding a noisy snowmobile to reach them. They might not have even had one at the cabin anyway.

"We have a quarter of a mile left to go," Casey finally said, "in answer to your question, Doug. Once we get back in, you folks can get warmed up, and then we'll eat. The others that I had dropped off started cooking the meal right away."

"Are you all right?" Alicia asked Judi, wrapping her arm through hers.

"Yeah, just scared and cold. I was so thrilled to see Casey suddenly appear out of nowhere. I thought I was going to be lost forever out there and worried any moment I'd run into a bunch of bears. Or wolves. And I worried about what had happened to the rest of you too."

"I'm glad Casey came back to help," Alicia agreed, but she had to know what had happened to Rob when he vanished in the snow and why Edward had left him out there to fend for himself.

CHAPTER 7

When Rob and the others with him finally spied the first of the cabins, the lights on inside, smoke coming out of the chimney, everyone in their little group cheered with excitement. One of the men was watching out the window and yelled for the others. The rest of the group hurried outside to help them, one of the men having been the lookout, staring out the window, when he saw them.

Those who had been waiting at the cabin appeared shocked to see Edward wearing a bloody bandage on his head. Rob had finally resorted to using the fireman's carry to get his brother there the rest of the way. He took him straight to their bedroom and laid him in the bed. Edward's eyes were open, and when Rob took off his hat, goggles, and face mask, Edward smiled at him, though he looked pale.

Rob began working on removing Edward's boots next.

"What happened?" one of the men asked, peering into the room.

"Grizzly attack," Alicia said. "It was horrible. I...I've never been so scared in my life."

"Me either," Judi said. "We all just took off running."

All except Alicia, who had stayed to take care of Rob's brother. Rob couldn't thank her enough for braving it out and caring for Edward like she had done.

"Can you eat some hot stew?" Casey asked Edward.

"Yeah, sure."

Rob was certain Edward just wanted to curl up in his warm bed and sleep like a bear in hibernation. Edward let on he was well enough to eat.

Casey moved them out of the bedroom and the doorway. The others began to serve up the meal in the dining room while Rob helped Edward out of his socks, gloves, parka, ski pants, and sweater, until he was only wearing his black long johns.

"Was it Gary?" Edward asked as Rob took care of his head, cleaning the wound, and then bandaging it again.

"Yeah."

"What happened?"

"I chased him off."

"How badly did he injure you?"

Rob wasn't sure. His skin was just now beginning to burn across his chest and on his neck and right arm. The adrenaline that had flooded his body while he was in fight mode, then desperate to find the others and get his injured brother and everyone else to safety, was now dissipating. He unzipped his parka. "Probably not as bad as I hurt him."

"Take care of it, Rob."

"I will." Rob pulled off his parka and laid it on his bed.

A knock at the door sounded and Rob answered it. Alicia was holding a steaming bowl of beef stew. She looked unsure as to what to do—offer to help Edward eat, or let Rob do it because he was his brother.

"I'll take it." Rob took the bowl of stew from her. "Thanks, Alicia. Why don't you eat with the others, and I'll be out soon."

"Okay. Everyone wants to know what happened exactly..." Alicia's gaze settled on Rob's chest, her lips parting and then her gaze shot up to his, her eyes wide.

He looked down. Sure enough, his pale blue sweater sported three bloody slash marks across his chest, in the same location that his skin was burning. Which probably thoroughly confused her because the bear hadn't clawed *through* his parka or the sweater.

Edward was watching the two of them, but he

didn't seem to understand the problem.

"I'll explain what happened in a few minutes," Rob said.

"Did you see what happened? I...I thought I saw a polar bear fighting off the grizzly, but the snow was blowing so hard, I might have imagined it. Edward said he was talking to you, but then he returned without you and the grizzly suddenly came out of nowhere and attacked Edward. Everyone ran off, including me, but then they kept running and I came back, slowly, afraid to catch the grizzly's attention, but I wanted to reach Edward. He had the medical pack with him. I hoped I could take care of him until you showed up. What happened to you?"

"The grizzly attacked Edward and I tried to chase the bear off so he wouldn't attack him again or anyone else in the group."

Alicia frowned at Rob, looking skeptical, then took the bowl from him, crossed the floor to the bedside table, and set it down. Then she rejoined Rob and gently lifted his sweater. "Take it off," she said, and found a long-sleeved T-shirt under that.

He sighed. There wasn't any way he was going to be able to explain the bloody claw and teeth marks, but he knew she wouldn't believe him if he said he got some of Edward's blood on him. The slashes looked just like a bear's claw and teeth marks and his parka didn't have any blood on it.

"I can bunk with Casey tonight," Edward offered.

Rob tossed his sweater on a wooden chair at the foot of his bed. Alicia stared at the same pattern of blood stains on his T-shirt.

"You took off your parka, sweater, and T-shirt to scare the grizzly off?" She lifted his T-shirt and stared at the angry claw marks on his neck, chest, and arm. And teeth marks in his neck.

He was just lucky none of the punctures hit any major arteries.

She gently pulled the shirt off, then looked up at him, waiting for an explanation.

"The grizzly clawed me. What can I say?"

"Hell, you have to look way worse than me." Edward frowned at Rob.

"And he bit you. Okay, sit. I'll take care of this, unless you want to show off your badge of courage to everyone before I clean your wounds and bandage you," she said.

"Hardly."

"We're going to see a doctor in the first town we get to, right?" Alicia arched a brow.

"If it's giving me trouble tomorrow," Rob said. "Otherwise, no."

She glanced at Edward. "Same here," he said.

She pulled out her phone and took a picture of

Rob's wounds. "Everyone needs to know how dangerous the bears are and what you did to protect us."

Rob really wished she hadn't done that. She probably would have thought he was acting too strange if he insisted she didn't.

She cleaned up his wounds with antiseptic, and he had to grit his teeth against the pain. "Really, you can scream out in pain, if you want. You might feel better," she said.

Edward laughed. "I did when she put that antiseptic on my head."

Rob smiled at his brother. "I didn't hear you screaming."

"Probably because you were too busy chasing off the grizzly."

She began bandaging the claw and bite marks, her touch gentle, so much different from when Casey or Edward took care of his injuries, and likewise when he did so for them. She grabbed up his clothes. "I'll wash the blood out of these. Can you eat?"

"Yes. I'll be out in a little while." He pulled another shirt on.

"I'll be right back." Alicia left with his clothes and her phone.

Edward smiled at Rob. "She is *so* the one for you."

"Not happening. Do you remember telling her I was

a polar bear shifter?" Rob helped his brother sit up. "Can you eat without any assistance?"

"Yeah, sure. I just need to sleep. I must have joked about you being a shifter."

"No, you didn't. It's a good thing she thought you were kidding or delirious." Rob handed him his bowl of stew. "Are you sure you don't need some help?"

"No, thanks. My head's killing me. After I eat this, I need to sleep. Why don't you join the others and have a meal? I'll have a bigger breakfast tomorrow."

"All right. Holler if you want anything." Rob patted him on the shoulder, then left the room and kept the door open just in case Edward needed something.

Rob walked down the hall and heard the shocked comments concerning what had happened to him when he tangled with the bear. "Omigod, the bear did that to Rob?" "How did Rob manage to survive?" "Hell, he's one lucky SOB." "Rob did that to save all of us?"

"Yeah, I would have been running the other way. Well, we did," Doug said. "Then Rob had to go looking for us in his condition, no less."

"Hey, I'm fine," Rob said, grabbing a bowl of beef stew from the kitchen.

"How's your brother doing?" Hamilton asked.

"Good. He has a headache, and he's finished his stew, but he wants to sleep."

"Are we going to stop at a town and have a doctor

look over the two of you?" Judi asked.

"Only if we feel we need it. Otherwise we'll be fine."

"What caused the bear to attack?" Hamilton asked.

"He was protecting his territory, possibly." Rob was thinking of Gary's girlfriend. They weren't even married. If they weren't engaged or married, the grizzly didn't have a legitimate reason to attack any other bear in the vicinity, whether it was a polar bear or otherwise. Gary and his girlfriend had come to Rob's aunt and uncle's tavern once and he'd been drunk and belligerent and they'd had to throw his sorry ass out of the tavern when he picked a fight with Rob's cousin Ben that time. Gary's girlfriend had seemed nice enough and Rob wasn't surprised she'd hooked up with another bear.

Rob suspected Gary had been drinking way too much vodka before he went on his rampage. That was the alcohol he'd been drinking the night at the tavern when he went ballistic, and it was hard for humans to detect the scent sometimes, depending on what he mixed it with. For polar bears, no. Even so, it hadn't registered right away that Gary had been drinking because Rob had been too busy avoiding his teeth and claws.

The way Alicia was watching Rob, he suspected she still wanted to know exactly how he could have fought off the grizzly bear on his own, and shirtless, without succumbing to the cold.

After the long day, the concern about the snowstorm and the grizzly trouble some of them had, everyone called it a night. Rob finished putting the glasses away in the dishwasher before he headed for bed.

"I'm taking a shower," Alicia said to him as if he needed to know where she was every second of the day. He was surprised she didn't begin grilling him again about chasing off the bear.

When he finished up, he turned off the kitchen light and headed for his room. He opened the door quietly so as not to disturb Edward's sleep. Then Rob stripped off his clothes, all except his boxers and climbed under the covers. Alicia left the bathroom, returned to her room, and shut the door.

A few minutes later, a light knock sounded on the door. He climbed out of bed, figuring it was Alicia, but he was surprised to see Judi instead.

"Yeah?" Rob wanted to get some much-needed sleep, his own wounds burning like crazy.

"I loved hearing your story, but I just wanted you to know that when I got separated from everyone, I was really turned around. I ended up heading in the wrong direction and nearly ran into the grizzly bear. I didn't see you anywhere, but I did see a polar bear fighting the grizzly. I didn't say anything because I knew you'd been injured as badly as your brother. I know the polar bear chased away the grizzly. Your secret is safe with me." She smiled. "Night, Rob." Then she returned to her room, and he just stared at the closed door for a moment.

"Hell." Rob closed the door and returned to bed.

Edward was watching him. "See? It didn't matter that I told Alicia you had turned into a polar bear shifter. Her roommate already knew that."

"Her roommate thinks I took credit for chasing off the grizzly bear when a polar bear did it instead."

"How are you going to explain that your garments had no claw marks?"

"I snapped the grizzly bear in the nose with my sweater and he took off."

Edward smiled. "Yeah, but you're forgetting about the polar bear that chased the grizzly off."

"Well, you know how eyewitness accounts can be. Completely inaccurate. Especially in a whiteout."

***

"Did you really see a polar bear fighting the grizzly?" Alicia asked Judi as they settled down in their room at the cabin to sleep. That sure confirmed what she'd seen too, but she had really doubted herself. What if that was the one she had seen in her vision, only somehow, she had gotten it wrong?

"Yeah. And as soon as they began to fight, I ran

away from there."

"You didn't actually see it chase off the grizzly."

"I assumed it did. It was a lot angrier than the grizzly."

"You didn't see Rob anywhere? Passed out in the snow, maybe, like Edward had been?"

"No. I didn't see any sign of Rob or anyone else for that matter. Just the two enraged bears. Scared me to death. I took off running and couldn't believe my luck at meeting up with Casey when he came looking for the rest of us."

No matter what had happened out there in the snow, as far as Alicia was concerned, Rob had been heroic. She knew he had tried to save everyone. Then she wondered, if she touched him again, could she see what had really happened to him?

* * *

Early the next morning, Rob and Edward were feeling better, not perfect, but better. They had to let on they were raring to go and didn't need any medical care. They had tried to call their aunt and uncle, members of the bear council, to let them know what had happened between Gary and them, but they still had no cell service.

Rob looked outside and saw a foot of snow. He smelled eggs and bacon and assumed the ones staying with them were making breakfast. He and Edward were supposed to be making it this morning, so he suspected the rest of the group felt he and his brother needed more rest.

"Smells like our cabin mates have taken over our tasks this morning," Edward said, climbing out of the bed to get dressed.

"We have to let them know we're doing fine. No groaning, even if you feel the need to."

Edward laughed.

After they dressed, they joined the others in the kitchen and everyone asked how they were feeling. "I'm great," Edward said, his bandage still on his head. The bleeding had stopped, but he was leaving the bandage to remove later, so it wouldn't look like he'd healed up too fast.

"What about you?" Alicia asked Rob.

He smiled. "I'm fine, thank you."

She raised a brow as if she wasn't sure he really was.

"Thanks for fixing breakfast." Rob took his seat with the others, and they enjoyed breakfast. He was going to help clean the dishes, but Doug and Judi took charge of them.

To Rob's surprise, Alicia touched his shoulder with a gentle touch and said, "Let me see your wounds."

He didn't want to show them to her, not when she'd seen how bad they were yesterday, and she would witness how much they had healed by this morning. It wouldn't be normal.

Edward raised his brows a little at Rob, but she said, "You too. Everyone's afraid you're worried about the tour group and won't seek medical attention because you're afraid you're going to ruin our excursion. We're all in agreement. I was picked as the person to check out your wounds, and if they look all right, we'll do as you say. If they don't…"

"This is really not necessary," Rob said.

Alicia folded her arms. "If the two of you get an infection, then what? You'll get sicker and we'll feel responsible."

"She just wants to get another look at your naked chest," Edward kidded Rob.

Rob laughed and her cheeks reddened.

"Okay, it looked worse than it was last night." Though he didn't want to show off his wounds, he would do so and then they could get on the road with everyone's mind set at ease. Though he suspected Alicia's wouldn't be when she saw the change. The thing of it was, she had pictures of his wounds, so it wasn't like she had to recall what she'd seen by memory either.

"Oh, and everyone asked if we shouldn't be reporting the bear that attacked the both of you?"

"No," both Edward and Rob said at the same time.

"Troopers could shoot the wrong bear," Edward

said.

"But what if it attacked more people?"

"In the same area, then they can report it. But as bad as the snowstorm was and as shook up as I was, I couldn't give a good description of the bear that would single him out instead of a dozen others in the area," Edward said.

"Same here," Rob said.

She removed Edward's bandage first and gasped.

"I told you they weren't bad." Rob pulled off his shirt. He hadn't even replaced his bandages.

She ran her fingers gingerly around the wounds. "They're nearly gone."

"Yeah. Are you going to certify us as ready for duty so we can pack and get on our way?" Rob asked.

She frowned at Edward's wound. "Why are you still wearing a bandage?"

"I didn't remove it. I didn't realize the wound was nearly gone." Edward looked in the mirror at the fading bruises and gash. Instead of red and bloody, the seams of the skin had knit together and the area was pale pink now, looking more like it had been a couple of weeks since the incident.

Rob's puncture wounds were deeper, so since he still needed a bandage, even though he hadn't put new ones on, she rebandaged them.

Then she glanced back at Edward, still looking

surprised.

Rob was already pulling on his shirt and then his sweater, wanting to get this show on the road before she saw him healing up even more.

After packing up the vans and Alicia reassuring the group that Edward and Rob were healing up fine—while Casey was smiling at them—they headed out.

"If you feel in the least bit sick," Alicia said, "one of us can take over the driving."

"Yeah, I'm originally from Minnesota and drive in snow a lot in the winter," Doug said. "I'd have no problem taking over."

"I'll be fine," Rob assured them, but he couldn't quash the concern he had that if the water incident hadn't occurred when he fought the grizzly, when was it going to happen? On the return trip, maybe?

They stopped at a park to have lunch, but when they saw moose standing in the lake, everyone got out their cameras to start snapping shots.

"Stay away from the water," Rob warned Alicia, who was so excited about taking the photos, he was worried she wouldn't heed the visions they'd shared.

***

"It's not snowing," Alicia told Rob as she used her telephoto lens to take long distance shots because she intended to stay well away from the water, just in case. The edge all around the lake was frozen and she suspected the water would continue to freeze further out, the colder it got.

"I wish it was snowing," Judi said. "I got some beautiful pictures of the snow falling before all hell broke loose when the grizzly struck."

Alicia had been wearing five more layers of clothing for every day, quickly discarding layers when they arrived at the place they were staying for the night, just so she'd be prepared if she ended up in the water. Not that the layers underneath her parka were waterproof or even water repellant, but she hoped they would help insulate her a bit until someone could come to her rescue. *If* someone was able to.

Everyone was excited about seeing the moose in person for the first time, even those who lived where moose were, but still had never seen one in their state.

"If any of them run this way, race around the vans. Even if you're not in the van, if you're out of their sight, that's usually all it takes to stop them from advancing and the best way to protect yourself," Rob explained.

Alicia had her tripod out and had just set up her camera when it began to snow. She felt an eerie shiver shoot up her spine.

Judi was smiling. "This is just perfect! Snow, moose, it's going to be my Christmas card for this year."

Casey offered to take pictures of Judi and the moose in the background, and he took several photos of her while Alicia moved from one location to another, trying to get the best shots. That was the thing with photography. She never knew which would turn out the best, so she just had to keep moving around to take advantage of several different settings and backdrops.

Sometimes the three moose watched her, sometimes they were observing others in the group, who were likewise moving around to get better shots.

Rob was sticking close to her, but then the sound of fireworks rent the air.

"Gunfire!" Rob shouted.

Alicia was furious, thinking some ass was shooting at the moose in front of her. But the moose turned and swam off across the lake and away from the tour group. A stampede of moose came from behind them. She was struggling to free her camera and her tripod, but the tripod's legs had dug into the mud. So she was trying to release her camera from the tripod instead. As expensive as the camera and lens were, she didn't want to lose them.

Someone fired shots close behind her as one of the tour guides began firing a weapon, trying to scare the moose to run off in a different direction. She heard running footsteps crunching in the snow headed straight for her, when the man plowed into her, and knocked her into the frigid lake.

CHAPTER 8

Rob was too busy to see what was happening behind him as he attempted to scatter the moose, to prevent them from running toward the tour group's location as some hunters fired on the moose. Rob couldn't see the hunters, though he immediately thought of the three men in the tavern who claimed they were going to kill a bear. Had they decided any game was fair hunting? He wouldn't be surprised.

Rob suddenly heard Alicia scream behind him. His worst nightmare, and hers, was realized. She was already in the water, four moose having raced between the vans, heading for the lake.

The snow was falling again, but not enough to hide Rob from the tourists' sight if he tried stripping and shifting there. He bolted for the woods, hoping the firs would provide enough cover for him so he could shift unseen, and that he would have time enough to save Alicia before he lost her for good.

No one else could reach her in time and there was only one way to save her, though she might hate Rob for what he was about to do. Unable to do anything else, he glanced in the direction of his brother, who was trying to get the attention of one of the moose to draw it away from the tour group. Casey was trying to protect them also, and had moved two of the women and two of the men into one of the closest vans.

Rob got as far from the group as he could and hidden, he stripped off his clothes, shifted, and raced to the lake in his polar bear coat. He dove in, swimming underneath the surface of the water with his powerful forearms, his legs steering him in her direction. He prayed he would reach her in time. His heart was beating like a jackhammer, his blood pounding in his ears as he finally reached Alicia. She was clinging to the ice edging the lake, too frozen to pull herself from the water. Her fingers slipped off the ice and she began to sink. She would soon be dead. She saw him then, right before he bit into her parka to get a hold of her. Her eyes wide with terror, she choked out a scream. But she could do nothing to fend off the polar bear—him. She was too frozen to make any more of a response than that.

He tasted blood, hating that he had to turn her, but

it was either that, or she'd die as her body temperature core dropped too low. They'd never be able to warm her up fast enough. Now he would have to take her someplace else, unsure as to how fast she would begin to shift, or how much control she would have over it, and how much she would want to kill him for it. He pulled her out of the water, her heartbeat so slow, he was afraid he'd still lose her. He wanted to kill the hunters who had caused the moose stampede and done this to her.

He dragged her into the woods where he'd left his clothes. Casey had already moved all the others into two of the vans. Edward was waiting for Rob, medical pack and blankets in hand to help Alicia and him.

"She's bleeding," Edward said as he began stripping her out of her sopping wet clothes and redressing her while Rob hurried to shift and get dressed so he could assist him. "You bit her," Edward accused, seeing the place where Rob's teeth had penetrated her shoulder, just enough of a puncture wound to introduce his saliva into her bloodstream.

"I had to. If I hadn't she would have died. She may still." Rob hurriedly pulled a pair of wool socks on her feet. "We'll bandage her in the van. We just need to get her into dry clothes at this point." After wrapping her in the emergency blankets, Rob carried her toward the van he'd driven. Her eyes were closed, and she appeared to be unaware of what was happening.

"You turned her," Edward said, as if he couldn't believe that Rob had made that decision. No one they knew had ever changed anyone.

"She would have died. She still might." They didn't know how being newly turned would affect someone. All of them were several generations removed from their first ancestor who had been turned.

As soon as Rob carried her into the van, Edward started the engine to warm up the vehicle. "Where will you take her?"

"Our cabin. It's peaceful and quiet there. That will give her a chance to shift and get used to being one of us. I'll do everything I can to help her get through this."

"What will you tell the others? Her roommate?"

"I'm taking her to the hospital. What did everyone see?"

"I saw her in the water and told everyone they couldn't do anything for her. Just to go to the vans. I was going to help you rescue her, but we didn't want them getting in the way or getting into trouble themselves. They're horrified, naturally. Casey's with them, reassuring them."

"Good. Did you get her camera?" Rob figured Alicia might be upset about losing it, besides everything else that had happened to her. He wanted to be able to reassure her that her camera had survived, at least.

"I'll check and see if someone got it and tell Judi that Alicia asked if she'd keep photographing the sites while Casey and I keep the tour going. Hopefully, Judi will agree. Hell, she's coming toward the van now, despite Casey trying to deter her."

"We'll let Judi see Alicia, that she's survived, and then I have to get moving before we have another disaster on our hands, namely, before Alicia begins to shift." Rob had finished bandaging Alicia's shoulder, pulled on a spare parka, and wrapped her up again in several blankets. He was glad her heart rate was normalizing and her color was turning from blue to a warmer peach tone. Her eyes were closed, her breathing steady. He still worried whether she had permanent cell damage from the cold.

"Here Judi is," Edward warned right before he opened the van door for her.

Casey looked apologetic that he hadn't stopped Judi from leaving his van.

"Judi can see her, but then she will be right out," Edward told Casey.

"Is she...is she alive?" Judi asked, tears streaming down her cheeks.

"She's doing well. I'm taking her to a facility to have her checked out. She wanted you to keep photographing the sites for her," Rob said. "She's sleeping right now. The shock of the cold on her system was too much. We'll know more later, but for now, her heart is beating normally, her pulse is good, and she's much warmer to the touch."

"I'll go with her," Judi said, running her hand over Alicia's wet hair. "Casey gave me her camera and tripod for safekeeping."

Rob had pulled a stocking cap over Alicia's head to help keep the heat in, but he couldn't do anything about her long, wet hair for now.

"She insisted you do her job for her," Edward said. "She was having a difficult time speaking, but that was all she managed to say. Judi—pictures. We need to let Rob get on the way with her. He'll keep us posted."

Judi wiped away tears. "Just, just take good care of Alicia."

"I will," Rob said, torn between feeling glad he had saved Alicia's life and guilty about how much he had changed it without her consent. "I'll keep in touch when I can."

"Thank you." Then Judi squeezed Alicia's hand and said, "I'll take the pictures for you, but only if you promise me you'll get better so you can edit them." Then she gave her a hug and left the van.

Casey eyed Alicia for a moment, then led Judi back to the other van. Rob suspected Casey knew what had happened.

Edward cleared his throat. "Are you going to be all

right with this?"

"Yeah. I just hope I changed Alicia in time. Hopefully she won't shift before I'm ready to deal with it. I'll keep you updated and you can tell Casey what happened when you're able."

"This will be a life changer not only for her but for you too."

Rob had known it from the moment he'd shifted to save her. Even in those harried moments, he had thought about Alicia's vision. The polar bear who was trying to eat her. And he had bitten her. Maybe she had even experienced that he had bitten her and that's why she was adamant that the polar bear was trying to eat her. It made sense. But her envisioning them making love had also made him assume he might have turned her to save her life. Otherwise that part of her vision would never have happened.

Edward slapped him on the back, then he and Casey grabbed bags out of the back of Rob's van belonging to Judi, and the others and they returned to their own vans.

"Alicia, you're doing fine. You'll be fine." But would she be? Rob had no way of knowing how this would really affect her and if they'd warmed her up in time. What if she was permanently brain damaged or injured in other ways that their enhanced healing abilities couldn't repair? Then he remembered them making love in their visions and he sighed with relief. She would be okay.

He made sure she was comfortably stretched out on the bench seat behind him. She was all bundled up and her eyes were still closed.

He didn't believe he would have done anything differently even if he hadn't learned of her visions. Just getting to know her a bit, in addition to the paranormal connection they had, he was certain *that* had sealed their fate.

Edward and Casey waited to drive off, ensuring Rob and Alicia were headed out first. Rob waved at them, and drove back the way they had come. No way could he take her to a medical care facility for now. They had always taken care of their own and if she began to shift, it would be a disaster for all of them. He drove back onto the highway, thinking of how his aunt and uncle and even his cousins would react. Unsure if Alicia was awake enough to hear his words, he decided to wait to call them later, once he and Alicia reached the cabin and he could talk in private.

The drive would take an hour and it was the perfect place for polar bears to run, while mostly staying out of sight of humans. Plenty of water, glaciers, trees, mountains, and a nice warm cabin for their human half.

Alicia was so quiet, Rob was still worried about her. "Alicia, can you hear me?"

Rob didn't know how he was going to tell her that she had to live with the other polar bear shifters—his family and friends—from now on. He wondered how the other shifter species would view what he'd done also, once they learned of it. As far as he knew, none of them in this area had ever turned anyone either. They'd all been born into the shifter world.

Alicia whispered, "The polar bear...tried...to eat me." She didn't sound upset, or shocked even. Maybe relieved the polar bear hadn't been able to devour her, and she was completely whole.

"He saved your life," Rob said, able to hear her soft words because of his enhanced hearing. "If he hadn't pulled you out of the water when he did, you would never have made it." Rob didn't think she had been aware of him shifting in the snow and dressing next to her as cold and out of it as she'd been.

"Everyone else?"

Rob was relieved to hear her thinking clearly. "Everyone is safe. Judi wanted to come with you, but Casey found your camera, safe and sound, and gave it to her to take more photos. We hope that's all right with you. We figured there was no sense in her missing the rest of the journey and you missing out on all those fabulous photos. We thought this was the best plan for everyone."

"Cold."

"Do you want to come up here with me?" He'd wrapped her in two blankets, and warm, dry clothes, but her hair was still wet.

"Should be...dead."

"If the polar bear hadn't pulled you out when he did, you would have been too far gone." Rob wanted to emphasize to her that only he could have saved her as a polar bear. That he'd had no other choice, once she learned he was the polar bear who had bitten her.

"You...saved me. You...and Edward."

"We wouldn't have been able to reach you in the frigid water. The polar bear pulled you out of the lake. You were already sinking into the water."

"My shoulder is burning like fire."

"One of the bear's teeth punctured your skin, but it should heal quickly. It was minor. You were blue at first when I pulled you out."

"The bear."

"I mean, the bear."

"Where did it go? Why didn't it eat me?"

"Edward and I came to your rescue." Rob didn't want to lie about it, but until he was at the cabin and she had recovered further, he wasn't about to tell her—unless he let it slip again—that he was the bear who had saved her. "Can you feel your extremities? Your fingers and toes? Wiggle them?"

"Burning."

"Just your extremities?" Rob was worried she was suddenly feeling the urge to shift.

It happened so fast he nearly ran off the road. She began yanking off her blankets and tearing off her clothes as if she instantly knew she had to shift.

"Fever. Burning up."

Glad the windows were darkly tinted, he pulled the van off the road and shut off the engine. They still had another thirty-five minutes to go to reach the cabin, and he had no idea how a new shifter would react. Would she be like a wild animal? No conscious idea of how dangerous a swipe from her paws could be? How dangerous her bite could be? As a polar bear, he could deal with it. But not as a human.

He was already out of his seat and headed toward her, her face a mask of terror. "You'll be all right. You're going to be all right." He began helping her out of the rest of the clothes, and she shifted just as he tried to pull the sweatshirt over her head. It was caught like a hood around her head. Her paws were swiping at the sweatshirt, and she was twisting her head, snapping at it, trying to shake it loose.

"Don't bite me or hit me with your paws or you could gravely injure me. I'll remove the sweatshirt for you as soon as you hold perfectly still."

He didn't dare move toward her until she was sitting still and staring at him, probably wondering what the hell had happened to her and why he wasn't shocked or terrified to witness her transformation from a human to a polar bear.

CHAPTER 9

Alicia stared at Rob, uncomprehending. Yes, she'd envisioned she'd be wearing a fur coat and knew beyond a doubt it had been a bizarre dream, not a psychic vision. Dreaming about things that had taken place that were disjointed or out of place was one thing. Like seeing a house number, a chain-link fence, a dumpster, dry, cracked earth, and a water source to reveal the location of where a woman had been murdered—each of the items was real. So though it seemed unreal, the homicide detective had found the woman's body in the area described.

This was nothing like that. And she wasn't imagining any of it. If she'd been having a dream, nightmare rather, this wouldn't be so real. Rob was frowning, looking worried, but he wasn't in the least bit terrified of her. She tried to speak to him, to ask him what the hell was going on, but all that came out of her mouth was a very scary growl.

She thought Rob's smile was meant to reassure her. But maybe not. Maybe she was scaring him to pieces like it scared her to be dealing with this nightmare in the flesh—or fur. Or maybe he was a bit amused.

The notion infuriated her. She growled even louder.

She couldn't understand how he could look at her in her current state and not be terrified!

He sighed. "If you want me to, I'll remove the sweatshirt."

She thought then how silly she must look, a polar bear wearing a gray sweatshirt around her head and neck. As if being a polar bear wasn't bizarre enough. Of course, she wanted the sweatshirt off her head, but she wasn't sure how she was going to indicate that if she couldn't speak. Then she pawed at it again.

"All right. Just don't paw at me. I'll get it off."

She was seated on the floor of the van and put her paws on the floor and lowered her head for him.

He pulled off the sweatshirt. "I know you're in shock over this whole situation. You're not alone either. You're not sick, cursed, or having a nightmare about this. I need to take you to a cabin we own. My brother and I, that is. If you feel you can manage the trauma over all this, I'll drive us the rest of the way there. Can you?"

She grunted. What was she supposed to say? A polar bear had bitten her, she was still feeling the pain in her shoulder where he had cut through the skin, and Rob and his brother were fine with it? Edward had to know what had happened to her also. And Casey? Probably. The rest of the MacMathan family. Gaelic for son of bear. Omigod. She couldn't believe this. Who else?

Before Rob could return to the driver's seat, she smelled him. Not only did he smell like a sexy male who had been out in the fresh Alaskan wind and snow for a while, he smelled like a polar bear, like she smelled. What the hell? She nudged at his back with her nose and shoved him forward. He caught himself before he fell, but she realized then, a little nudge from a polar bear could be dangerous for a human. She didn't know her own strength.

"Gently," Rob said, turning and then to her shock, he wrapped his arms around her and gave her a warm embrace. "You're beautiful and no matter what you might be feeling now, you're alive and well, and you'll learn how to live like we do."

He had been the first on the scene to take care of her. But had he been there earlier? As a polar bear too? Why would he smell like one otherwise? Not her polar bear scent, but different. Why would he not be terrified of what she had become?

"We're polar bear shifters," Rob said, "in case you hadn't figured that out. Except we were born this way. I saved your life. I was the bear who pulled you out of the water. I'm now responsible for you. None of us have ever known a newly turned shifter. I can't imagine how you're feeling. But we'll show you how we survive, how we love our polar bear halves. I just want to get you to the cabin so you can enjoy the outdoors as a bear. I'll discuss everything with you. I'll join you, protect you, and show you the ropes. I'm sorry. I never imagined doing this to anyone. But I couldn't let you die."

She finally nodded. She realized that having the van parked next to the highway, while Rob waited for her to agree, wasn't a safe thing to do. What if someone came along and stopped to see if they were having car trouble and needed some assistance? And then what would they see? A polar bear sitting in the van.

Rob returned to the driver's seat and got back on the road. He began to explain how the family had shared their oral history for generations about the first polar bear shifter in their family. "One of our ancestors, a Robby McNaughton, who was from Scotland, was always looking for a better way of life, or at least more adventurous. He settled in the Alaska wilderness way before it had become a state. At least we believe that's what happened. A pretty, Scottish lass named Mari had joined him, and he gave up hunting for pelts to set up a tavern when the gold rush hit the area.

"Before this, he had tangled with a bear. A polar bear. Everyone just thought he was lucky to have survived. Then he would take off for days and Mari wouldn't know what had happened to him. By all accounts, he had tried to avoid turning her. Then a grizzly attacked Mari.

"Looking for food, the bear had broken into their cabin. Robby returned home to find her near death. He turned her to save her life. They had two sets of twins two years apart and they started the polar bear shifters known as part of the MacMathan Clan bears.

"You might wonder what happened to the polar bear that had bitten Robby. The polar bear had two cubs and had been protecting them when he came across her on a hunt. He was hunting seals, not bears, but she was too. Elizabeth McConnell later became friends with Robby and Mari. She'd lost her husband to hunters earlier on. One of her daughters mated one of Robby and Mari's sons. Another daughter married another of their sons a couple of years later. Ben's and my families descended from Robby, and their offspring. We're not the only shifters though."

Alicia couldn't believe it. In no stretch of the imagination could she make sense of any of this. A truck approached and she scooted down so the driver wouldn't see her.

"Arctic wolves and gray wolves—like you saw on our trip—live in the area. Snow leopard triplets, all male, frequent the tavern also. Oh, and the grizzly who attacked me? That's Gary Spitzer. He was pissed off because a polar bear had relations with his girlfriend. Not me though. Someone else. But we don't know who."

Omigod, a shifter had attacked them?

She thought back to when the grizzly had attacked Rob, and Edward too. And Judi's claim that she'd seen a polar bear fighting the grizzly, but she hadn't seen any sign of Rob. Now Alicia knew why he had the claw marks on his body and no tears in his clothing. He hadn't been wearing any. Just a polar bear's fur coat instead.

"We heal much faster than humans," Rob suddenly said. "Not only couldn't we reach you in the frigid water like a polar bear could, even if we had just pulled off your wet clothes and dressed you in dry ones like we did, wrapping you in blankets, you most likely wouldn't have made it. Your core temperature had dropped too much. Our healing genetics helped to revive you quickly. Though I wasn't sure the change would work quickly enough even then."

That's why he had bitten her. But now what? She had to stay here forever? She realized the story of his ancestor was like Mari and Robby's story, except he had loved her. This meant what? That Rob wanted to marry her? Every time she thought of one problem with this whole scenario, she thought of more. Like Judi. If Alicia couldn't return home to San Antonio, how was she going to explain staying here? She had suddenly fallen head over heels for Rob and decided to stay? She'd have to leave her job. Running as a polar bear in San Antonio wouldn't be a viable option.

She just couldn't fathom being a part-time polar bear, even in her wildest nightmares.

"We don't know how this will affect your shifting. Whether you will shift just at any time or if you will have some control over it. Unlike with the wolves, the moon doesn't affect us." Rob pulled off onto another road. "I can't apologize to you enough for changing you without your consent, but I had to save your life, Alicia. I couldn't lose you." He paused for a time. "I think you'll like it here. I need to contact my family and let them know what happened. We've never set up any kind of protocol for something like this happening."

What would she have done in his place? If she'd been a polar bear shifter and seen Rob in the water, succumbing to the cold? Knowing him like she did, she would have saved his life in much the same manner, risking his wrath. She wouldn't have let him die.

She glanced out the windows at the tall firs and the snow-covered mountains. How different would it be, running as a polar bear in the wilderness as compared to a human all bundled up in multiple layers of clothing? She wondered if she'd have any warning at all, or if it would just hit her at once like it did this time when she'd shifted. Rob seemed to be able to shift at will if the way he had come to her rescue and the group's rescue when the grizzly struck was any indication.

Nestled in among the fir trees a log cabin with a steep alpine-styled roof came into view. "Several of us have bear cabins out here. We call them that because we usually come out to them when we want to get away from civilization and swim and see the area as bears." He parked and got out. Then he opened the side door for her. "I'll gather your wet clothes, the spare ones you were wearing, and your bag and take them inside the cabin. Feel free to explore. I'll start a fire and join you in a few minutes."

Alicia bounded out of the van and landed on the snow. Without wearing hiking boots, she was expecting her feet to be cold, or to slip, but when she sat down on her rump and looked at her paws, she realized fur protected them. She felt...weird. Her body not moving like her brain said it should. They had been born like this, so they were used to it. This was so new to her she felt really out of her element.

Rob smiled at her, then took the clothes to the cabin and opened the door.

She was adventurous by nature, but this was a little

more than she could wrap her mind around. Rob disappeared inside the cabin. She wanted to see what it looked like, but she wanted to check out the surroundings as a polar bear, though the concern that hunters or grizzlies might be about, after the last encounter, made her hesitant. But then she went exploring first, the urge as a polar bear overriding the desire to see the cabin, or to hide away. She traveled cautiously through the trees, cognizant of the fact that a grizzly had attacked Rob. She wasn't sure she could fight off a bear like that, but she couldn't live her life in constant fear either.

Then she saw a beautiful blue lake, glacial ice floes floating in it, some of the chunks of ice on shore. She had the greatest urge to dive in, but she couldn't shake loose of the last memory she had of being in the water. Nearly freezing to death, drowning, and being bitten by a huge, ferocious-looking polar bear.

What she hadn't expected was to see a polar bear running to join her. Was it Rob? Another shifter? Or a full polar bear? She realized she didn't know how to react. It wasn't completely an instinctual response for her because she hadn't been guided as a child or cub to learn their way. One thing she knew, animals fluffed up their fur or feathers to appear larger, more formidable. And bears stood up like a man to show off their height.

She was scared. Who wouldn't be when faced with

an approaching polar bear that looked every bit as wild as the ones in the wild and that could be extremely dangerous? It didn't matter that she was one too right this minute. She still had a human's mindset. She might be bulky and tall like a polar bear, but she still felt like a human in a bear suit.

But that's what she did—stood up to look more menacing to the approaching bear.

***

Rob knew this was going to be difficult for Alicia, but he wanted to show her what it would be like for them to be together as bears, and how to communicate and enjoy the wilderness. Her posturing said she was scared, that she didn't recognize he was the bear who was approaching her.

He sat down on the snow to show she had nothing to worry about with him, so she would sit and not stand in a confrontational way. If she bit him, he'd let her, until she realized he was not going to fight her.

She finally sat too then.

He rose to his feet; she did too. He joined her then, nuzzling her face and neck, and rubbing his body against hers in a way to show he was a friend and not a foe. But also, to let her recognize his scent. He hoped she would be able to distinguish him by sight soon. She probably thought all polar bears looked alike.

For her well-being, she needed to catalog the polar

bears by scent and sight, both those who were in his family and those who were friends. But touching her aroused his keen need as a polar bear to procreate, to mate, and have his offspring with her. He hadn't expected that at all.

***

Alicia waited to see what he was up to at first, recognizing Rob's scent, feeling some relief, allowing him to nuzzle her and affectionately rub his body against her—she thought in friendship. Maybe this was really a courtship in a bear's way. She smelled his sexual interest and realized that she was smelling scents she hadn't been able to smell before. The annoying thing of it was, without her express permission, she was giving off a scent that said he was arousing her too! What if he took that to mean she wanted to have a little bear sex? She could see it now. Suddenly, she would be carrying a cub or two.

If he even considered doing that with her, she was biting him. And *not* affectionately.

Then he walked toward the water. Didn't he remember what happened to her the last time she'd been near the water? She kept telling herself the cold wouldn't affect her like it had when she was a human. But she couldn't convince herself that it truly wouldn't.

He reached the water's edge and turned to look back at her. She assumed he intended to get in the water and that he wanted her to follow him whether she wanted to or not. She realized he was attempting to teach her something about their world. Her new world.

He slid into the water and floated there for a moment. Just watching her.

She didn't move toward him.

He dove underneath the water and she moved closer to the water's edge to see if she could see him. The water was cloudy, so she couldn't observe where he'd gone to. Suddenly, he came up just below the surface of the water and looked up at her. She stepped back. She wasn't sure if he'd planned to get out and push her in, so she'd get over her fear of the icy water, or not. She wasn't having any of it right this instant. If she wanted to, she'd go in on her own when she could convince herself she wouldn't freeze to death.

He floated in the water for a moment and looked expectantly at Alicia. When she didn't join him, he floated on his back and looked up at the cloudy sky. She thought of how she would have been riding with the others on the next phase of their journey if Doug hadn't accidentally shoved her into the water. And about how this was now her home. She would no longer be a tourist. She needed to call him and let him know she was fine and there were no hard feelings.

She realized she'd never hesitated to jump into a new adventure before and so despite the reason for her reluctance before, she gritted her teeth, and decided to take the plunge. Rob knew she would be safe or he wouldn't have encouraged her to join him.

She needed to accept what she was, though she was certain it was going to be rough and that she'd most likely have years of ups and downs while she learned how to cope with this. Seeing Rob floating on his back like this as a polar bear, he looked cute and cuddly, whereas seeing him in the pool swimming as a human, he'd looked hot and muscled.

Casting her doubts aside, she dove in and found herself submerged in the icy cold water, expecting to be freezing and near death at any moment. Instead, she felt invigorated and buoyant. Rob was watching every move she made as she swam toward him. He waited, as if giving her space and letting her come to terms with this on her own. Which she appreciated. It was amazing and fun, if she would get over how bizarre all of this was. She bumped into him, and he nipped at her ear. She couldn't believe how gentle he could be. He wrapped his arms around her in a hug and bit her on the neck and cheek in a gentle way. She mouthed him back as gently as she could, afraid she'd bite him and draw blood, not knowing her own strength.

It wasn't going to be easy getting used to being what she was now. Especially since, by Rob's own account, no one knew how it would affect her. How difficult would it be for her to keep her human shape? Would she just shift at any time, day or night? And how long would it be before she could get it under control? Would it take days, weeks, months, years? Since no one knew, that wasn't reassuring either.

For now, she played with Rob, swimming beneath the water, swimming after him, coming around and tackling him, while he tackled her back. She loved this side of being a polar bear, the swimming, and playing with Rob part. Down here, they were in their own private world, safe from everyone else.

Then she had to go up to the surface of the water for air, and she shook off the excess water just like a dog would, sending the water droplets flying. Rob immediately tackled her again, and she retaliated. She'd always loved to swim before, but having the ability to swim in the frigid waters was invigorating. She wasn't sure dealing with any of the rest of this condition would be much fun.

They played forever, one getting out of the water and diving back in and then the other. Each of them tackling the other. Or just swimming around each other. And then Rob finally got out and she waited, but when he didn't return to the water, she climbed out too. He shook off the excess water, and then she did, getting him wet again. He bit her playfully on the neck, and then moved toward the cabin. Now she was beginning to get worried. What now?

It was one thing to be a polar bear and doing polar bear things, but to sit as a bear in the cabin for who knew how long? And damn it! She was getting hungry. No way was she going to go fishing for seals or raw fish for her meal.

She followed him to the cabin where he shifted outside, all naked, pure muscled beauty, then opened the door for her and went in. Inside, he was already starting to pull on his clothes. As soon as she entered the cabin, he closed the door. He was standing there in boxer briefs, and she again wondered how he'd look in a kilt. Sexy, she thought.

Then she moved around the spacious cabin, exploring in her bear form while Rob dressed by the fire. "You're probably hungry. I'll make us something to eat."

She realized then he had enough food for several days in the van, and probably more in the cabin already that wasn't perishable. So how would she eat? Licking her meal from a dish like a dog?

She considered the loft bed and the two bedrooms off a short hall. She smelled Rob's scent in the one room that was decorated all in forest greens. The other bedroom was all in browns, and she smelled Edward's scent in there. Casey had been in the place too, and others. But she didn't know their scents...yet.

"I enjoyed playing with you in the water," Rob said,

pulling out a pan to cook something. "Playing with you is a lot different from roughhousing with my brother, cousins, or Casey. You can sleep in any bedroom you'd like."

She grunted. How was she supposed to sleep on someone's bed as a polar bear?

"Yeah, normally we all shift when we're in the cabin. In your case, we don't have any idea when you're going to change, so you pick where you want to sleep. The beds are big enough. Just think of it like 'Goldilocks and the Three Bears.' Just choose a bed and it's yours. Edward's is the brown bedroom, and he won't mind you sleeping there. Same with me as far as you sleeping in my bed."

She'd sleep in Edward's bed. It seemed silly to make Rob change beds for no reason.

He fixed her halibut and she set aside her human need to be civilized and hungrily licked the plate clean, thinking that as a bear, she got to do things she'd never consider doing as a human.

It was getting dark out and Rob sat down by the fire. She joined him. "Our grandfathers built this cabin and two others like it. They needed a place to go to get away from the civilized world. I've got to call my aunt and uncle and let them know what's happened. They'll pass the word along to the other polar bear shifters."

She worried how they'd react to the news. She

could endanger all of them because of her inability to control her shifting.

He got on the phone and she sat next to the fire, just staring into it as he spoke. "Hi, Uncle Ned, I have some important news I have to share with you."

Bad news, she was thinking.

"Hunters were illegally hunting at one of the locations where we stopped to take photos. The hunters caused the moose to stampede in our direction. One of the men on our tour group knocked one of the women into the lake. I had to pull Alicia Raycroft out of the water. Yes, sir. As a bear. She wouldn't have survived as chilled as she was. I made the decision. Yes, sir. I turned her. She's at my and Edward's cabin with me for now. Casey and Edward continued with the tour. No one else saw me shift."

Rob reached down and rubbed her head. "She and I were just swimming as polar bears. No, sir. She shifted right away, but only after we were alone in the van. She hasn't shifted back. We'll stay here until we know she has some control over her shifting."

He looked down at her. "I don't know about her family. Her assistant went with the tour group. Yes, sir. We'll have to say we had a whirlwind affair, and she's decided to stay here in Alaska with me. I hope she's agreeable."

Alicia grunted. As if she had any choice! But she was

grateful Rob had saved her life, and she was none the worse for wear—except she seemed to have a permanently affixed polar bear coat. It reminded her of the story she'd read as a child: "East of the Sun and West of the Moon," a Norwegian tale where a man was turned into a polar bear by day and was a man at night. He married a woman who was never to see him as a man, but when she did, he left her. But she came after him and together they took down the evil troll that had cast the curse on him.

Alicia guessed there was no fixing what she was though. She would just have to learn to live with it and pray she could soon get the shifting under control. She couldn't imagine living out her days and nights as a polar bear.

"Yeah, we'll all take good care of her. I told her we would. She's the dark-haired beauty. The one Ben was trying to hook me up with." Rob laughed. "Yeah, well, now that she's one of us, he can't have her."

Alicia looked up at Rob. He smiled at her, and she wondered if he was thinking that they could really date. Now she knew why he had been reluctant to become intimate with anyone on the tours that he guided. Not just because of the distant relationship business. The guests were human and that wouldn't have worked well in the long run for any of the bear shifters.

"Okay, thanks. I'm sure she'll appreciate it once she

feels more settled about her new abilities. She's still in her bear form. Okay, call you later. Night." Rob said to Alicia, "Well, they're not happy that I've put you in this bind, but they're glad you survived and are doing well. And they welcome you with open arms into the MacMathan clan. Others will be interested in courting you once they learn of you, I'll warn you right now, but the family will fight to keep them away."

She stared at Rob, not understanding. Did his family think one of the MacMathan bachelors should marry her? Or because of her uniqueness, being turned and not born as a shifter, which could cause all kinds of trouble for them, they felt they should keep her in the family? Which made her wonder why they would want to. Wouldn't it be easier to let someone else deal with the problem? Or maybe it was because Rob had bitten her, so they felt she was his responsibility.

In any event, she had an unusual connection with Rob because of the paranormal business and he had saved her life. Now he was teaching her how to be a polar bear and taking care of her, so she didn't think anyone, who wore a polar bear coat part time, should have any concern about her seeing them.

She hadn't had any visions while being in this form and that made her wonder if she couldn't have them as a polar bear. Did Rob have his visions as one?

It had long since grown dark and Rob finally said,

"Did you want to go to bed?"

She shook her head, but she curled up by the fireplace and closed her eyes. She hadn't meant she didn't want to go to sleep, only that she didn't want to sleep in a bed as a bear.

"All right. If you need anything, just come and nudge me and we'll figure it out."

Bathroom break? Ugh. She figured she better make a pit stop if she was going to manage to make it through the night. She'd had plenty of fresh cold water to drink and though she felt all right now, she didn't want to have to wake him in the middle of the night to have to go outside to pee.

She got up and headed for the door.

He rose from the couch and followed her, then opened the door for her. "Do you want me to go with you?"

She shook her head. She didn't need him to watch her while she squatted somewhere in the woods. This was just too weird. Yet, it was just a natural part of being any kind of animal, she reminded herself. She thought if she was a wolf shifter, she could have a doggy door, and wouldn't have to bother Rob with this, but as a polar bear, she'd need a human door practically. And then any bear could enter at will.

"Just roar if you need me. I'll be out there in a heartbeat."

She made another noise that sounded like a huffing sound to her. She didn't know what she was saying to him, but he said, "Good. With our enhanced hearing, I'll be able to locate you quickly and come to your aid."

She went outside into the dark then and found her way through the trees. She startled a white hare that bounded off. An owl hooted from a nearby tree. Everything, including the movement of the hare, sounded so much more vivid, and the cold crisp air smelled so clean and bracing. She couldn't imagine coming out here to relieve herself as a human, so in that respect, she was glad for her winter coat. Where they were going to backpack into the wilderness area and set up tents with the tour group, they didn't have restroom facilities either.

As soon as she finished outside, she sprinted back to the house, and Rob was waiting for her the whole time, door open, watching for her. She had to appreciate he was taking his job to care for her seriously. When she entered the house, he shut the door, and she rubbed up against him, showing him her appreciation. Then she curled back up before the fire for her long winter's nap. Though polar bears didn't hibernate.

"Night, Alicia," Rob said, crouching down and running his hand over her head. She licked his hand, and then laid her head back down, exhausted.

She didn't think playing in the water as a polar bear would have worn her out that fast, but she figured it had something to do with the trauma of being turned, the loss of body heat when she had fallen into the water, and the injury to her arm. Which, she realized felt fine now.

Rob headed into the back bedroom and she heard him get into the bed, then the light went out and she closed her eyes again. She hoped she would turn back into her human form soon, and stay that way for a while so she could ask Rob some questions. Which was the last thought she had before she woke up completely naked as Rob carried her to his bedroom, placed her in his bed, climbed in with her, and covered them with the blankets.

She guessed he'd decided she didn't need to make a bed choice. That he was making it for her. As tired as she was, she didn't care. She was only glad he'd come to get her when she had turned or she would have been freezing, probably confused, and not snuggling against his naked body under the comforter and blankets.

But how had he known when she'd shifted?

CHAPTER 10

Rob hadn't been able to sleep, not with worrying that the fire would die out, which, for Alicia wearing her fur coat probably would be preferable. As a human lying on the faux fur rug on the wooden floor, not. He'd grabbed a pillow and blanket and stretched out on the comfortable couch, ready at a moment's notice to wake and move her to a bed in case she shifted. Two hours later while he was catching some z's, he heard her moving a little and opened his eyes, just in time to see her form blurring into that of a human's. He'd quickly left the couch, expecting the shift to wake her, but it didn't. She only slightly stirred in his arms when he lifted her off the rug and carried her into his bedroom. For an instant, he'd thought of depositing her in Edward's bed, but he quickly discounted that notion. She was his responsibility, and he didn't want to have to worry if she changed back again into a bear, felt disoriented, and he wasn't there to reassure her.

Besides, he really didn't want her to leave her scent in his brother's bed. Rob much preferred smelling her sweet scent in his bed, and wrapping his scent around her that said she was his. She might not appreciate it, though for now, she snuggled closer, her leg propped over his, making him feel as though she was comfortable being with him. He supposed he should have at least worn a pair of boxers, but he had wanted to be prepared if she got all growly with him, and he could shift and deal with a bear better as a bear without having to pause to strip.

He'd noted when he had lifted her, her shoulder was completely healed, which he was grateful for. He just hoped she could hold her form until after he fed her breakfast tomorrow, and longer, of course, but he suspected she'd prefer eating as a human. She was sure to have questions to ask of him too that she couldn't until she was human again.

He'd had so much fun playing with her as a polar bear in the water that he wanted to do that again if she shifted. He thought they could go exploring also, and he'd show her how she could move as a bear, though he figured she'd learn that on her own quickly enough.

Rob was sleeping soundly when he felt Alicia's hand caressing his chest. At first, he thought she was just moving in her sleep, yet all his senses were attuned to her and he was hoping she was reaching out to him for more.

She pressed her mouth gently against his shoulder in a soft kiss, stirring his cock to full arousal. He stroked her shoulder, wondering just where she wanted to take this, and was eager to do whatever she wanted.

He kissed her forehead and wrapped his arms around her, hugging her. "How are you feeling?" he asked, his voice low, not wanting to wake her fully if she wasn't ready to get up.

"I still can't believe everything that's happened. It just seems like I'm living some fantasy, not reality at all. It's like yesterday was all just a dream." She let out her breath. "I'm coming to grips with making a home with you, with your family. I mean, I really don't have any choice."

"I'm sorry." He meant it as far as not giving her a choice in the matter, but he wasn't sorry about saving her life. He continued to caress her shoulder in a reassuring manner, but her naked body pressed against his couldn't help but stir his libido.

"You didn't have anything to do with what happened to me. Doug knocked me into the water and you rescued me in the only way you could. And I know, despite all the hurdles I'll have to overcome, I need to embrace what I've become. I take it your story that you chased away the grizzly bear was correct and what Judi saw was you in your bear coat."

"Yes."

"I couldn't imagine how or why you would have stripped off some of your clothes to fight off the grizzly, until I learned what you were. What do we do now?"

"Play, eat, just learn what it's like to be one of us. Whatever you want to do, I'm game."

"Make love?" She was stroking his chest with her fingertips, her gaze steady on his.

It was his fervent desire. But he didn't want her to regret anything later. "Hell yeah. If...if that's what you want."

"No worry about birth control. I have it covered." She kissed his shoulder again, her lips warm and soft against his skin.

"Good." Rob's voice was already husky with need. He couldn't help it. Touching her, smelling her, listening to her steady heartbeat, her light breathing, seeing her in the soft morning light, he wanted her and needed her. He ran his hand over her cheek, felt the silky softness, and kissed her there. She sighed.

He moved her onto her back so he could kiss her mouth, slowly deeply, his hand brushing over her firm breasts. "You're beautiful."

"Hmm, so are you."

Smiling, he moved his mouth over her nipple and

began to suckle, making her moan with pleasure. She ran her hands through his hair, the touch of her fingers stroking his scalp making his cock twitch. He began to lick her nipple, teasing it with his tongue, the pad of his thumb rubbing over the other nipple, enjoying the way they pebbled. She slid her smooth leg against his, her scent triggering his craving for her to fully, sexually aroused, which helped to stimulate his own interested scent.

She was warm and soft beneath him as he licked a trail to her navel. She grasped hands full of his hair, her breathing ragged. Then he slipped his finger between her legs, deepening, stirring, wringing a gasp from her. Her eyes were half-lidded, her hands stilled on his hips, as if she was lost in his touching her until he began to stroke her clit. She was a dream, responsive, melting under his ministration, eager. She grabbed the mattress in her clenched fingers, and he slipped his finger inside her, pushing as deep as he could.

He felt her tensing, barely breathing, her heart beating hard. And then she cried out as she came, her muscles clenching in orgasm.

"Are you sure about this?" he asked, praying she didn't stop him now. He felt like a randy teen, unable to control his need to finish this with her.

"Yes, do it." She stroked his waist, encouraging him to enter her.

He didn't hesitate to press his cock between her legs. He seated himself all the way into her heat and began to push into her silky chasm. She locked her legs around him as if claiming him for her own. He rocked into her, feeling the primitive need to have and hold as she ran her hands over his arms. Then he leaned down and kissed her willing mouth, and she tangled her tongue with his, her hands combing through his hair again. Everything about the way she touched him said she wanted him and wanted this just as much as he did.

He hoped she wouldn't regret it when she thought about it later. That it would make her feel more connected with him than even before. The electricity sparked between them before he climaxed and continued to rub against her until she cried out in exaltation. "Oh. My. God."

He collapsed on the bed next to her and pulled the covers over them, his hand stroking her breast, wanting the intimacy to continue between them. Just like he wanted everything else to continue between them. The playfulness as bears, the learning to live with this, the getting to know each other better even, and meeting the family, and hoping Alicia would accept all of them.

"That was *un*believable."

"Good, huh?" he asked, kissing her throat.

"Nothing has ever come close to making me feel that way." She licked his nipple and ran her hand over his chest.

"I think it has something to do with the bear in you."

She laughed. "God, like the primitive side of us was unleashed? *Beautiful.*"

"You made it so." He had to learn if she had family too, and what to do about that. He hoped they'd be right for each other. Here he thought it would be years before he'd ever find the right woman for him, but Alicia made his world complete in ways no other woman ever had.

In the bear world, the bears weren't monogamous and the bear shifters weren't like the wolves who mated for life. Even so, most of the bear shifters still took a mate for life. He knew that's just what he wanted too, with her.

***

Alicia was quickly getting used to the idea that what had just happened between her and Rob was meant to be—the natural progression of their relationship. The intimacy that would draw them even closer, to connect on a different level, on a closer, more endearing level.

She was usually an upbeat optimist no matter the situation. But whenever she needed reassurance she was on the right path, she would think of some of the philosopher William James's comments on life: that if you could change your mind, you could change your life;

or that no matter where you are, friends make your world—was exactly the place she was at right now.

One of her favorite quotes by William James: "If you believe that feeling bad or worrying long enough will change a past or future event, then you are residing on another planet with a different reality system"—summed up her current situation in a nutshell. She often reminded herself of that quote when she had a particularly bad vision, and wished she hadn't and even wished she didn't have the ability at all. Yet she'd been able to assist in solving criminal cases because of her ability, helping to put the criminals behind bars even.

She realized now, she didn't just have a psychological paranormal gift, but a physical one too. Just like the quote William had made about altering your life if you altered your attitude was all so true in this case. She could see being a polar bear shifter as a gift or a curse, just like how she viewed her ability to see happenings through touch. It was her choice how she viewed her extraordinary abilities.

She still doubted herself sometimes. She knew she would with being a polar bear shifter too, especially until she was more used to being one.

She wrapped herself around Rob even more, hoping he wouldn't see her move as clingy, but just a way to say she was comfortable being with him like this, enjoying the intimacy, and hoping he did too. The way he was gently caressing her back ensured her he was fine with the way things were—relaxed, contented, not tense and pulling away.

"We made love like that in my vision. I never expected it to be quite like this though," she said.

"As a shifter?" Rob asked, his voice soothing.

"Yeah. I didn't know it would be this hot either."

He smiled down at her.

"Just that we'd be naked and making love. Not where or when." She ran her hand over his chest. "It was beautiful, nothing I could have imagined."

"Do you normally see the visions of something that hasn't happened? Somehow I thought you would only see those things that had already occurred by touching a person or object."

"You're right. That's usually how it works. Our abilities seemed to have somehow synched and then I began to see your future visions."

"When you first touched me."

"Right."

"Do you have to always touch me to see them?"

"I'm not sure. Both times I had. I haven't had any visions since then."

"This feels right to me, being with you like this," Rob said, kissing her forehead.

She snuggled closer. "I don't want you to think I'm clingy. I never am."

"Ditto, Alicia. This just feels right. If I were crazy and didn't appreciate being with you like this...that's how I might view it. But that's not the case or I'd be leaving the bed, not wanting to stay here with you. Being with you has changed my whole outlook on life. I have family and friends, but the relationship between a man and woman goes so much deeper. At least for me it does with you."

"Because of our paranormal connection?"

"I believe so."

"And now our shifter connection." She kissed his chest and wanted to make love again. She could already feel his erection at full mast, and the way his voice was growing rougher, he was interested.

They stopped talking then, and began kissing, enjoying this deeper connection—a man and woman with common grounds—needs to be satisfied before she turned back into a bear.

CHAPTER 11

Rob basked in the dreamy sensation he felt after making love to Alicia. He loved how affectionate she was.

"Do you have visions as a polar bear?" she suddenly asked.

"Yeah. Have you had any since you've been turned?"

"No. I wondered if, when you shifted, you could still see visions."

"We're still the same people, just wearing a different outer form. But our brains are still ours."

"Okay, I just wondered. What do your aunt and uncle feel about all this? About me being an unreliable shifter among you? Really?"

"They're worried about you, about how you feel more than anything. Even if you seem to be fine with it now. After the initial shock, will you feel differently days or weeks from now? How difficult will it be for you to maintain your human form? Where will you stay until you have more control over it? They just worry about how you feel, not how it will affect us. They welcome you as part of the family, no qualms about it."

"Okay, I worried that they might be anxious or upset about you turning me."

"They understand the situation."

"About our paranormal abilities too? I mean, besides the shifting part of it."

"No, they don't know about that, but I intend to tell them."

"About me too?"

"Do you have any trouble with it?"

"No. Not if you're going to share about yourself."

"I told Ben and my brother. They're good with it."

"Okay."

"Want to get up and shower, then eat?"

"Yeah, sure."

After they showered and dressed, Rob fixed them eggs and sausage links while she made toast and coffee for them. He had never had any long-term, fix breakfast, and hang around girlfriends before. He could get used to this. "Ben will be bringing supplies out here. One of my cousins, Ben's brother Craig, has a seaplane. He'll land on the water, drop off the supplies, and they'll return home. If there's anything you want, we'll let them know and they can make another drop later."

"Clothes?"

Smiling, Rob served up the eggs and sausages. "I thought we might not need them a lot."

"If I'm a polar bear?"

"And otherwise. I've got your bag and mine in the van still, but he can bring more clothes if we're going to be staying here longer than anticipated."

She sighed. "I admit this is really nice, but what about Judi?" Alicia coated her toast with butter and blueberry jelly, then stared at the jelly.

"What's wrong?"

"I never liked blueberries or blueberry jam before."

"Your polar bear half likes them. As to Judi, you're marrying me. That's what you can tell her."

"Right. She wouldn't believe that in a million years, not as cautious as I am about relationships. Which has a lot to do with a recent breakup. And then there's the issue of my paranormal abilities. It's not something that goes over big with some people."

"Does she know about your abilities?"

"Yes."

"Tell her I'm like you then. What better way to convince her that we were meant for each other? You can even say you envisioned we were getting married."

"Then she'd want to come to the wedding. I'm sure

she'd believe that I feel more connected to you through our abilities though."

"What about your family?"

"Mother and father, no siblings. Grandparents are gone. No aunts or uncles."

Rob was immediately concerned about the parent issue. "How close are you to your parents?"

"Not very. They never believed in my paranormal abilities. When I helped the police to solve a couple of cases, my mother said I sure had them hoodwinked. You know, it's hard enough dealing with the issues that come up with this. It can be even worse when your family doesn't believe you and calls you crazy. I was never so glad as when I left home and was on my own."

"Would you consider helping the police locally?"

"Maybe. It depends on the situation."

"I understand. With me, I just never share with anyone. I figure if I don't, I avoid all the naysayers. Well, a few times I did when I realized what I could see would come true and that it wasn't some figment of my imagination. I can't see visions of anyone close. I just had a couple of visions around people and couldn't believe it, shared what I'd seen and was scoffed at. After all these years, I just told my brother and Casey about my abilities. I was surprised they believed me. If I had known they would, I would have told them years earlier. Like you, my talking about it resulted in such negativity,

I just kept it to myself. It's a real relief to me to know someone who understands what I see, just as well as I can understand what you envision."

"Yet you were still reluctant to get close until I was really like you."

"As in being a shifter? Yes. I can just imagine what you would have said to that if I'd told you beforehand."

She smiled at him, and her expression was devilish. "What if I'd said I believed you, only you had to show me your big, cuddly polar bear form first to show me just how beautiful you were?"

"At the house when the rest of our tour group was gone? I could have shown you."

"But you wouldn't have. You would have smiled in that wicked way that just makes me all hot and bothered and makes me want to know about all your dark secrets."

He laughed.

Then she grew serious, refilling their coffee mugs. "Do you have any regrets about turning me? I mean, at first you reacted on instinct, shifted, and came to rescue me. After having done so, do you feel in some way you might have made a big mistake?"

"Are you kidding?"

She set his coffee mug on the table before him.

He took hers and set it on the table too, then pulled her onto his lap. "Does it seem to you in any way that I regret this?" He kissed her neck and cheek and lips. "Admittedly, I did worry how you would feel about it and that's *all* I worried about. I was certain if you could see it as a gift, not a curse, we could get through this. And hell, this is one damn wonderful way to get through this."

She laughed. "I have to admit you are one cuddly, hot polar bear in the flesh."

He smiled at her, glad she felt that way about him. "You are too. Just my kind of bear." He meant it too. He knew that he wasn't giving her up for anything. She was fun and spontaneous and taking this whole upside down world in stride. He hadn't known how she would react, but he was glad she wasn't angry, growly, or inconsolable about the whole situation. If she had been, he would have done everything in his power to make her feel better, to help her get through this, but he was glad she was more accepting. He suspected it was because she had unique abilities and had learned to make the best of her unique situation concerning that too.

"When you had to shift the last time, did you have any forewarning?" he asked, hoping she could recognize the trouble before it occurred.

"I was burning up."

"Our muscles, tendons, cells warm during the shift. It clues us in. I was worried the cold and the bite wound was the difficulty. That you were feverish."

"I guess not because after I shifted, I was warm, but only because of the fur coat."

"We instinctually know when we're going to shift. Hopefully you will too soon, if you don't right away."

They heard a plane flying closer and Alicia immediately got off Rob's lap.

"Ben?" she asked.

"Most likely." Rob wasn't sure how his cousins would react to seeing Alicia now that she was a bear shifter too. "I'm running out to help with the supplies."

"Me too."

He was glad she wasn't reluctant to be with others of their kind, afraid they might not accept her. They grabbed their parkas and quickly put them on. Then pulled on their gloves and hats and headed outside.

Ben was all serious looking while he was already carrying a box of groceries to the cabin. He smiled then at Alicia, a warm, welcoming smile, not a hungry-bear look that said he was interested in a romantic liaison.

The pilot, Rob's cousin Craig, had a couple of bags in hand and was grinning at Alicia. He *did* have a hungry-bear look.

"Hey, thanks, Ben, Craig, for bringing us all the stuff," Rob said.

"Hell, if you want to continue on with the tour group, I can stay here with Alicia and teach her all about being a bear shifter," Craig said.

Rob knew his cousin was only partially teasing.

"She's Rob's. He saw her first, wined and dined her—" Ben was saying.

"Bit me," Alicia said, grabbing a couple of bags from the shore while Rob lifted another box of groceries and they began to walk back to the cabin. "Which meant he saved my life."

"Debt of gratitude," Craig said. "Gets them all the time."

"Hey, Mom and Dad want Alicia to come see them as soon as she feels comfortable doing so," Ben said. "Because, you know, she's part of the family now."

"We will." Rob didn't know how long it would take. He figured he could take her at night so if she shifted, the van would be nice and dark and no one would see he was carrying a polar bear inside.

"What about your roommate?" Ben asked Alicia.

"Rob and I are getting married."

Ben smiled, but Craig's jaw dropped.

"Sorry, man," Rob said, setting the box of groceries on the kitchen counter. "You know how that goes. Ben is a matchmaker extraordinaire."

"For real? I mean, you're really getting married?" Craig asked.

"Ben asked about my roommate. We're telling her we're getting married." Alicia walked back to Rob's room with the bags.

"Your room?" Ben whispered to Rob.

Rob suspected Alicia might have heard, as good as their hearing was. "Yeah. I told you you're good at your matchmaking job. I was serious."

"Besides," Alicia said, returning to the dining room, "we both have a unique talent."

Rob guessed she wanted to let his cousins know that they both had unusual abilities to prove they truly did have something in common. And maybe to say it so that Craig might not be so eager to get to know her if he realized she was different.

Both of his cousins looked from Alicia to Rob, probably wondering what his unique talent was that he had never mentioned to them before. Playing a special instrument? Some other talent? He was sure they wouldn't guess anything about them having a paranormal ability. Unless Edward or Casey had let it slip. He was certain if one of them did, his cousins would have said something before now.

Everyone took seats in the living room before the fire, Rob making sure he sat next to Alicia. Rob explained what they both could do, and his cousins looked from Rob to Alicia to see what she had to say about it. Neither appeared to believe it.

"Okay," Alicia said. "You believe you're polar bear shifters, right?"

"Uh, yeah, but that's a given," Ben said.

Craig nodded.

"Right. But I envisioned what would happen to me when Rob came to save me, only I believed he was going to eat me."

The guys both smiled. Rob knew just what they were thinking. He cleared his throat. "I did bite her. I saw the grizzly attack in the blizzard. I knew it was going to snow before there were any weather reports indicating it would."

"When I touched Rob, I saw what he saw, so we had some kind of real connection. I've worked for the San Antonio police department as a...well, consultant a few times. It's hush-hush."

"Because you can help them, but they don't want to ruin their reputations by saying you helped them," Ben guessed.

"Exactly. They appreciated my help, once they got over the skepticism, but they didn't want to advertise what kind of actual aid I was giving them."

Ben shook his head.

"Okay, well, I'm a believer, so if you want to date me, I'm ready to take you to some nice places." Craig winked at Alicia.

Ben slapped Craig on the shoulder. "I already made the match between them. You don't stand a chance. They probably already had seen they were together in their future. Can't beat that."

Craig gave an elongated sigh, then rose from his seat. "Well, if you see anything differently, you know where I'll be."

"Thanks, Craig. I appreciate that," Alicia said.

Rob shook each of his cousin's hands and they both gave Alicia a hug. "Welcome to the family," Ben and Craig said at the same time.

"If you need us for anything," Ben said to Rob, "just holler and we'll come." He was ultra-serious now, and Rob appreciated his offer.

"Thanks, Ben. Will do."

They saw them out the door, but Alicia suddenly excused herself.

Everyone watched her disappear back inside the house.

"We're serious. If this takes longer than you can afford to stay here, we'll all help. Even Mom and Dad said they'd take turns coming out here. Whatever we must do to help Alicia get through this," Ben said.

Rob thought his cousins were going to leave then, but they waited until Alicia came out in her polar bear fur coat, wanting to see how beautiful she was.

"Aw, just great," Craig said. "She has to be beautiful in her fur coat too."

Rob laughed. "As if she wouldn't be."

"We'll see you soon," Ben said to Alicia, and then

he and Craig got into the plane and took off.

And then Rob headed back to the house. "I'll change and be out in just a second."

When he went outside as a polar bear, he didn't see any sign of her. Not near the cabin, in the lake, or the woods. Though he knew he shouldn't panic, he couldn't help worrying about where she'd disappeared to.

He took off through the woods, saw her bear prints in the snow and began to follow them in haste.

***

Alicia jumped into the water, loving this part about being a polar bear best. She swam down several feet beneath the surface of the water and saw a seal. Excited, she swam after him before she had to come up for air. When she surfaced, she saw a grizzly catching fish nearby and nearly had a heart attack. Since polar bears weren't normally in this territory, just shifters, she feared this might be the grizzly's territory. Then she wondered if he was a shifter—maybe even the same one who had attacked Edward and Rob. Despite that she was a female and a lot smaller, she wanted to bite him for attacking her friends. If he was the one who had.

She realized then how quickly both Edward and Rob had healed from their wounds, not a scratch on Rob's chest, neck, or shoulder when she'd made love to him. That was one good thing about being a shifter.

She slipped underneath the water and swam back

in the direction of the cabin. When she had to surface, she found she'd swum beyond where the cabin was. She peered back and saw the grizzly still catching fish. And then she saw Rob. He was watching the grizzly, unaware she was in the water. She came up on the bank, not wanting to catch the grizzly's attention, but she didn't want Rob confronting the bear for no reason either.

Rob saw her then and began to move backward toward her, keeping an eye on the grizzly. A single wolf had no chance against a bear, but a pack of wolves could chase off a bear. Would the same be true for two polar bears against one grizzly?

Rob indicated to her with his head that he wanted them to return to the cabin. That worked for her if that would stop the grizzly bear from attacking. He was watching them now, wary. Just as wary as she felt. This situation made her realize just how vulnerable they were against other bears or against man also.

They moved away from the bear, making a wide circle back to the cabin. The grizzly stood up in a menacing way. Her heart beating triple time, she wanted to race to the cabin. But running might trigger the grizzly to take chase. So she moved just as cautiously as Rob did. When she finally reached the open door to the cabin, she hurried inside. Rob followed, shifted, and shut the door. He slid the bolt across it, and walked across the wood floor where she was sitting and gave her a hug.

She loved him for it. She had half expected him to scold her for going off on her own, but instead, he smiled at her. "Did you like the water this time? I thought you might still be reluctant to get in. When I didn't see you at first, I figured you were in the woods, which is where I found your paw prints in the snow. Until I saw they led to the water, and observed the grizzly catching fish there."

She was disappointed that she had to stay in the house when she really wanted to play in the snow. A rifle report shattered the quiet outside. A second round was fired and Rob hurried to dress.

"Whatever you do, don't come outside. If they're hunters, they could shoot and kill you, saying you were attacking them. Stay in the bedroom if you like. Just stay out of sight, no matter what."

She fervently wished she could shift, and didn't want Rob to go outside when hunters were about. Why would he go out to speak to them anyway?

She tried to get around him, to stop him.

He sighed. "They're most likely illegally hunting the grizzly. It's winter, no hunting allowed."

She growled at him. If they were lawbreakers, what if they decided to shoot Rob to cover up what they were doing?

"Alicia, I need to get rid of them. If they hang

around here, we can't even leave the cabin when you're a bear."

She still didn't want him to confront them. It would be easy for the men to kill him, dump Rob in the water, and let the animals feed off him. No one would ever be the wiser, except for her.

He gave her a hug, then headed outside, leaving the door slightly ajar. Despite what he'd told her, she went to the window in the living room and peered out. The men were near the lake, and she didn't see any sign of the grizzly. Despite how dangerous they could be, she was glad the grizzly had run off.

Three men in white and brown camo parkas and matching ski pants watched as Rob went out to speak with them.

She would kill them if they shot Rob. She wouldn't hesitate to protect him.

CHAPTER 12

Rob hurried outside and hollered at the three hunters, wanting to get their attention so they wouldn't shoot him accidentally. "Hunting season's over!"

"What's it to you? The bear was attacking," the bigger of the two men said. "We have every right to defend ourselves." They were the same damn men from the tavern.

"Show me your ID," Rob said.

"Who the hell are you?" the black-haired man said.

"Wildlife Management official." Rob pulled out a badge. The men showed him their IDs, though they were damn slow about it. He wasn't really with Wildlife Management, but he and the other shifters who lived around here, had badges professing they were with the organization to discourage hunters from killing any of their kind, especially when it was past the hunting season, so illegal to do so. "Were you shooting at moose near where a tour group was, causing a stampede in their direction?"

The men looked stony-faced. From experience, Rob knew that men who were innocent of a crime would have said they hadn't had anything to do with it. But he still couldn't prove anything. He hadn't seen the men who were shooting. He'd only heard their gunfire.

"I'll let you off with a warning," Rob said to the men, memorizing their names and addresses. Homer and Reefer Johnson. And Hanson Baldwin. "But if I learn you've killed any bears in the area, or anything else, for that matter, I'll turn you in myself." He handed their IDs back to them.

The men started to snowshoe it out of there and Rob turned to head back to the cabin. But he heard them turn, and knew before they fired a shot that one of the men was going to try and shoot him. Rob dove for the snow as a round was fired and went off where his back had just been, the bullet buzzing above his head.

Bastards!

Before they could shoot at him again, Alicia shot out of the cabin as a polar bear, sprinting at about twenty-five miles per hour toward the hunters. The men would shoot her, damn it! Rob was on his feet in an instant, chasing after her as one of the men fired at her, but his rifle jammed. The other two took off running, trying to distance themselves from the enraged polar bear.

"Holy hell," Hanson shouted as he turned to escape her.

She struck him in the head with her paw, knocking him out cold. Then she ran for one of the others as he was trying to run in snowshoes, but he tripped and fell, planting his face in the snow.

Rob raced to catch up to her, grabbing the first man's rifle and tossing it into the lake. She roared at the man and swiped at him too, knocking him out. The last man was still running and Rob reached him and took him down. Alicia grabbed the second man's rifle with her teeth and carried it to the lake and dropped it in. They had a choice: dump the men into the lake, letting the cold take its toll, take them into the cabin and let them recover and try to get the troopers out here to take care of these men, or let them go and they could find their way home without their rifles.

If the men hadn't tried to kill Rob, that would be one thing. But if they were tried in court, he'd have to be a witness, and so would Alicia. What if she couldn't hold her human form? He couldn't trust that she would be able to. Even though, she'd been a bear the whole time, once she turned, if the men were still here, the police would most likely question her as a witness.

Rob checked the men over further and found drugs

on all three of them. Hell, so not only were they illegally hunting bear, and attempting to murder him, they were in the possession of drugs. To sell? Most likely. And that could very well be the reason they didn't want him to tell the troopers what they were up to. They probably had been in jail before. Rob tossed the third man's rifle into the lake.

Alicia paced back and forth, looking like a highly agitated polar bear.

Rob got on his cell and called his uncle and was glad he got through. "We have a situation here. Three men tried to shoot a grizzly near my cabin and then tried to kill me. Alicia knocked them out and I threw their rifles in the lake. They're also in the possession of illegal drugs."

"We'll send the plane to pick them up."

"Andy?"

"Yeah. He's on leave, and the only one of us with a legitimate badge. He can arrest them, say they tried to kill him, everything you told me, except he'll claim they said it to him instead of you."

"All right. I'll drag them inside so they don't freeze to death, and Andy can take it from there."

"Was the grizzly bear they attempted to shoot Gary?"

"No. I didn't recognize the bear. Probably not a shifter, but I'm not sure." Rob started to drag the first unconscious man toward the cabin.

"Your aunt already has a call into Andy."

"Thanks, Uncle Ned."

"How's the young lady?"

Rob glanced back at Alicia. She had taken his cue and was dragging one of the other men toward the cabin.

"Alicia changed back earlier. When one of the hunters fired at me, she raced out to stop him from shooting further, saving my life. She controlled her strength when dealing with the men. I wouldn't have stood a chance if she hadn't come out to help me."

"Genevieve wonders when you're going to settle down with her. Sounds to me like she's the right one for you."

Rob smiled. "We just met."

"Okay, I'll remind your aunt of that."

"I've got to go. One of the men is stirring."

"All right, son. Good luck, and call me if you have any more trouble, and let me know when Andy gets there."

"Wil do." Rob finished pulling the first man into the cabin when Alicia suddenly pushed at Rob to get him to move out of the way. She'd left the other man back in the snow and then raced into the house and disappeared down the hall. If Rob had to guess, he'd say Alicia was getting ready to shift. Sure enough, by the time he'd pulled the last of the men into the house and tied them up, Alicia was coming out of the bedroom, her hair tied back, and she was dressed in ski pants, a sweater, and socks.

"Omigod, Rob, I'm so sorry." Tears filled her eyes.

Rob pulled her into a hug. "You saved my life. Nothing to be sorry for."

"What are we going to do about them now?"

"I have a cousin who is a trooper. He's on leave, but he's flying in to take care of them."

"Arrest them?"

"Yeah."

"They tried to kill you."

"They did. Andy will handle it. Thanks for coming to my rescue. You nearly gave me a heart attack, though," Rob said, speaking quietly to her while he rubbed her back.

"You didn't stand a chance. I didn't think I could move that fast as a bear though. I was glad I could. I never really knew what seeing red meant until I saw the one man aiming his rifle to shoot you."

Rob hugged her tight. "Thank you."

"We're even now." She looked up at him, her eyes still misty with tears.

For an instant, he felt as though she meant that she didn't owe him her life any longer. That she was free of him. He realized just how much he wanted her in his life for the long-term. That he'd been thinking that way all along—not as in a planned way, but just taking it for granted that she had nowhere else to go now that she was one of them. That she needed him and he would be there for her while she learned to be what she was now and beyond. He was looking forward to it, not as an obligation for turning her, but because she added so much to his life.

He thought about how he could be with his brother and Casey with the other members of the tour group right now, doing all the things he normally did, or be with Alicia, playing as bears in the snow and water, making love to her in the warm, cozy cabin, sharing meals and stories, and enjoying each other's company. He didn't want to give that up. To go back to the way it was. He wanted to come home to her when he was through with an assignment. And he wanted her to go with them when she could get her shifting under control.

He didn't want her looking for someone else to share her days and nights with.

What were they going to do? She would always have to stay with his family if he was going to keep her safe when he took groups on tours. He couldn't leave her alone in the cabin out here. She'd need someone to watch out for her.

His aunt and uncle would take her in at a moment's

notice. Insist on it even. Well, any of his cousins would too. Which didn't sit well with him. "You did great with using restraint and not injuring them severely or fatally."

"I will admit it was hard to do. It would have been so easy to take them out after what they tried to do to you."

"But you didn't, and I admire you for it. I'm sure I would have had a harder time with it had you been the one they were shooting at."

"What the hell," one of the men said, coming to enough to realize he was lying on the floor inside the cabin near the door, tied up.

Rob imagined the guy would be sporting a couple of bruised ribs and a bunch of other bruises. He also realized that he'd tossed the men's rifles into the lake and Andy wouldn't be able to use that as evidence that the men had been shooting at the grizzly bear illegally, or that they'd shot at Rob. Except...yeah, they'd have residue on their fingers from firing the rounds. And the casings from the spent rounds.

"Do you want to have some hot cocoa?" Rob asked Alicia.

"Yeah. How long before Andy gets here?"

"An hour from now." Rob wrapped his hand around hers and walked her into the kitchen.

"Hey, let us go," the alert man said. "You have no

right holding us."

"You tried to kill a trooper while he was doing his duty. We have every right," Alicia growled.

By the time the cocoa was ready, the other two men were stirring, and trying to wrench free of their bindings. "A polar bear tried to kill us."

"I didn't see any polar bear, did you, honey?" Alicia asked. "Just the grizzly bear you two were trying to illegally kill."

"Nope. If we'd seen a polar bear taking off after the three of you, you wouldn't be alive to tell your story. And, you were firing rifles. Any self-respecting polar bear would have run the other way, not run into the face of danger. Have the three of you been drinking? Using some of the drugs you have in your pockets?"

The men glowered at him.

"My ribs hurt like hell. I think one or two of them are cracked. How in the hell did that happen if a polar bear didn't attack me?" the man growled.

Hanson agreed. "We both saw what we saw. And hell, we have the injuries to prove it."

"You all had an accident? Good thing for the three of you that you didn't fall into the lake like your rifles did or you wouldn't have survived." Rob drank some of his cocoa.

"Do you want me to make some sandwiches for us while we're waiting for the other police to arrive?" Alicia asked.

"Sure," Rob said, watching the three men. They had tried, unsuccessfully, to get out of their plastic bindings when they thought Rob and Alicia didn't know what they were up to. With his enhanced hearing, he heard all their movements. His keen sense of smell told him they were scared to death of what might happen next, if Rob decided to get rid of their sorry asses instead.

Despite being on the cool floor, all three of the men were sweating profusely.

"Is that the smell of fear?" Alicia asked, carrying the tuna fish sandwiches on plates to the table.

Rob set out glasses of water and a bowl of potato chips. "Yeah. They're tough men when they're armed with rifles. Take away their weapons and tie them up? Whole different story."

After they ate their sandwiches and cleaned up, Rob and Alicia heard the seaplane.

"Can you watch the three of them?" Rob needed to tell Andy exactly what had transpired so that he could say it happened to him instead. Or, at least part of the story. The polar bear part was just a figment of the men's imaginations.

"Yeah." Alicia brought out a big butcher knife. "I'll be fine."

Rob hoped everything that had happened to her hadn't traumatized her to the extent she was someone entirely different.

She smiled at Rob, but her expression was more devilish than sweet. "Go. We want these men gone. *Permanently.*"

"All right. We'll be inside momentarily." Then Rob stalked outside to greet Andy and Craig. Rob wanted to make this quick, not trusting to leave the hunters alone with Alicia for too long. "We're sure glad to see you."

"Where are they?"

"Tied up in the house. Armed with a butcher knife, Alicia's watching them."

Andy raised his brows, his lips curving up slightly. "Okay, tell me again exactly what happened."

CHAPTER 13

Alicia peeked out the window for a moment to see what Andy looked like. He was tall, bearded, well-built, so he looked like he could handle these men. Rob was explaining what had happened, pointing to where he'd thrown the rifles.

Craig was waiting with them, listening, glancing back at the cabin. The three tied-up guys were trying even harder to break free of their bindings. She glanced back at them, thinking they couldn't get loose, but one of the men had managed to stand.

Damn!

He ran at her and though he had his hands secured behind his back, if he hit her with his big body, he could knock her down. She didn't want to really cut him because then Andy would have to explain how that had happened.

She let out a startled scream and jumped out of the path of the raging bull of a man. He turned and ran at her again, but she dove behind the couch. The other men were frantically trying to stand also and she was certain that they thought to join the other hunter and knock her down, get the knife, and somehow slice off their bindings.

Then she realized the other man had worked his tied hands underneath his butt, and his hands were now in front of him. He quickly got to his feet and raced to reach her.

She sliced at him to keep him away when the other man came up behind her and hit her with his stocky body, sending her sprawling to the floor. She lost the knife and scrambled for it, her heart thundering. The man with his hands tied in front of him slammed his foot on top of the knife and reached down to grab it at the same time.

Rob, Andy, and Craig barged through the front door and rushed to take the men down.

Rob tackled Hanson and took him to the floor, a fist to the guy's temple, knocking him out cold.

Andy had his gun on one of the other men. "Make my day, buster. Just make a move, and we can end your life of crime right here."

Craig had the remaining guy pinned to the floor.

Rob pulled Alicia off the floor and held her tight,

kissing her cheeks and mouth. "Are you all right?"

"Yeah. I was afraid to cut them and mess up the story Andy had to tell." Not having expected the guys to come after her, she was shaken up, her heart still beating like crazy, her hands trembling.

"Okay, let's get these three out to the plane." Andy woke up the knocked-out guy. He read all three of the hunters their rights, and then he, Casey, and Rob hauled them out to the seaplane while Alicia followed after them—just in case they needed her assistance. Andy pulled a hypodermic needle out of his bag and jabbed one of the men in the arm with it and did the same to the other two men. "Something to make them more manageable while we transport them to Anchorage."

"Thanks, guys, for helping out so quickly," Rob said.

"She's a real keeper," Craig said.

Rob wrapped his arm around Alicia's shoulders, and she swore he was declaring to the other men that she was his, and she liked it where he was concerned.

"These guys have warrants out for their arrest already. Thanks for helping to apprehend them so I can bring them in," Andy said.

"As long as you're considered a hero in all this, and we're kept out of it, we're grateful," Rob told him.

"Absolutely. Well, before those three wake up, we need to take off."

After they said their goodbyes, Rob and Alicia

returned to the house, and Alicia collapsed on the couch. "Now what?"

"We can't stay here forever. I've been thinking of taking you back home and the family will be there to help out too."

"What if I change forms when I'm there? I can't be running around as a polar bear." She wasn't used to being in her polar bear form, but she wanted to do the things a polar did when she was wearing a coat.

"The house is bigger than the cabin and we'll have more of a support group there."

And Edward lived there, which, if she was going to have a hot, steamy relationship with Rob, would make it more difficult. "You mean, if you have to leave—to do your job, for instance—others in the family can babysit me." She didn't like the idea that she had to be watched over, and she didn't want people to feel obligated to look after her either when they had to be busy with their own lives.

"Yes. But we'll come out here too so you can be a polar bear also. I'm thinking we could stay out here for a couple of more weeks, and see how it's going with the shifting. After that, Craig can fly us back to town. Actually, he would have to take you back in, and I'll drive the van home."

"Why don't I just ride in the van with you?"

"Or that too, though it would take longer. Also,

there's the concern that people might see you in the van, or if we got stopped for any reason, same thing."

"We'd have to go at night. You'd have a problem with someone picking me up at a dock if I went by seaplane too, whereas in the van you can just drive me into the garage."

"True. We'll decide which way to go when we feel we need to leave."

"I couldn't ask you before, but the grizzly we saw fishing at the lake wasn't a shifter?"

"Not that I know of. We can't tell the difference between whether a shifter is the real deal or not. Unless we've met him or her before or can get downwind of the animal or be close enough to smell his scent, but again, only if you already know the person as a human and know their scent."

"Okay. I've got to text Judi and let her know I'm all right. And I want to reassure Doug that I'm fine in case he's feeling guilty about knocking me into the water."

"Go ahead. I'll check with Edward to see how things are going without us."

Then Alicia called Judi, instead of texting her. She wanted her to hear Alicia's voice, to know for certain she was okay. "Judi, I'm fine. I have no major complications from falling into the frigid water, but they're keeping me here for observation."

Rob smiled at her. "Hey, Edward. We had some

issues over three men shooting at a grizzly and I had to stop them. Then one of them shot at me. Not shifters. Yeah, we're both fine. Andy and Craig picked them up. How are things going for you?" Rob paused. "Good. I'm glad to hear it. No, we won't be joining you. Just tell everyone that in a case where someone has been that hypothermic, she can't go back out in the cold for a while."

Alicia said to Judi, "I hope you're taking great pictures and I miss going with you, but I believe I'll be having a private tour when I'm cleared to go back out in the cold." She suspected when she got her shifting under control, she would be visiting all the sites one of these days on a specially-guided tour with her favorite tour guide.

"Are you joining us? Maybe near the end of the tour?" Judi asked, her tone of voice hopeful.

"They say I've had too much exposure to the cold for now. So no. And I can't tell you how great Rob has been about checking on me and getting anything for me that I need. I don't know if anything will happen between us, but I think I might be staying here longer. I mean, after the tour is done."

"You're kidding. For real?" Judi sounded surprised.

"Yeah." Alicia looked at Rob, who was still on the phone to his brother, but he was listening to her, smiling a little.

Well, she had to make up a story, didn't she? Especially since she wasn't returning on the flight back to San Antonio. Not when she had this polar bear shifting issue to deal with.

"How long are you going to stay for? Did you want me to stay too?" Judi asked.

"Uh, no. You go home. I'll return later." Never, Alicia thought because of her bear shifter status, but everything was happening so fast that she didn't know what else to say.

"This is serious. I mean, between you and Rob. Wow. I thought there was something going on between the two of you."

"He's clairvoyant." Alicia figured telling Judi that would help convince her that Alicia had more of a reason to stay.

Rob wrapped his arm around Alicia and she smiled at him.

"Seriously? Omigod, are the two of you making a psychic connection?"

"Yes, we are. It's nothing like anything I've ever experienced before. I need to see how this will play out between us."

"Why didn't you say so before? Oh. I know when it happened too. Just when he was serving drinks. Your hand touched his, didn't it? You both had such shocked expressions. I was afraid you'd seen something about him that was scary. I wasn't sure why he was worried about the connection. But now I can see why. Omigod! Did you see that this was going to happen to you?"

Alicia had forgotten she'd told Judi about that. "Yes, through his visions, not mine."

"How could you, I mean you couldn't do anything like that before, could you?"

"No." Alicia still wondered if it had been a one-time occurrence or if her own psychic ability had been altered or expanded.

"Isn't that scary to witness something new like that?"

"It was bizarre, to say the least. I had years of dealing with past visions since I was a child. It was part of who I am. Just something I grew up with so it seemed natural. I'll have to get used to this, if it happens again." Along with the shifting. "Anyway, so I'm going to stay here for a while."

"I completely understand. I've got to take some pictures of the whales right now. I'm so sorry you can't see them, but I'm sure you can later if you're going to stay in Alaska longer."

"I will." Alicia wished her well and then they ended the call.

Rob said to Edward over the phone, "Yeah, I will. Glad everything is going fine without me. Catch you later." When he ended the call, he rubbed Alicia's back.

"You know something is happening between us."

He pulled her close and kissed her, rubbing his body against hers, and already was becoming aroused.

"Wow, is this the human side of you, or the polar bear?" Alicia loved his sexy moves. The raw power of his touch. His eagerness to make love to her.

"The bear and human are one and the same. Both halves make us whole. But you are the one who inspires me to feel this way. Only you."

"Hmm, well, I sure like both sides of you." She kissed him long and hard and deep. She smelled his interest in her and hers in him in a purely sexual way.

It was amazing to have the heightened animal senses that gave her such a different perspective, an intensity that made everything more amazing and she did love it. Having the uncontrollable urge to shift was another story.

She broke free of the kiss and held him close, listening to the rapid beat of his heart, feeling his warm breath as he kissed the top of her head.

"I know it's going to be hard to live with the changes in your life, but I'm glad you're here with me."

"You didn't plan this, did you? Just to get me alone with you?" she teased.

He laughed. "Making the change? Convincing Doug to knock you into the frigid water? No. but I try to make the most of a situation and turn it from dire circumstances to something incredibly wonderful."

"Make love to me," she said. "I was so scared I could have lost you when that one man tried to shoot you." She hastily brushed away tears. She hadn't meant to cry, or show how upset she'd been that the hunter had tried to kill Rob. Now that they were gone, she finally could acknowledge the way she'd felt in that devastating few moments before she was able to start taking the men down.

"Aww, Alicia, honey, I'm okay. We took care of them." He held her close for several moments, just hugging her and kissing her.

"Make love to me," she said, wanting the intimacy between them again.

"Nothing I'd love to do more." He swept her up in his arms and headed back to the bedroom, and she was glad she'd only slept in his room since that's where she would be until they left anyway.

He set her on the bed, and then began stripping her out of her clothes. She ran her hand over his jeans, enjoying the swell of his arousal. "You sure have a great body."

"I could say the same about you."

"When you got out of the pool"—she licked her lips—"your swim trunks showed off just how hot you were. I don't think I've ever seen anyone that intriguing in a swimsuit before."

He chuckled, and unfastened her bra. "Being close to you in the pool, fantasizing about what you'd look like out of your zebra bikini, that's what made me that way."

She tugged at his belt. "You were fantasizing about what I'd look like naked?"

"Hell, yeah. Even from the beginning, you had my attention." He combed his fingers through her hair. Then he pulled off his sweater and shirt.

She stood and pulled off her pants and he tugged his off. Then he slipped her panties down and ditched his boxer briefs.

He held her tight to his body, her flesh in contact with his groin. "You are so hot," she whispered against his mouth, her hands sliding up his sculpted abs.

"So are you." He nuzzled her neck and face, nipping at her ear as if he was in his polar bear form.

She loved the sensual sensation and nuzzled him right back. She was keenly aware of everything about him, the way his heart was beating like crazy, his pheromones were ripe with raw need, the hardness of his sculpted muscles, and the softness of his skin, the heat of his body, and his fresh, cool scent.

He brushed his lips against hers before settling her back against the mattress and joining her. With one leg propped over hers, he spread her legs for him, running his fingers through her short curls, until he found her clit and began to pleasure her. But his mouth sought hers at the same time, kissing, their tongues tangling, her body on fire.

She needed this. The physical release after the emotional trauma they'd experienced. The closeness to reassure herself he was whole and fine. He was sweeping her up onto that peak that would claim her, rocket her around the world, before she crash-landed in a burst of flames and then basked in the climactic glow.

He rubbed his hard cock against her thigh, kissing her deeply, before he settled between her thighs and thrust into her. She locked her heels against the back of his legs, met his thrusts with her own, gently clawed at his back, with rife need, and soaked up the essence of him.

Rob loved making love to Alicia. She was perfect for him in every way. He couldn't have asked for a better sexual partner as he brought her to climax and then thrust into her with renewed gusto. He tucked his hand under her buttocks and pressed deeper inside her, reaching for the end, and gave into the orgasm.

He finished, then laid back against the mattress and encouraged her to curl up against him.

They had no words for each other, completely content to snuggle until they fell asleep, and he wasn't aware of anything more than her soft breath against his chest sometime later.

"Rob, what happened after your parents died in the avalanche?" Alicia asked.

"Edward and I grew closer to our aunt and uncle and cousins than ever before. I'm not sure that we would have started the tour group if our parents had still been alive. They wanted us to be troopers like them. Though we all rely on tourists to keep us afloat, my dad wasn't a huge fan of them."

"Humans, you mean?"

"Yeah. He felt they didn't respect the wildlife like we do." Rob hugged her closer. "It's our home, not our dumping ground. We need to appreciate it, not take it for granted. He'd seen too many humans disrespecting the animals and the environment."

"He wouldn't have liked me then. Maybe not even after I was turned." Alicia caressed Rob's bare chest with her fingertips.

"Dad would have loved you because you would be one of us. And if I didn't take care of you, he'd have been all over my case."

Like that would have happened. "You said your parents were both on the police force?"

"Yeah. Dad tried to keep the criminal population in line. My mother did too. She would have adored you. And she would have been hopeful that you would stay with us."

"And you?"

"Hell, yeah. If we can be happy together while living in the same place, enjoying each other either when we're humans or bears, I think it's a sure thing. But we'll wait so we'll have more time to get to know each other better." Though he thought they had a damn good start already.

"Are polar bear shifter's laws completely unique? Do they not have to—oh crap. I've got to shift. Can you check on the grizzly situation for me?" Then she began jerking aside the covers and blankets as fast as she could. He would have helped her, but she was so wild, he climbed out of bed instead. He wanted to be with her as a polar bear, enjoying the snow, playing with her, being with her as a bear would anytime she had to shift. So she wouldn't feel bad about it. He needed to show her how to play fight as a polar bear and how to wrestle a bear, both in case she had to fend off another bear herself.

Though he never intended to leave her alone to have to deal with an issue, he knew that it was best to always be prepared.

Gloriously naked, she stood before him in her human form, then her body blurred into her polar bear. And she was just as beautiful then.

She sat on her rump and waited for him, her gaze going to his waist. And yes, he was fully aroused. He couldn't help himself whenever he was around her.

CHAPTER 14

More than a week later, it was almost time for the tour group to return to the lodge where they'd started the tour and Rob and Alicia decided they needed to go back to the house in town so that they could enjoy the farewell dinner and celebration before everyone flew out the next day. Rob had waffled about it for days as he and Alicia settled into a routine of sorts at the cabin. It was more like a flexible routine, one that revolved around Alicia's shifting difficulties. They'd only had one instance where they were making love and she had the urge to shift. They'd hurried up to finish and she'd jumped out of bed right afterward to shift. Man, had she been one growly bear. But he'd taken her outside to play in the water and she'd gotten over it.

He was concerned that she couldn't manage without shifting while they were visiting those in the tour group.

His family had pushed him though, saying they'd all help to conceal what she was if it came to that and that she really needed to find closure with her friend and the others. Alicia had wanted to say goodbye to Judi in person, if she could at least manage that. They'd have to just do the best they could about everything else.

"We'll be okay," Alicia assured him as she got into the van. "I'll just see Judi briefly, if I feel any urge to shift and skip the goodbye dinner. She's bound to think there's something terribly wrong with me if I don't see her otherwise. The same with the others."

"If you must bite her," Rob reasoned, because he wanted Alicia to know that if she shifted in front of Judi she'd have to turn her, "is she close to her family?"

"Very. I won't bite her. I'm getting an earlier warning now."

Removing a polar bear from a hotel would be impossible, not like with the wolf shifters who could somewhat pass as dogs.

Another call came in. It was Andy this time. "Hey, I know my brothers and Mom and Dad have all called, wanting to see Alicia and welcome her to the family. I'll have a pizza party at my place this weekend. Put it on your calendar. Dress code optional."

"Thanks, Andy," Rob said, glancing at Alicia to see what she wanted to do.

"Sounds like fun." Alicia settled back against her seat. "As long as I can wear my bear coat if I have to."

"Absolutely. And one of the wolves has a swimming pool and wants to invite you to his house for a pool party. Believe me, he usually never opens it to the polar bears because we take up so much space. But he wants you to feel welcome in the shifter world if you have to shift while you're at the party."

Alicia laughed. "I can just see all the polar bears in a small swimming pool at the same time. I'd like that."

"I'll let Rory know you want to do that. Well, I'll let you go. Just call when you get in."

"Will do," Rob said. "And thanks about the pizza party."

"Damn," Alicia muttered and quickly unfastened her seatbelt, and climbed into the back.

They were driving under the dark of night so unless they had car trouble, they could get into town without anyone seeing what she was. Rob still had wanted to put off visits for a little while, but if Alicia was ready, he was glad. He just hoped she wouldn't be upset if she had to shift during a party. He knew everyone would do whatever they could to make her feel fine about it though.

He hadn't even discussed with Edward how they were going to handle the living arrangements for the time-being. He called Edward then. "Hey, brother, we'll be at the house early in the morning."

"Good. We haven't had any other difficulties on the return trip. The remaining time on the tour, everything has gone per the plan."

Rob was relieved to hear it.

"Hey, how are things going there?" Edward asked.

"Alicia's a bear again. Everyone wants to see her, but I wanted to wait a couple of days until she feels more settled. We're on our way back to our place right now and she's sleeping in the back. Rory's invited us to a swim party."

Edward laughed. "You've created a celebrity. He never invites us to his swimming pool."

Rob smiled. "I agree. I figure if Alicia shifts, maybe one of us can shift to keep her company, but that's it. Andy called to say he is having a pizza party this weekend."

"Okay, he hasn't called me yet. Guess he wanted to make sure Alicia could attend. Sounds good. About the living arrangements, I'll see if Casey doesn't mind me staying with him for a few weeks or so, to give you and Alicia more time to get to know each other better. Or if that doesn't work, I'll stay with our aunt and uncle or one of our cousins."

"Thanks, Edward. I wasn't sure how to arrange this. I'm going to go out and pick up some groceries after I leave her off at the house because we don't know how long she'll be in her bear form and I need to pick up some things. Just keep me informed on how the trip is going. And I'll do the same here as far as what's going on with us."

"Sounds good."

When they ended the call, Rob felt Alicia's bear nose poking at the back of his neck. He glanced back at her and she was sitting on the floor looking glum. "We're pulling into the garage now. If you think you'll be all right, I'll run into town to get some groceries. I can have someone from the family come and sit with you if you'd like."

She grunted and shook her head, looking growly now.

He was certain she was feeling out of sorts because of not being able to control the shifting, maybe tired of still being a bear, but she'd slept through the drive home. He closed the garage door and let her out of the van. He grabbed their bags and once she was in the house, he set the bags down and gave her a hug. "Would you like me to turn on the TV for you?"

She nodded.

He turned on the TV and flipped through the channels until she poked at his hip with her nose. "*Alien Invasion* it is. Okay. I'll be back in a little while. Unless you'd rather I asked someone else to get us some groceries."

She shook her head.

"Okay, then, I'm off. Be home soon."

As soon as Rob pulled out of the garage, he called his aunt. "We're here and Edward's hoping to stay with Casey for a few weeks until we can sort out living arrangements when he returns home with the tour group. They're on the return trip now."

"Your uncle and I have discussed it. You'll need a home of your own now and one of these days, you'll have cubs. So, you really need to have your own place. We'll help contribute to it. You just decide where you want to live. Probably out of town a ways so your kids can run as bears. We wondered if they'd have the same issues with shifting as their mother. Well, of course they will early on because they'll shift when their mother does, but I mean, later."

"We'll have to see when it happens. Or if it happens. I'm just trying to get her through today, a day at a time. She's been really accepting, though she hasn't had much choice. I'm sure some people would be upset or angry about becoming what we are, if they hadn't had a choice like that." Rob couldn't say enough about how he admired Alicia for how she was dealing with all this. He hoped it wasn't because she was in shock, and she hadn't really had time to begin to deal with it.

He already knew he wanted Alicia in his life from now on. He couldn't imagine her not being with him there. But he wasn't for sure if she would want to be his bear mate. In any event, if she did, he didn't know how long they would have to wait before they could actually get married because of her shifting difficulties. He figured they'd have to have the wedding at one of the cabins, just in case. But he was ready to ask her if she'd even consider marrying him. They could be engaged for however long she wanted, if she wanted this. That way, she could decide if he was really the one for her.

Hoping he could convince her that he was, he parked at the grocery store and saw one of the snow leopards, Jasper Wright, headed for his van. "I'll call you later, Aunt Genevieve. I'm at the grocery store to pick up some things."

"Is she by herself?" His aunt sounded worried about it.

"Yes, and she wanted it that way. As hard as it is for us, we need to give her some space."

"All right, dear. Oh, and the other shifters know what happened now so I imagine you'll be hearing from a lot of them about what's going on. I hope no one is upset with you about it. We couldn't tell. Most every one's been really quiet."

"Andy said we're invited to Roy's pool party."

"Oh my, that's good news."

"Jasper Wright looks like he wants to talk to me about it. I'll call you back later."

"Just let us know when it would be a good time to come over and welcome her. And if you have any trouble with anyone over this, just let your Uncle Ned or me know."

"I will." Rob finally ended the call and greeted Jasper, his blue eyes fixed on him, his dark hair mostly covered by the pale blue hood of his parka.

Jasper shook his hand in greeting. "Hey, Rob, my brothers and I heard the news, and we'll be happy to help you and the lady out anytime. We can't imagine what it would be like for her or you or the others of your kind to have to deal with it. If you ever need our help, we're all here for you."

"Thanks, Jasper. You don't know how much that means to me. I didn't know how everyone else would react. I sure hadn't intended to create problems like this for anyone, and certainly not for Alicia."

"You had to save her life. I would have done the same thing. All of us would have." Jasper frowned. "Your aunt said you have a...gift. And that Alicia does too."

"Uh, yeah. I didn't know that she knew."

"I think Edward told her. Apparently, you predicted that Ben would have a broken arm when he and Edward were wrestling." Jasper shrugged. "It sounds to me like you already have something in common with her. From what Edward's telling everyone, the two of you are great together. Ben said he brought the two of you together."

Rob smiled. He figured that if he and Alicia tied the knot, Ben would always claim it was his doing.

"And she's beautiful, so as far as the way are animal halves are concerned, she seems perfect for carrying your offspring."

Rob laughed. Alicia and Rob both had been physically attracted to each other from the beginning, so Jasper was right about that. It was just something that they were instinctively born with.

"We're good with what's happened, and about learning you and she have special gifts. Could be a good thing. I know you need to run, but we heard about Gary and his going nuts. We haven't seen any sign of him around here, but his ex-girlfriend moved in with her new boyfriend, the father of her twins, and they're all up north now."

"You know who the guy is that she hooked up with?"

"Someone by the name of Wilbur Covington, but none of us really knew him."

"He's not from around here. Neither were she and Gary either though. How's Gary handling it?"

"He's got himself a new girlfriend and he's moving further east. Way out of our territory. And way out of hers. Your uncle said Gary has been banned from our territory because of what he did to you and your brother and the way he terrorized your tour group. He could have injured even more, or killed several of you if you hadn't stepped in to fight him as a bear."

"Did Edward tell you all of this?"

Jasper smiled. "Yeah. He wanted everyone to know what a hero you were in case we were upset about you turning Alicia. We'll all help to enforce Gary's banishment."

Rob loved his brother. "Good."

"There's one other thing. I thought Cam Wessington was banished from the entire state of Alaska."

Rob felt his stomach tighten. "He was. He hasn't returned, as far as I know." Rob didn't know how to feel about it. Cam had been only sixteen when he'd caused the avalanche that had killed Rob's parents and nearly killed him. His parents had arrested Cam several times, so he had the motivation to eliminate them. But some on the council had felt Cam had been too young to try him as an adult. Rob saw right through the tears Cam had shed. He had been upset for the council members catching him in the act. Not for having killed Rob's parents. "Have you seen him?"

"I might be mistaken, but I thought I saw him at that Commodore Hotel. I dropped by there because they have great cheeseburgers on the grill, but when I saw this guy, he was older, sure, but he still looked a lot like Cam. Just wanted to give you a heads up in case it is him. I haven't told your aunt and uncle yet. I'll do that next."

"Thanks. I'm sure they'll send some people over to check on it." His cousins. Rob would have gone himself, but he had to return home to ensure Alicia was all right. He didn't want to leave her alone for long, though he knew she might feel she needed some alone time.

Rob hoped that Jasper was wrong and that Cam hadn't shown up back here, defying the bears' order never to return to Alaska.

***

As a bear, Alicia was pacing in Edward and Rob's home, wishing she could shift back, feeling more alien than the aliens in the movie. Even though she would need her space from Rob and the others, and he would likewise need some time away from her sometimes, for now, she felt better when he was with her. She felt a kind of peace that she didn't feel when he was gone. She hoped she would be more comfortable about being a shifter soon. And she was trying her darnedest not to let on that it bothered her when she was left alone. She kept worrying someone would suddenly enter the house and find a polar bear sitting in the middle of the living room floor. Then what?

Not that anyone would just walk into the house who wasn't a bear, she didn't think. But what if someone broke into Rob's house looking to steal. She smiled. Then she'd be one hell of a guard bear. Forget needing a guard dog.

She tried walking through the living room again, but this time she misjudged her polar bear's size. She bumped into the coffee table and knocked off a hand-painted pottery vase picturing a family of polar bears. Her heart nearly gave out as she swung out her paw to try and stop the vase from falling as if she still had a pair of hands. In her bulky bear form, she could do nothing but hold her breath and watch the vase bounce against her paw. The vase fell onto the faux polar bear rug and rested there. Staring at the vase, she hadn't heard any cracking sound and prayed it was wholly intact.

For the longest time, she studied the beautiful piece of artwork—four grown bears and five cubs, and she wondered if they were Rob and his extended family. Irritated with herself for her clumsiness, she was damn thankful she hadn't broken the precious vase.

She felt like a kid who had to live in a child-proof home. Or a clumsy cat or dog that couldn't move around without wreaking havoc.

Frustrated, she didn't move from her spot and fell asleep, the TV still playing in the background. Until she felt cold, woke, and smiled to see she had finally turned into her human form and was glad she didn't have company right this moment.

***

Rob and Jasper said goodbye and Rob stalked toward the grocery store to get this done as quickly as possible.

As soon as he was inside and grabbing a loaf of sour dough bread off the bread aisle, he got a call from Ben. "Jasper said Cam might be in the area."

"Uh, yeah. I need to get home to Alicia or else I'd head over there."

"I'm going with Craig to check it out. Andy said he'd meet us there to give us backup. We'll let you know if we discover Cam's been there."

"Okay thanks. I'll be home with Alicia in just a little bit."

"Okay, out here."

Rob was trying to get everything on the list that both he and Alicia needed and wanted, but he was trying to do it in a rush so he could get home to her soon. He was also anticipating a call from his cousin to confirm whether Cam was in the area or not. The hotel was an hour away from here, so it would take a little time for them to get there. He assumed Ben and Craig had been at the tavern.

Suddenly, he got a call from Alicia, and he was thrilled she had changed back, and it was even more reason for him to return to her quickly. "Can you think of anything else that I need to get?"

"I hate to ask."

He grabbed a package of steaks. "Anything."

"Feminine pads. Sorry, Rob. But I wouldn't have needed them until well after I returned home and since I'm not going home, and I can't shop right now…"

He smiled. "Yeah, sure. No problem. Any particular brand?"

"No, just any. Just go to the aisle where they have them and read off a couple of size descriptions. Off the top of my head, I don't remember what the sizes were."

"Sure thing." He went to the aisle where they had the products, and a woman shopping there smiled at him, probably thinking he was so nice to pick up these items for his wife. "Okay, Alicia, there are wall-to-wall packages of this stuff." He hadn't expected that. She told him to pick out a package of three of the sizes, and when he dumped those in the basket, he asked, "Anything else?"

"Probably. For now, that's all I can think of."

"We're going to have to make arrangements to move your things from San Antonio to here."

"Uh, yeah, you're right. Though I doubt I'll wear as many of my hot-weather clothes up here."

"We'll get you some more clothes for here. Okay, I'm on my way to check out of the grocery store now. I'll call you as soon as I get in the car." Rob wanted to tell her about what Jasper had said concerning their help and that they were accepting of what had happened to her. He just didn't want to talk about it in the grocery store. He didn't intend to mention anything about Cam, unless his cousins discovered he had truly returned.

"I can't wait to see you. I love you no matter what form you're in, you know, but...well, I can't wait to see you." And he wanted to ask if she wanted to get engaged because Rob felt in his heart, she was the one for him.

CHAPTER 15

Rob called Alicia back a few minutes later, and she was thrilled he was so happy that she had shifted back to her human form. Almost as much as she was. She really was trying to take this shifting business in stride, but she was having a difficult time coping. Sometimes. Especially when it took her so many hours to turn back. But she couldn't believe he'd told her he loved her and it gave her a warm, fuzzy feeling that he felt that way about her.

She moved the polar bear-painted vase to the dining room table so that she wouldn't accidentally knock it over again if she shifted.

"I'm almost home," Rob said. He was so cute, worried, she thought that he'd left her alone for too long.

She was glad he was nearly there. "We're going to

have to bear-proof your home so I don't break anything." She wiped away a tear and then another. She couldn't help it. She still felt awful that she could have broken the polar bear vase.

"Hey, don't worry about it. Everyone has accidents sometimes. And you're not used to your size as a bear. We'll do whatever it takes to make this work. There's nothing I can't replace—except for you."

That was the second time he'd acted like he wanted to take their relationship to the next step. And she was feeling the same way, but had been afraid to let on in case she was pushing for something he wasn't ready for. She didn't want him to feel obligated to provide her a home for the future just because he'd turned her.

"I almost broke your polar bear vase. Is that your family that's painted on it?"

"Yes, but like I said, anything like it can be replaced. Don't worry about it. All I care about is ensuring you're happy with us. We can rearrange furniture, move stuff out, whatever you'd like to do to make this work for you."

"I moved the vase to the dining room. I just feel so clumsy. I can't seem to remember that I'm not able to catch things with my hands when I'm a polar bear. I can't even swear when I get upset."

He chuckled. "You'll get used to it. It will take time. You've only been one for a very short while. When

Edward and I were kids, we knocked over so much stuff, Mom finally put everything she felt was valuable away until we were in our teens. This is all so brand new for you. Just give it time."

She heard someone pulling up into the drive and thought it was Rob. "I hear you pulling up."

"It's not me."

She peeked out the window and saw a red pickup truck with three men inside. "Someone just pulled up in a red pickup. Three men. The sunlight's reflecting off the windshield so I can't make out their details, but it looks like those three hunters that Andy and Craig took into custody." Her heart pounding, she watched as the engine cut off. She realized that she could hear things she couldn't before. Not from inside the house. Like when Edward had driven back to the house that first night, she hadn't heard his vehicle when he had returned. "It can't be them, can it?"

She knew if it was, it wouldn't be good news.

"I'm nearly there. Just a couple of more minutes. Get their license plate number in case they drive off."

"They're getting out of the truck." She gave Rob the license plate number. "Alaska plates. It's them. What are they doing here?"

"Nothing good, I suspect. They must be out on bail. But what the hell they would be doing at the house, I don't know. Trying to intimidate us? I'm just at the end of the street. Don't leave the house."

"Believe me, after what they tried to do to you, I certainly wouldn't. All three of them are coming up the walkway to the front door."

"I don't want to end this call to get hold of Andy, but as soon as I pull up behind their truck, I'll call him to let him know we may be in trouble."

"They're pounding on the door and ringing the bell like they know we're here."

"I am here. I just parked behind them. Sit tight. I'm calling Andy before I leave the van."

What did these men hope to accomplish by coming here? Andy was the one who swore out the complaint against them, not she and Rob. And Craig was serving as his witness. Luckily, Andy and Craig had been together when they'd received the original call to come and arrest them, so that part of their story was true. And they'd been out in the wilderness at the time, so no one could say they hadn't been at the cabin at the time.

Rob engaged the men outside, all three of them turning to face him. He told them they were trespassing and to leave his property, that the police were already on their way.

She opened the door and stepped outside to hear their conversation so she could let the hunters know Rob wasn't alone, when her cell phone rang. She looked at the caller ID and saw that it was coming from the

Commodore Hotel. She thought maybe that was one of the hotels the tour group was staying at so it could be Judi calling while they were settling down for the day.

As soon as she answered the call and heard Bill's voice, she was startled.

"I'm in town. I want to talk to you in person. We can't do this on the phone. I'm here. With you. Or soon. As soon as you agree to meet me," he said, insistent.

She couldn't believe it. Then again, as controlling as he was, she could. Now she had a little bear issue that changed everything between them to an even greater degree than before. Not wanting to talk to Bill, she was trying to watch Rob in case anything bad happened. She didn't have any weapons on her to deal with the hunters if they pulled out a gun or another kind of weapon, unless she shifted into a polar bear. And that would be a disaster. *If* she could even do it. She really didn't have any control over shifting or not shifting.

"I'm sorry you came all the way here for nothing. I'm not seeing you while I'm on my tour," she said, wanting to make it clear that just because he had come all the way out to see her, it didn't change anything between them.

"I discovered you went with the MacMathan brothers' group. I'll wait here for you for when you return. We can sightsee before we take our return fights and go home together. We just need to start over."

Hanson, the hunter who looked like he oversaw the others, appeared as though he was going to shove Rob as he walked in his direction, his fists clenched, but then he began to raise his hand. She started moving toward the men as if she could stop them. But she wanted them to know Rob wasn't alone and she was a witness. "Yes, there are three men here who are threatening my fiancé. They were out on bail, I guess, officer. So now they're physically and verbally assaulting my fiancé. Yes, do hurry. We'll swear out complaints against them," she said over the phone.

"What the hell's going on?" Bill sounded confused and angry. "Are you in trouble?"

She was trying to let on to the hunters that she was on the phone to the police. She called out to Rob, "The police are on their way."

He nodded to her.

Just then she heard the sirens wailing, and she suspected Rob must have reached the police before he left the van, like he said he would. "Okay, the police are here, thanks." She hung up on Bill, but pretended to be talking on the phone or listening to the police. But really, she was concentrating on Hanson's tirade.

"Listen, all you've told about us are lies," Hanson said. "You won't get away with it. You know a polar bear attacked us. You tossed our rifles in the water. Trooper MacMahan didn't have anything to do with it. Nor did his brother, the pilot. What are *you* hiding?"

"It's amazing how the crooks who were illegally hunting and carrying around illegal drugs could project their criminal shortcomings on innocent people," Alicia said. "You should be grateful to us for chasing off that polar bear—if you really believe he was there."

"That polar bear ran into the house. And when is having a polar bear for a house pet legal anyway?" Hanson asked.

"We were all in the house. I didn't see a bear at all. And if we had a trained bear, as if anyone could train one, I would have had him watching the three of you, making sure you sat nice and still. So why didn't I? Because there wasn't a polar bear in the house. Tell that to the judge, and I'm sure he'd believe you were using some of the drugs you had on you at the time."

The other two men looked at Hanson, and she smiled. "You told the judge and he didn't believe you either."

Two patrol cars pulled up curbside. Andy was driving one of them, and he hurried to exit his car. "Are they trespassing?" he asked Rob, stalking up the drive to join them.

"Yeah. I told them so too. I ordered them off the property even. I thought these three men were going to stay in a jail for a while." Rob sounded highly annoyed that the hunters were out on bail.

Alicia had thought the same, but no way had she believed the hunters would end up at Rob's house. Nor that Bill would be in the area now too. She was glad Bill thought she was still with the tour group though. She hated to think he might try to track her down here. When the tour group returned to the lodge that they'd stayed at the first night they were here, Bill would find she wasn't staying there. She just had to make sure Judi didn't tell him where she really was staying and hope she didn't run into him while she was trying to say goodbye to her friend.

Andy threatened to arrest the men if they didn't leave Rob's property immediately. The hunters got into their pickup and backed out of the driveway with a squeal of their tires, then took off.

"Are you folks all right?" the other trooper asked.

"Yeah thanks," Rob said.

"I'll take their statements," Andy told the other officer.

He tipped his hat and left while Andy asked Alicia, "How are you doing?"

Rob led them inside out of the cold. Alicia was glad. She might be a polar bear shifter now, but she hadn't acclimated to the weather in Alaska yet when she was in her human form.

"Better. I'm having a little more control over the shifting."

"It'll get better," Andy assured her.

She knew neither Andy nor anyone else had any idea how long this would take. "I don't think anything will come of this, but I have a situation with my ex-fiancé."

Frowning, Rob fixed everyone a cup of hot coffee and they took their seats in the living room. "I thought you were blocking his calls."

"I am. He called right when we were having all these issues with the hunters and said he's in the area. He was calling from the Commodore Hotel, and I didn't remember which place the tour group was staying at for the night. Judi keeps me apprised of the schedule. I thought Judi was calling me from the hotel."

"He's stalking you," Rob said, all growly.

"I can't believe he flew all the way out here to see me. He just won't let it go between us."

"What's his name?" Andy asked, getting ready to write it down.

"Bill Hollinger."

"I'll head on over there and see what's going on," Andy said.

"Thanks so much, Andy. Tell him I'm getting married and staying here."

Andy smiled and glanced at Rob. He was smiling right back. "Hey, she's the only one for me. Tell your brothers that."

Andy chuckled. "Somehow, I got that impression already."

"Did you see if Cam Wessington was at the hotel?" Rob asked him, wrapping his arm around Alicia's shoulders. "I didn't hear back from Craig or your brother Ben. I wasn't sure if you made it over there or not and had any information."

"I didn't make it over there. Then we got your call and had to come here. According to Ben, Cam wasn't there. Of course, they smelled around for his scent. I wouldn't be surprised if he was hiding it though, since he's been banished. We don't have any current pictures of him to show to management either. I'll head on over there and tell Bill Hollinger that Alicia filed a nuisance complaint against him, and if he pursues this further, I'll make it a stalking charge."

"I really hate to go this far, but…" Alicia said, really wishing Bill would have gotten the message a long time ago.

"But, it's dangerous, not only because he's already followed you all the way here, not believing you mean it when you say no, but also because of what you are now." Andy patted her shoulder in a brotherly way. "I'll make sure he knows I mean business."

Alicia was glad for his help and told him so.

Then Andy wished them well and left. Alicia said to Rob, "Who is Cam? And why was he banished, and by whom?"

***

Feeling ill at ease that Cam would be back, Rob got refills on their coffee, needing to tell Alicia all about him, and they took their seats in the living room. "Cam was sixteen at the time he was living in our community as one of us, and had been in a lot of trouble up until that point. My mother and father both had hauled Cam in on several different occasions from petty theft and vandalism to selling illegal drugs. His dad had killed three men in cold blood over the illegal sale of drugs when Cam was twelve. By order of our council, Cam's dad was eliminated for the murders he committed. Hunters shot and killed Cam's mother when he was fifteen. He lived with another bear family, but he was continually in trouble from the age of twelve, taking up where his dad had left off. The year Cam turned sixteen, the council had decided that Cam should serve jail time based on my parents' recommendations after he'd broken into a home and caused an elderly woman to have a stroke. He stole four-hundred dollars and some of her jewelry and pawned it, feeling no remorse for any of it.

"We assumed he had a vendetta against my parents and brother and me because my parents kept arresting him and they were testifying against him at the trial. They'd let him off so many times before that, and they knew they had to finally make him accountable for his actions. They felt that hopefully through tough love, he'd turn his life around. He probably would have been convicted and gone to jail that time, but he was out on bail until the trial. Edward and I were spending some family time together with my parents, my cousins, and aunt and uncle, something we rarely could do except on the holidays. We were all close.

"Early that evening, we were making our last ski trip down the slope before the resort closed. A light snow was falling. Every one of us had seen Cam up on the slopes, all alone. I think all of us had been keeping an eye on him at one point or another. For the most part, he'd been skiing just like us. If he was staying out of trouble, we had no problem with it.

"Then we heard the sound of the massive amount of snow breaking away from high above us up on the slope. I turned and looked and saw Cam above the avalanche, raising his ski poles in victory, yelling, and screaming his excitement."

"Omigod." Alicia's face paled and she looked stricken. "I know they can't be the same man, but I saw a vision once that involved Bill. He'd witnessed an avalanche that had buried some people. I thought that he was reluctant to go up north because of the traumatic experience he'd observed on the slopes.

"Three months earlier, he had a brochure lying on

his coffee table about your tour group, which was what gave me the idea to even come up here. I'd gone to his place for dinner, saw the brochure, and became really interested in it. I thought he'd picked it up to share it with me. I believed he wanted to deal with his experience in the snow. I tried talking to him about it— not telling him I'd envisioned what he'd seen—but just related it to his not wanting to go to Alaska, maybe because he'd had some traumatic experience with snow.

"To my surprise, he became angry. He threw the brochure into the trash, and then tried to act like nothing was the matter, but he couldn't pull it off at that point. That was really the turning point for me. I thought he had too many issues, and we weren't meant to be together. I thought about that brochure for a couple of weeks, and then I asked Judi if she wanted to go with me. She was delighted. Then we made the plans. I like to go to places that are unusual. And I'd never been up here before. I'd been to the Amazon earlier this year, but I guess I won't be going back there ever again. Not that I'd planned to."

Rob couldn't believe it. "But he didn't try to stop you from coming here."

"I didn't tell him I was coming here. We weren't together any longer. He didn't know I'd signed up until I was flying out the next day. We'd already broken up shortly after that night that was such a disaster. Judi lives closer to the airport, so I stayed with her the night, and we just drove her car to the airport parking lot. No sense in taking both cars. He couldn't physically come by to stop me then either. He didn't know I was going with Judi, or where she lives." Alicia took hold of Rob's hand and squeezed. "Cam caused the accident?"

"Yeah. Our family was skiing together. The snow buried my parents and me alive. It partially buried Edward. He managed to free himself and then freed me. By the time we could both reach our parents to dig them out, they had been buried for far too long. They had suffocated. Several of the elders on the council, including my aunt and uncle, voted to ban Cam from the state."

"I'm so sorry that Cam killed your parents. I can't imagine anyone doing something so...cowardly and being so vicious. Or how that could have affected you."

"I agree." As far out as the notion might be, Rob couldn't let go of the notion that Cam might have changed his name. What if he was this Bill Hollinger? "Do you have a photo of Bill?"

"No. I got rid of them." She sighed. "Unless I missed deleting one when I was cleaning the pictures off my phone." She pulled out her phone. "You said Cam was banished from the state of Alaska."

"That's what the council had decided. The polar

bears are self-guided. Their council is made up of the elders who decide the fate of the polar bear shifters who commit premeditated murders. Since Cam had only been sixteen at the time, he'd been banished from ever returning to Alaska instead of being eliminated. It would have been a hardship on him to live where he couldn't shift, but we don't have to shift unless we choose to."

Alicia let out a little snort.

Rob rubbed her back and kissed her cheek. "Not those of us who were born shifters. Though it could be possible he moved to Canada. Much more likely than further south. Jasper, one of the snow leopards, said he thought he saw Cam at the Commodore Hotel."

"But Andy said he didn't smell him there."

"Right. If Cam has come back, he'd have to use hunter's spray to disguise his scent. None of us would know he had returned."

"Why in the world would he come back? Wouldn't the council vote to eliminate him at this point?"

"The council would determine if he's done anything wrong wherever he's been living for the past fourteen years. If he's continued his life of crime, and now broken our laws by returning here, then they could very well decide he's a threat and will never be able to live with our kind. Or anyone else's. But they'll have to talk to him. It's possible, he's been living up here all along, just staying far away from us, under the radar. But why he would come to a location only an hour away from where we live now means he either wants to make amends, believes now he can set things right with us, or he is up to no good."

Rob got a call and said to Alicia, "It's Andy. I'm putting this on speaker so you can hear what he has to say."

"Bill's not here," Andy said. "No one is registered by the name of Bill Hollinger. Eight single males were staying here. If he was here, he was going by another name. I didn't think to ask Alicia for a photo to show the management because I figured the guy would just be here under his own name."

Not liking this whole scenario that her ex-fiancé had assumed an alias, Rob said to Andy, "Hold on. I'll see if Alicia has found a photo of him."

Alicia was still looking through the photo gallery for one of him. "Oh, here, I have one. I really thought I'd deleted all of them." She handed her phone to Rob.

He took the phone and looked at the picture. *Damn it to hell and back*. Cam had his arm wrapped around Alicia in a possessive way. She wasn't smiling, like she felt...confined by his posture. "That's Cam," he told her.

Her lips parted in surprise.

When he saw Cam, Rob couldn't believe his eyes. He sent the picture to Andy, who cursed. "Okay, so that means Cam's back, only he's going by the alias of Bill Hollinger. Let me show it to the hotel management." Andy said to someone else, "Do you recognize this as Bill Hollinger?"

"Yes, sir. That's the man all right. He checked out of here a little while ago."

"Thanks, sir." Andy said to Rob, "We need to find the bastard and now."

Rob knew beyond a doubt that if Cam didn't already know that Alicia was with Rob now, he'd learn of it soon enough. No telling what he'd do.

"I'll get the word out right away," Andy said. "I'll forward this photo of him so everyone knows what he looks like today."

"I'll call Edward and Casey to let them know," Rob said, wanting everyone to be on the lookout.

Then they ended the call.

Cam could target anyone in the family. Even though Rob's aunt and uncle both had voted to send Cam away, they could have just as easily voted to terminate him instead. Rob suspected that wouldn't matter to Cam. He already was obsessed with wanting Alicia in his life. If he learned that not only was Rob marrying her, but that he'd turned her also? Rob knew the guy would go ballistic, and want her even more.

"Okay, what's going on?" Alicia asked, rubbing Rob's arm.

"I'm afraid if Cam learns you're one of us and that I'm marrying you, all hell will break loose. If he wanted to make amends, he could have written someone on the council first. By not doing so, I don't believe he intends to do anything but get into further trouble. Why wear hunter's spray to come up here also? He's a loose cannon."

CHAPTER 16

Alicia would do anything to protect Rob from Cam or anyone else, like those hunters, who would have killed him. She just couldn't believe any of this was happening though. Just when she thought she was getting her life under control, just a little bit, now this? She couldn't believe what Bill, or Cam, had done to Rob and his family and that she'd even thought of marrying the man. "No wonder he was so against coming here in the beginning. No wonder he said he hated the cold and wouldn't ever come here. What will happen now?"

Cam had been a polar bear shifter all along. She realized she hadn't even known the real man who had asked her to marry him.

Rob kissed her head. "I think he will come for you. And I suspect I'll have to kill him."

She looked up at Rob, not thinking he was joking.

She was right. He looked dead serious.

"Do you think he could have turned his life around?" Rob asked, running his hand over her shoulder in a gentle caress, considering her eyes, maybe worried she would hate him if he killed Cam.

But she knew Rob wouldn't take him down if he wasn't forced to do it. "I think some can. I think there's some good in every man, no matter how bad they've been, or can be."

"If he were to see you, do you think he would go away willingly then?"

Alicia let out her breath on a heavy sigh. In truth, deep down, she didn't think so. "None of us can know for sure, but given his obsession to keep our relationship going, I would say he won't willingly give up wanting me. Has it anything to do what with you are? The bear's territorial nature? If so, maybe he can't help himself."

"There could be something to that. Our human halves normally control our wilder bear instincts. In the wild, the bears must kill to survive. They must find food where they can. That means establishing and protecting their territories."

"And a female to mate within that territory."

"For wild bears, yes. Again, we can't allow our bear half to rule that part of our behavior. And truthfully, people who are not shifters, can have the same obsessions for people."

"But it's unnatural."

"Right. It's borne out of a need to control." Rob was quiet then, but suddenly said, "He wouldn't know that you've been turned, would he?"

"How would he...*Judi*. If he called her to try and talk to me, she might have told him I was no longer with the tour group and was injured. In a hospital, even, because you said I was being checked out."

"But he didn't mention it when he talked to you."

"No, you're right."

"If he believed you were one of us, that we had gone to save you in the frigid water, that might have been the reason he flew all the way out here."

Alicia glanced at the clock. "I'll call Judi and if he hasn't called her, I'll let her know that she can't tell him what happened to me." As soon as Alicia reached her friend, Judi was so excited.

"We're watching the polar bears feasting on the whale. You wouldn't believe the size of those bears. Five of them! They look cuddly and cute. Not dangerous. But, of course, Casey and Edward are keeping us out of harm's way. How are you doing?"

"I'm doing fine, but Bill called me from a hotel nearby, and I thought it was you calling or I wouldn't have answered the phone. He's got a past we didn't know about. His name is really Cam and he started an avalanche here that killed Edward and Rob's parents."

"Omigod. That's terrible. Wait, you said you had a vision of him witnessing an avalanche. That was it? And he caused it? How awful. You said you wanted to help him get through it. Before you broke up with him. Oh, oh, that's why he didn't want to come here on this trip. But he had the brochure on the MacMathan's and Casey's tour group."

"Right. He nearly killed Rob in that avalanche. He left the state, but he's come here to try and convince me to return with him. Have you talked to him? Did you tell him I was injured and am no longer with the tour group?"

"Yeah, omigod, Alicia, I'm so sorry. He said you and he were in touch and then something happened to your phone. He asked if he could talk to you on my phone. Then I told him you weren't with us. And I told him about your accident.

"He just kept questioning me about how cold you'd been, how fast they'd pulled you out of the water, and if you'd been bitten. Seriously! He was certain a polar bear had bitten you. I told him you hadn't been. Wait, you said a polar bear tried to eat you in your vision. Did a polar bear bite you?"

"No. I wasn't bitten. I'm sure I wouldn't have been alive to talk to you about it if I had been. Edward and Rob pulled me out of the water, and I was out of it for a while. But then I warmed up and I was fine."

"Did Rob use that technique of getting naked with you to warm you up?"

Alicia smiled. "No."

Judi sighed. "Okay, well, I'm sorry. I didn't mean to cause trouble for you. I can't believe Bill, or Cam, flew all the way out here just to convince you to go home with him."

"We're getting married. Rob and I. We're not sure when, but it's over between Cam and me. And he's not even the man I knew anyway."

"Oh, oh, you're really doing it. Marrying Rob is awesome. As far as Bill goes, I'm blocking him."

Alicia was afraid it was too late.

"Let me know more when you learn of it. I should go. The bears are getting snarly."

"Stay safe," Alicia said, then they ended the call.

"Do you want to get married? To me?" Rob said to Alicia.

"Well, I think I'm going to have to marry one of you, and because I see it happening to us—"

"Wait, I didn't envision it. You only see past events unless you're touching me." Rob was hopeful she had seen it come to pass.

She smiled up at him. "Not in a vision. I just see that this is where we're going. Unless you think I should play with the other polar bears a bit first."

Rob lifted her off the couch. "I'll prove I'm the one for you and no one else." He carried her back to his bedroom, fully intending to make love to her. "Besides, my aunt and uncle are already planning to help us with buying a home and everything."

"Edward would stay here?"

"Yeah. That way we have more room for you to explore and less traffic where we'll be. We'll need a place of our own. And for the kids."

"We'll need to wait on the kids."

"You don't feel your biological clock ticking?" Rob asked.

She smiled. "Do you feel yours is?"

He laughed. "My aunt does. She'll be just like an ecstatic grandmother and my uncle will be just as thrilled. He's already said he's in charge of wheels for the kids when any of us have them. I don't think he meant cars, though. But yeah, I'm all for waiting, of course, so you have more time to get used to shifting. The babies would shift at the same time as you until they're older and can shift safely on their own. We also homeschool our kids."

He was pulling off her sweater and she was struggling to unfasten his belt, his voice already husky with desire when he said, "I don't know how I ever got so lucky. When here I thought we were both doomed with facing the issue of the grizzly and you with the cold water and a ferocious polar bear."

"Instead, it meant a whole new beginning for us— in the most unpredictable way."

Then Rob smiled down at her. "Which, considering our paranormal abilities, makes sense for us."

"Hmm," she said licking his chest. "Are you tan all over because your black polar bear skin absorbs the heat?"

"Yeah." He cupped her face and kissed her mouth. "Like your bikini tan is fading and your skin is tanning all over."

She glanced down at herself; he cupped her breasts. "See? Glorious."

She ran her hand over his arousal. "Yeah, I see."

He fondled her breasts, and leaned down to kiss her again, glorying in the scent, taste, and feel of her. She was his. A wedding and marriage license was a human condition. For them, the agreement to be mated bears meant making love to her this time went even deeper, a commitment to each other.

Since an earlier time when she had shifted so soon after he'd made love to her, he'd been torn between hurrying, and trying to draw out the pleasure.

He realized she must have known something about needing to shift the other time, because she'd been more frenzied before, trying to push him into climaxing sooner.

This time, she was stroking his arms, his waist, her mouth slowly kissing his, her tongue sweeping over his, but not in any rush. Yet the way she reached down and caressed his cock made him feel hot and reckless. He swept her up and set her on the bed.

Before he could move her legs apart, she bent her knees and pulled him in, cradling him between her knees. Her hands swept down his back as he plunged in between her legs, afraid when she took the initiative, she was getting ready to turn. He covered her mouth with his and plundered her, before nuzzling her cheek, and jaw. They moved against each other with purpose, her pelvic thrusts deepening his thrusts. He felt the ending coming, and was afraid she wouldn't have enough time to climax before he was through. He leaned aside and began to coax a climax out of her, rubbing her clit, licking her nipple, keeping himself still.

He was desperate to make this right. But he was afraid he was going to fail.

"Hurry," Alicia pleaded.

Hell, he was hurrying.

***

Alicia didn't want to have to stop in the middle because of having to shift. Since that one time, she'd feared the same thing happening again. Her blood was sizzling from the way Rob was kissing her and thrusting inside her. Which had happened before, well, every time she made love to him, which had disguised the need to shift that one time. So now she didn't know when it would happen.

Poor Rob was hurrying, trying to pleasure her before he climaxed and she was so close now. He was delicious, so focused, sexually intense as he worked diligently to make the orgasm happen, his finger working pure magic. She about hit the roof, the spine-tingling thrill to the center of her core erupting when she came. She cried out, "Yes, yes!"

He began thrusting inside her again, kissing her as if he was going to lose her any second now.

She loved him for wanting to make every moment count. He finished up fast and hard, groaning with spent pleasure, then held her tight in his arms as if to keep her from shifting.

"You are amazing," she whispered against his cheek.

"You are incredible." He finally moved over and pulled her into his arms. "Are you okay?"

She knew he meant about having the urge to shift. "You make me so hot."

He smiled. "You weren't sure if you were going to shift."

"Yeah." Alicia sighed. "If we're really going to do this, I don't want to wait to get married. This trouble I'm having with shifting could take months, years before I have any real control over it. I'd love to return to your cabin for the wedding. And if I shift, we'll go swimming there."

"I love the way you think and I'm all for it. I'll see when everyone can come."

"No fancy gown or anything. I have a nice sweater and slacks and that will suffice."

"We'll have to wait until my brother returns with the tour group."

Alicia let out her breath. "Of course. And Casey too. We can do it before we attend a lot of the parties that friends and family want to give and then we'll be a couple."

Rob frowned at her. "Are you worried about Cam still?"

"Yeah. Aren't you?"

"When it comes to your safety, yes. I don't believe our being married will make any difference to him, if you think it might deter him."

"No. I agree with you about that. I just feel there's no sense in waiting."

"I'll start making arrangements right away. I know a lot of shifters would like to come, but given the circumstances, it's completely your call."

"You mean my unpredictability with regards to shifting. It's bad enough when I can't control my shifting just around you."

Rob took her face in his hands and said, "You're amazing to me. And beautiful and precious. I don't want you feeling bad about not having control over your shifting. Everyone understands and wants to help you through this. No worries, okay?"

"Easy for you to say."

He smiled and kissed her mouth, then pulled his mouth away from hers. "We do have a problem coming up. Everyone from the tour group is going to want to see you. To make sure you're doing all right. We've talked about seeing Judi. But we can say you're still recovering, or we could have you meet the group briefly and if you're doing all right, enjoy our final celebration and picture taking and then return home. If you feel you need to shift, we can leave and say you weren't feeling well."

"I don't want anyone to think I've died or am near death. Particularly, because Doug might feel guilty still for knocking me into the water."

"I agree. Judi might be more of a problem. I could see her wanting to visit with you for longer because you're good friends."

"Then let's hope we make it through this party without a hitch. I'll tell Judi goodbye, and tell her I won't be able to make it to the airport to see her off."

"Hopefully, that will suffice. I'll call my family and let them know about the wedding. I'm sure my aunt will want to meet you to make some of the arrangements."

"Really simple."

"We have to have a wedding cake." He smiled.

"Yes, absolutely."

"Is there somewhere that I can go swimming?"

"The lodge?"

She frowned at Rob. "I can just see myself diving into the pool in my zebra bikini and come up for air as a polar bear."

He laughed. "I would love to see you in the bikini again."

"The next time I'm a polar bear, I want to go swimming. I love it. Being confined to the house isn't fun."

That had Rob worried though now. What if she turned back into a human while swimming in the ice-cold water as a bear? "When you were swimming as a bear, did you have the urge to shift?"

"No. Not once. Maybe the bear's body craves the cold water. I wonder if the first time I shifted was because I was still so cold from being submersed into the water. I couldn't get warm no matter what. Then I turned into the bear and I was toasty warm all at once."

"But you shifted at other times with no rhyme or reason."

She sighed. "I want to go swimming. I'd love to go back to the tavern and swim with you as humans too."

"That place is usually packed with people. It was amazing that we had it all to ourselves until Judi arrived."

"Almost like fate."

"I'd build you a swimming pool, but the summers are only about sixty degrees so it would have to be indoors."

She smiled. He was so ready for it.

"Listen, because Cam knows about the business with your accident—"

"I might as well unblock his calls so we can get this over with. Maybe he'll listen to reason when I say I'm marrying you." She retrieved her cell phone from the nightstand and had barely unblocked his call when she received one from him.

She put the phone on speaker so that Rob could hear Cam talking too. "Your name wasn't even Bill Hollinger," she accused.

"Who have you been talking to?" Cam sounded like he was wondering how that had happened.

"Rob MacMathan. He said the council banished you and you have to leave here."

Cam didn't say anything for a moment, probably surprised she knew Bill was Cam and a bear shifter. "What council? What the hell are you talking about?"

They'd only assumed Cam knew she was a shifter like him now. She just wanted him to go and not bother

her or Rob. Would he believe she was meant to be his if he learned she was a polar bear shifter too?

"Is Rob there?" Cam asked.

"Yeah, listening to every word. You really don't want to hang around and get yourself into more hot water. The council already knows you're here and they're having an emergency meeting," Rob growled, feeling protective of Alicia.

"You've told her about the council? You turned her, didn't you? You son-of-a-bitch," Bill said.

"You murdered my parents and were glad to have done it. *You're* the real son-of-bitch and you were banished. You can't be here."

"That was an accident. I'll leave as soon as Alicia agrees to go home with me."

"She's one of us now. She can't control her shifting. She has to stay here. And you're not welcome." Rob couldn't believe the bastard was pushing to be with Alicia still. And no way in hell was the avalanche Cam had caused the result of an accident.

Alicia was getting dressed, frowning. Rob didn't blame her if she was worried about Cam. After a few years of dealing with the pain of losing his parents, Rob had never wondered what had become of Cam. He had just been glad Cam was no longer in the area. His being here now brought back the painful memories. Now Rob was ready to take care of him personally.

"Alicia, I want to see you and make this right between us. Now that you're one of us, it'll be perfect."

"I'll never be like you or married to you. Give it up. After what you did to Rob's parents, I can't believe you have no remorse. Why would I even be interested in someone like that?" Alicia asked.

"Fine. Then if this is what you want, then...fine." Cam hung up on them.

Rob began pulling on his clothes. "I still can't believe he was the one you were dating."

"I'm sorry, Rob. I can't believe he murdered your parents, but he obviously wasn't sorry for it." She frowned at Rob. "Do you think he sounded too agreeable? Or do you believe he's finally realized he's putting his life at risk by being here for no good reason? I mean, what can he hope to achieve?"

"He sounded too damn agreeable to me. It reminds me of when he was like that, very nice to my parents, right before he caused the avalanche. He was belligerent and rebellious before that. Now that I look back on it, I'd say he was up on the ski slopes that day because he'd been stalking my parents and his whole change of attitude was because he'd decided how he was going to exact revenge."

She shook her head. "What will they do now that he's returned if he doesn't leave?"

"Kill him, if he doesn't leave voluntarily." Rob got a

call from Aunt Genevieve then and he explained that Cam had just called Alicia. "What are we going to do about it?" Rob meant what was the council going to do about it. It had been fourteen years since Cam's banishment. Would the council feel that had been enough time for Cam to make amends? Rob knew that the guy would cause more trouble, especially if he thought he could get Alicia back. Now that she was one of them, Rob imagined the notion would appeal even more.

"What does Alicia want?" his aunt asked.

"We're engaged. She already told him to take a hike. He just doesn't take no for an answer well. You know how he is."

"We're calling an emergency meeting of the council. Since you and Edward were so keenly affected by this, I'm certain they'll want to hear from you both. And of course, Ned will speak on behalf of his brother, your dad. We'll let you know when that will happen, but it will be soon, I'm certain."

"Thanks. I can come anytime. Edward is still on his way home with the tour group."

"If it needs to be before he returns, you can ask him how he feels and speak on his behalf."

"Okay, thanks."

"When are you getting married?" his aunt suddenly asked, as if she had just realized he'd told her he was engaged to Alicia.

"As soon as we can do so."

"Omigod, congratulations to the both of you."

When they ended the call, Rob felt completely blindsided. Not that he could have foreseen this business with Cam coming.

"Didn't you worry about him shifting somewhere else where polar bears don't live?" Alicia asked.

"In his case, no. He wouldn't have wanted to get himself into *that* kind of hot water."

CHAPTER 17

A couple of days later, Judi called Alicia and she hurried to pick up the phone as Rob was clearing fresh snow off the driveway. "Did you get back to the lodge?" Alicia had been worried how she was going to put off seeing Judi if she was having trouble with shifting. But she didn't want Judi to think she didn't care about her now that Rob was in her life.

"Oh, yes. Can you come over so I can show you all the great shots? I think you're going to love these, and you'll find some great ones for articles and magazines. I've just had a ball. But I missed you the whole time," Judi quickly added.

"About that. You took the photos. They're your creative endeavor. I want you to have them. Use them however you'd like."

Judi was silent for a moment. Then she said,

"Omigod, I'm so sorry, Alicia. What was I thinking of? You must feel just awful that you missed out on over half of the trip."

"No, no." Alicia felt terrible that her friend thought she was upset about that. About controlling the shifting, about Cam being in the area, about wanting to see Judi to share in her thrill of what she'd been through, but worried about shifting in the middle of the visit—that's what Alicia was concerned about most of all. "I'll be able to see all of it with my own personal tour guide. And with living here, I can see even more, and more often." And from ways that she couldn't as a human. She wished she could carry an underwater camera with her as a bear and take some shots. "I'm sure your photos are great, and I can't wait to see them."

Rob came in from outside, and began to pull off his gloves when he saw Alicia was on the phone. "I'm talking to Judi. The tour group got in and are at the lodge now."

"Oh, good."

"Can you come over now? I'm just repacking my bags, and we'll have the final dinner in an hour. You're coming for that, aren't you?" Now Judi sounded worried that something was wrong with Alicia that she didn't want her to know about. Which was so true.

"Sure, I'll be right over."

Rob frowned at her.

"Rob's coming with me too. If that's okay, since we'll all be going to the dinner and party afterward."

Judi didn't respond immediately. Alicia knew Judi wanted to see her alone for a while before the party. They'd been the best of friends and Judi probably felt she couldn't talk about stuff like she'd like to in front of someone she didn't know that well, and in mixed company.

"Are you still feeling poorly?" Judi asked cautiously.

"Yeah, sometimes. I might have to leave right away if I start feeling bad."

"Okay, sure, uhm, are you sure you're feeling all right to come over now?"

"Yeah, for a little while. I might have to cut short my visit with you all at the party. But I want to see you."

"Okay."

If Alicia had to leave and shift in a hurry, she figured it would be better if she spent more time with Judi than with the tour group since she really didn't know any of them like she did Judi. "We'll see you in a few minutes."

Rob rubbed her back. "I know you have to do this, and I'm sure she feels the need to talk to you alone, so you've got my cell. Just call or text if you have the urge to shift."

"I usually start feeling like I'm going to shift about twenty minutes to half an hour now before I do, so that should be enough time for you to get me out to the van and take me home. I can't believe how out of control my life is." She hadn't meant to say that, but she'd been self-sufficient since she was sixteen and having to rely on Rob all the time to get her out of fixes just upset her.

He pulled her into his arms and hugged her tight. "I'm sorry, Alicia. I'll do whatever I can to make you feel better so that you can get through this until you're more able to do things on your own and not worry about shifting so much."

"It's okay. Just know that sometimes it's going to bother me. Like now, when I'd like to see my friend without worrying about this."

"I understand. I may just stay in the hall outside her hotel room in case we have an emergency."

"I hate to ask it of you."

"Don't ever feel bad about asking for assistance. Like I said, I'll do anything to support you through this until you have more control over it." He helped her on with her parka, and then once they were all bundled up, they headed in the van to the tavern.

***

Rob was sure hoping everything would go all right while he drove Alicia to the lodge. She looked as apprehensive as he felt. "Have you had any visons of shifting?" He quickly added, "Sorry. I keep thinking your ability is more like mine, and you see glimpses of the future, because you have before."

"Only when I touch you. But no, I haven't. Hopefully I'll be okay."

"I'll say I'm going to the pub, but I'll be right outside Judi's door in case you need me."

"Thanks, I appreciate it, Rob."

He knew the way she didn't tell him she'd be okay and he didn't need to stick that close meant she wasn't sure of this at all. He wished he could assure her she'd be fine, but he worried she'd be making a wild dash out the door, and he'd be hurrying to get her to his van before she had to strip and shift.

After they parked at the timber lodge, they both got out, and Rob put his arm around her shoulders to shelter her from the cold wind. She always looked like she was freezing whenever they went outside, as if she was trying to appear smaller like an animal that would curl into a ball to get warm despite how bundled up she was. She wore more layers of clothing than anyone he knew. But she hadn't had time to really get acclimated to the cold weather up here yet.

He opened the door to the timber lodge. Judi was waiting there for them, all smiles, yet she looked a little apprehensive also as she looked Alicia over to see that she was physically fine. She raced forth to hug Alicia, tears filling her eyes and spilling down her cheeks. Rob hadn't realized how hard Judi had taken Alicia's accident.

Alicia was just as teary-eyed and she hugged her friend back. "I'm fine, Judi, really."

"Go ahead and visit. I'll just get a drink at the bar," Rob said.

Judi looked relieved that she would have alone time with Alicia. Alicia frowned at him, but he had every intention of coming up to the room and hanging out in the hall, just in case Alicia had trouble.

"Are you sure?" Judi asked.

He thought she was just being polite and in truth appeared completely relieved he wasn't going with them. Just the opposite of the way that Alicia appeared. Then Casey and Edward headed their way, looking at the two women and then at Rob, and he knew they were surprised he'd brought Alicia here.

"The ladies are going to visit for a while. Why don't we get a drink?" Rob asked.

"Seriously?" Edward sounded like he thought Rob had forgotten Alicia had trouble controlling her shifting.

"Yeah. You can tell me all that happened on the tour this time." Rob gave Alicia a hug and a kiss, and then she and Judi headed for the elevator.

"Well, we saw a lot more polar bears than we normally do," Casey said as Edward and Rob and he walked toward the bar.

***

Alicia assumed Rob would be nearby if she

desperately needed him. She was glad the three men could help also, if needed. She'd never had any secrets from Judi, so it seemed strange to have this one that was such a life changer.

Judi took her up to the fifth floor, room 504, and then Alicia texted Rob the room number while Judi got them a couple of sodas.

Then Judi dug around in Alicia's camera bag and brought out Alicia's camera. Judi hooked it up to her laptop to download the pictures so they could view them.

"These are beautiful," Alicia said, considering the great job Judi had done of framing her subjects, using the rule of thirds, the sharp, clear objects, and the beautifully blurred backgrounds. "Just beautiful. You should be able to sell these."

"Thanks, Alicia. I've learned so much about photography since working with you. I owe it all to you. Are you certain you don't want to use these for your own?"

"I'm sure. They show your unique style, and I couldn't use them even if I wanted to, you know, because they're yours. From the heart. I couldn't sell them as mine."

Judi had such a funny look on her face, Alicia realized that the guys had told her that Alicia had wanted her to do the photo shoot for her. She was certain Judi wondered why Alicia would have said that if she really hadn't wanted her to do that.

"I'm sorry. I was so cold and confused, I'm not sure what I told the guys to say to you."

"To take the pictures for you."

"Oh, okay. Well, yes. I wanted you to be sure to enjoy the trip and take all the beautiful pictures you could."

"Okay." Judi repacked the camera and cord into Alicia's bag. "Tell me what really happened when Doug accidentally shoved you in the water. You look great, by the way. Not like you are recovering from the effects of being in that icy water."

"Thanks. I don't remember a whole lot. I remember us all trying to get out of the moose's way. And seeing Doug in my peripheral vision headed my way. I'd only glanced a little in his direction because I thought he was another moose. Then he slammed me into the water and I was freezing initially. I tried to get out right away because I knew the colder I got, the harder it would be for me to climb out of the water. All I could do was grab onto the ice edge of the water, and I was losing my grip, succumbing to the cold. The next thing I knew, Edward and Rob were rescuing me."

"You left out the part about the polar bear trying to eat you."

"I was so cold, I couldn't remember what happened

after that."

"I saw the bear. The polar bear."

Alicia felt her whole body tense. What else had Judi witnessed?

"He grabbed you with his teeth, bit into your jacket, it looked like. I nearly died. I was trying to keep from screaming out, afraid he'd turn and come after me. I knew he was going to eat you like you said you had envisioned. Then he dragged you out of the water and toward the woods. Edward hurried to join you and the polar bear. I couldn't believe my eyes!"

Alicia couldn't believe it either, and she didn't say anything. She was too stunned, and she needed to come up with something that was completely plausible to explain what Judi had seen. "Where were you? I was too out of it to be conscious of much of anything. Are you sure that's what you saw?"

"I had seen Doug knock you into the water and keep on running away from the moose. Then before I could race to the water to try and help you, the polar bear lunged out of the woods, headed straight for you. I stayed hidden in the woods. He dragged you to the closest woods that he'd come out of initially. I couldn't believe what I was seeing. I wanted to scream and chase off the bear, but then Edward was running toward the bear, and I expected either the bear to kill him, or take off. I was farther away in the woods."

Alicia's hands grew clammy. What had Judi really witnessed? Rob shifting? It seemed she'd had a view of all of it.

"So, of course, I was shocked, to say the least, when Edward didn't yell at the bear, or take a gun and shoot at it. And I was surprised that Rob wasn't anywhere nearby since he'd been with you constantly on this tour. Edward just began pulling off your clothes. I don't know what happened next. It was all a blur. Suddenly, Rob was there. Naked! The bear had vanished. Rob was hurrying to get dressed in clothes that were sitting on top of the snow. Then he helped dress you in dry clothes. So, you tell me what was going on."

"I...I...I don't know. I wasn't aware of anything except for a few minutes in the van. Then I think I was out of it again. I just don't remember."

"I don't blame you. But the question was rhetorical. You were totally out of it, which was understandable. We have one man unafraid of the huge, male polar bear, and was in fact ignoring it as if it wasn't there. Then another man, naked in the freezing temperature. He was getting dressed in a hurry, and the bear was gone! What had happened? Earlier, Rob had vanished while a polar bear chased off a grizzly. Right? And Rob was wounded, but he hadn't been there. When the grizzly wounded Rob, there were no marks on his parka. I know, because I really paid close attention because he'd claimed to have chased off the grizzly, and I had seen the polar bear chase it off. Do you know what I think?"

The impossible! "No. What?"

"The brothers raised a polar bear from a cub and it saved you the one time and protected Rob the other. You know, wolves will adopt people and then when they return years later, they recognize them and welcome them back to the pack. There was a case of two lions greeting the man in Africa who had raised them as cubs. So maybe that can happen with bears too, or any wild animal that imprints on humans. Has Rob mentioned anything like that to you?"

"No. Wow. I'll have to ask him later." Alicia was so relieved that Judi had come up with a story that would help her to accept what she'd seen. Except for the Rob being naked part.

"Are you really all right? I kept thinking you'd join the tour group as soon as you could, if you were okay." Then Judi smiled. "Oh, you've been having too much fun with Rob. Tell me about him. Any more shared visions?"

Of making love to him, but Alicia hadn't shared that with Judi before, and she wasn't going to now. "No. All quiet on the paranormal front." She hoped that meant that nothing bad was going to happen to Cam and that he was going to leave the state right away.

"Rob's good for you."

"He is. We both love to swim and fish. He wants to

show me all of Alaska when we get the chance. And his whole family is excited about me becoming part of the family. You know, I never had many relatives. And they didn't approve of what I could do with my abilities. Rob's family is completely accepting and that makes all the difference in the world to me."

"You've always wanted that. I'm so happy for you." Judi gave her a big hug. "I'm so thrilled you're okay also. Tell me what's going on with Bill. You say his name is really Cam? I can't believe he killed Rob's parents. So why did he have the brochure on the tour group up here? You thought he was hoping to get the courage to deal with what he'd witnessed in his past. If that wasn't the reason, and he'd caused the catastrophe to occur, why would he have the brochure?"

"Planning revenge? Rob and Edward were only fifteen and Cam was sixteen. So, the brothers hadn't started their tour group at that time."

"It sounds to me like Cam's been researching what they've been up to. Why would he want revenge? It seems to me they would be the ones who have a reason to seek revenge against him."

Alicia couldn't tell Judi he'd been banished. How could anyone banish anyone? "Maybe he was angry that he couldn't live in the area still because they said he'd murdered the MacMathans instead of believing it was an accident."

"They threatened him to leave the area and never come back."

Alicia said, "It could be."

"Well, it sounds to me like Cam's dangerous. I'd be wary of meeting him if he tries to convince you to come see him."

"I have no intention of doing that."

"Good. You'll keep in touch with me after I return home, won't you? Maybe I could come up here later and visit you? And you could come down to see me. Though after this long trip away from Calvin, I think he's ready to propose marriage."

Alicia laughed, but she was glad for her. "Sounds like being apart was definitely a good thing then. And yes, I definitely will keep in touch." Alicia couldn't agree to have Judi come up and stay with her or for Alicia to visit Judi if she still had issues with shifting. "I want to know how you make out with the photos."

"Oh, of course. I can't wait to show all of them to Calvin. And we could even plan trips together like this, though I suspect Calvin would want to come along."

"Yeah, if I don't have any babies."

Judi smiled at that.

Alicia figured that was a good way to get out of trips with her friend. Well, not that she planned to have any children right away, but when she did have them, it would mean she couldn't really travel and leave Rob home alone to take care of them.

But she also suspected Judi might be married and having her own kids one of these days.

Alicia glanced at the clock, glad she'd been fine as far as not feeling the urge to turn while she visited with Judi. "Oh, looks like we need to go downstairs and join the guys so we can head to the tavern for supper and the final farewells."

"Oh, absolutely. I'm just so thrilled I got to see you beforehand and that you're feeling all right."

Alicia texted Rob before they left the room so he'd have enough time to leave before they opened the door. Then someone knocked on the door and before Alicia could tell Judi to check to see who it was first, she opened it.

Rob was standing there and Judi said, "You are so considerate. Missing Alicia already?" She smiled.

Alicia was relieved that it was just Rob and not Cam.

Rob kissed Alicia. "How are you feeling?" He looked anxious, like he was afraid she would shift soon since she hadn't in a while.

"I thought you were okay." Judi sounded worried that she hadn't learned the whole story.

They headed down to the lobby where they joined Edward and Casey.

"I still get really tired. I'm good for now, but I might need to leave early if I begin to feel poorly."

"We'll take everyone over in the three vans so you and Alicia can leave early if you need to." Edward gave her a hug like a brother would.

Judi was smiling at them. Alicia loved him for it. Then she and Judi and the rest of those who had been with them during the first part of the tour rode together in Rob's van.

"I'm so glad to see you're fine." Doug was frowning. "I'm so sorry I pushed you into the water. The moose was chasing me, and I thought if I pushed you out of the way and kept running, he would come after me instead. I tried to reach a tree, and he raced after me until I dove behind the spruce. He kept going. I didn't realize that you had fallen into the water. Not until Judi told me later. I didn't even know right away that I had done that. Judi had seen everything. The bear included."

"I understand completely," Alicia said, trying to reassure him she didn't feel any ill-will toward him. Then she gave him a hug and he hugged her back. From his relieved expression, she thought that meant more than anything in the world to him, and she was glad she could reassure him before he left for home tomorrow.

When they arrived at the tavern, Ben was ready for them. They all took their seats at a long table in the back of the tavern. The staff prepared fish stew, steaks, shrimp, and drinks for everyone, though Alicia stuck to water, just in case she had to shift. She didn't know how alcohol would affect her and she hadn't had any since she was turned. What if she couldn't recognize that she was shifting in time if she was drinking alcohol?

Rob sat next to Alicia, while Casey sat on the other side of her and next to Judi.

Ben appeared a little worried to see Alicia there. So did Rob's aunt and uncle. But she knew they'd all help her leave there quickly if she needed to.

After eating dinner, Judi was drinking her third glass of wine and motioned to Casey with it. "Alicia wanted to know if Eddie and Robbie had a polar bear cub they had raised."

Eddie and Robbie? Judi had already consumed one too many drinks.

Alicia heard, despite all the conversations going on because of her enhanced hearing, but also because Judi was trying to be understood above the noise so was speaking louder.

"Bear cub?" Casey asked.

Alicia quickly said, "Judi saw the bear rescue me and chase away the grizzly earlier. She assumed that Rob and Edward raised him as a bear cub, that he was the same one, and he recognized them and knew we needed help."

"Ahh, yes, of course. Didn't he mention that story to you?" Casey asked.

"No. He hasn't yet."

Rob was listening in and Alicia wished she'd had time to warn them about what Judi had seen. But it looked like the guys were good at improvising when it came to their shifter deception to protect their kind.

"Hunters had killed the mother bear. She had only one small cub. Rob and Edward and I had to rescue it. The cub was really young and we raised him until we could take him out to hunt."

"What was his name?" Judi asked, waving her half empty wine glass around.

"Wilbur."

She smiled. "Wilbur. That's a cute name. I thought a mother would have to teach her cub to hunt or the baby couldn't be released out into the wild."

"We were able to teach him."

Alicia realized that if that had truly happened, they could have taught a bear cub while they were in their polar bear forms as if they were really his family.

"Oh, wow, so then whenever you see Wilbur, the polar bear, it must be like homecoming. But we were so far from where he had been earlier."

"Polar bears can swim two-hundred miles from land. They can travel a long distance across snow also. Though they mostly amble, they can gallop as fast as a horse for short distances," Casey said.

"Oh, okay. I guess since he couldn't know us, we wouldn't have been safe around him. But then why was he okay with Alicia?"

"We were just lucky," Casey said. "What was your favorite part of the trip?"

Alicia was so glad Casey had changed the subject. As soon as Judi began to tell Casey about what she liked most about the trip, Alicia whispered to Rob all about what Judi had said she'd witnessed.

"That's the reason for the bear cub story. She saw the bear vanish?"

"Yeah. What would have happened if she knew what had really occurred?"

"Nothing. No one would ever believe her."

Alicia felt mixed emotions when she said farewell to Judi. This meant the beginning of a new life for Alicia, but she'd miss her old one too.

***

Rob was so relieved that Alicia made it to the party and dinner, and could say farewell to her friend without having any trouble with the end of the tour gathering, but he was shocked to learn Judi had seen everything, as far as what had happened with the polar bear shifting business.

The family decided to add the story of the polar cub to their history, just in case they needed to use that again. And that's how a fake Wilbur bear was born.

CHAPTER 18

Three weeks later, the MacMathan family had the wedding at the cabin, finally able to get everyone together at the same time.

Aunt Genevieve reminded Alicia of Mrs. Clause, a white-haired, sweet, full-figured woman, who wore a perpetual smile. She'd been so busy helping with the wedding, Alicia cherished her, as if she was the mom she should have had. Aunt Genevieve couldn't tell her enough that Alicia was the daughter she'd never had.

She'd bought Alicia a winter white, angora sweater to go with her white slacks and white snow boots, and helped fix her hair with white roses and big white ear muffs.

Uncle Ned was just as loving, also white-haired and bearded, and thrilled to have a daughter when all he'd raised were rough and tumble boys. Alicia knew she'd be spending time with her new aunt and uncle when she could.

They had a quick wedding service outside and took pictures out in the snow for a little while, even a couple of them with Alicia and Rob throwing snowballs at each other, before Alicia was too cold. They worried her polar bear half might want to take over and warm her up. So far, she'd been fine.

Arctic wolves and gray, and the snow leopards, all came to the polar bear wedding. But everyone was on the lookout for a polar bear who didn't belong. Cam had disappeared and they didn't know if he'd returned to San Antonio, or if he was still in the area.

Though the cabin was crowded, they had the reception inside, filled with white roses and bows where they served halibut, shrimp, scallops, and lobster for the reception. What Alicia loved best was the three-tiered white frosted cake covered in berries: strawberries, blueberries, and raspberries, with two polar bears on top, one wearing a wedding veil, and a little carved wooden heart sign between them: The hunt is over!

Rob pulled Alicia into a hug and kissed her soundly. "It sure is."

"And you weren't even hunting for a mate."

He laughed. "I didn't think so until I saw you at the lodge and afterward when we made the physical connection."

Everyone toasted champagne to the newly married couple.

"To many years of mated happiness," Edward said.

"Here, here!" Everyone cheered.

After everyone had eaten, had cake and champagne, Uncle Ned said, "Okay, we need to let the newlyweds have their honeymoon."

Everyone cheered them again, and began to leave, all but the MacMathan family, who pitched in to clean up the place in a hurry. She hadn't wanted them to feel they had to, but she was glad they had. After hugs and kisses, the family left and Rob pulled Alicia into his arms and kissed her soundly.

"Thank you for bringing me here," Alicia said, loving Rob for wanting to make her happy.

"I never really thought about getting married, or taking a honeymoon with my new wife. I'm sure a trip to the Hawaiian Islands or some other island paradise wouldn't have appealed. Had you planned a honeymoon with Bill?"

"No. As soon as he asked me to marry him, and I said yes, he became super controlling. I realize now that by agreeing to be his mate, he felt he owned me. Do you think he would have wanted to go to an island paradise when he's a bear?"

"Somehow, I wouldn't think so. When had you planned to marry?"

"In the winter. Even so, winter in San Antonio doesn't get that cold."

"We really should thank him," Rob said.

"Because he brought us together. If he hadn't had that brochure on his coffee table, I might never have taken the tour with you."

"And been in all the trouble that you were."

"I won't deny that some of this is frustrating. The business with not having any control over the shifting and the worry people will learn about us, but I admit I love my enhanced senses, being able to swim in the cold water, seeing the world from a whole different perspective. It's really opened my eyes. Oh, and the enhanced healing abilities—that's wonderful." She paused, remembering something that had happened to Bill, and she had been surprised. "Bill cut his hand, but he wouldn't tell me how or how badly. He was bleeding a lot, and I was worried. He just wrapped a towel around it and said it would be fine. And it was. He canceled our date and he said he'd see me the next day. I wanted to see his hand, and he showed it to me then, and told me he said it wasn't anything."

"I guess he hadn't intended to turn you." Rob ran his hand through her hair.

"I don't know. Maybe he thought I was a good choice because I was estranged from my family. Then again, he would know how hard it was to shift as a polar bear in San Antonio."

"What if he'd been considering returning here, to see if he could be accepted? Maybe that's why he had the brochure. But he didn't want you coming up here yet. He had to make amends to us first."

"But he didn't."

"Right, because he learned you came up here and had an accident and realized you were now one of us."

Then Rob began kissing her again and nothing else mattered but being with him.

They quickly made love, afraid she'd have the urge to shift, but she was fine. Then they snuggled. "You haven't shifted in so long, I thought maybe you'd started to get it under control somewhat," Rob said, hopeful.

She thought about being a polar bear, trying to bring the shift on, then shook her head. "Nope. I don't seem to have any control over it. But I'm perfectly happy like this for a while." She was thinking that after they slept, they could make love again. She was glad that she wasn't shifting right now. "Sleep, make love to me, eat supper, and then we can plan for what we want to do next."

"Eat, then make love."

She laughed. "Need some energy food?"

"Yeah, and you too."

But she understood he worried she might shift

again and she wouldn't like having to eat like a dog.

***

An hour after eating, Alicia rushed to take off her clothes. "Not getting ready for sex," she said, though she was certain Rob had figured that out.

Rob began to strip too. "Part of the wedding festivities. Our polar bears want equal time to celebrate."

She was glad he could see it that way. And she agreed with him.

Both naked now, she threw her arms around him in a hug. "Love the way you look at life." But then she was standing tall as a bear and she looked down at him.

He shifted and gave her a bear hug right back and she loved that too. He nuzzled at her cheek, but she bit his ear in playful fun. He shifted then to open the door for them. Once she was outside, she waited for him, and he hurried outside, shut the door, and shifted. He raced after her as she galloped for the water. She dove in head first, and he followed.

They were soon playing in the water, and she realized she really couldn't stay under for very long. She really loved being so buoyant and the water felt just perfect, temperature-wise. Rob was underneath the water again and came up afterward to join her. Then she saw something moving across the snow in the distance and it kept her attention.

Rob floated next to her, watching it too. Then he nudged at her to leave the water, she thought. She hadn't quite gotten bear speak down yet. She climbed out, always amazed at how easy it was to pull herself onto the ice so effortlessly, despite being a big bear, and then Rob climbed out next to her. He nudged at her again, urging her to go toward the cabin. She thought the object growing closer moved like a polar bear, white against the white snow, but growing.

Again, Rob insisted she go inside. She started to walk toward the house, watching the object turn into a bear, a polar bear, and he was headed for them. She didn't know what everyone in Rob's family looked like in their polar bear coats. She wasn't sure if Rob could tell from this distance either, or if he knew the bear was trouble, and he wanted her inside for that reason. Rob wasn't coming with her and that concerned her.

She headed for the cabin, but Rob had shut the door. She wanted to shift and find Rob's rifle. But she couldn't even go inside without being able to shift.

He saw her dilemma and ran for the cabin. He shifted and opened the door. "Stay here, whatever you do. That's Cam, and I'll have to deal with him in my own way now."

She wanted to go back outside with Rob. To help protect him. Two against one. Or call his family so they could send backup.

As if he knew what she was thinking, he said, "You're too small and if you get involved, he could kill you. Just stay here."

Then he shut the door and she ran to the bedroom window to look out. She pleaded with herself to shift. If nothing else, she needed to call his family and ask them for help, if Cam seriously injured Rob.

No matter how much she tried, she couldn't shift and watched with horror as the two bears clashed, looking ready to kill each other, teeth bared, growling, and slashing with their wicked claws.

And she concentrated even harder on shifting.

***

Rob was afraid Alicia might be upset if he killed Cam. He didn't want to have to kill him, but Cam hadn't shown any remorse for murdering Rob's parents. He knew if Cam got the upper hand, he'd kill Rob in a heartbeat and feel no ounce of guilt for that either.

Rob just prayed that Alicia stayed in the house, safe from Cam's tirade. He hoped he'd win the battle so that Cam couldn't do anything to Alicia, if he had a mind to next. For now, Rob attempted to stay focused on Cam, on his teeth mostly. Cam was big like Rob, but most likely he hadn't play-fought another bear in years. It appeared he lacked the fighting skill because of it. Cam made up for his lack of skill with pure aggressiveness. Cam kept trying to get hold of Rob's neck with his teeth to make a quick kill of it before they both became too worn out.

Rob bit into Cam's neck and the bear twisted around, slashing out with his forearm in retaliation. He knocked Rob down. *Hell.*

Cam jumped onto Rob's back, intending to make the final kill, but Rob rolled over and fell off the shelf of ice into the water. He went under. Cam dove in after him and began tackling him beneath the water, biting and clawing. With his paddle-like feet, Rob swam away from shore and waited for Cam, ready to pounce. If he could only hold him down and drown him, but he couldn't. Cam came at him under the water, and Rob went to meet him, except Cam had miscalculated. He had to go up for air. Rob bit him hard in the leg, then went for his throat before Rob had to surface for air.

He had nearly reached Cam when shots were fired. *What the hell?*

Both bears came up for air and they saw three hunters. The same three damn hunters who had come here before. Rob suspected they believed they might kill the polar bear that had been here before, thinking this was its territory, as unusual as that would be. He and Cam dove under and began swimming farther out so the hunters' shots couldn't reach them. But now Rob worried about Alicia in the house. He was certain she'd be watching out one of the windows. What if one of the hunters saw the polar bear observing them through the window? Rob was certain they'd attempt to kill her too.

One of the men headed for the house.

Damn it to hell.

"See anyone? The van's here," Hanson called out.

"No, but if they're here, they'll call this in again."

Hanson and the other hunter were watching the bears now. Cam was no longer interested in fighting Rob. Thank God. They had bigger trouble to face right this moment. Maybe Cam was even worried about Alicia too.

The man tried the door knob and of course it wasn't locked, though Rob had hoped that Alicia had shifted and could have locked the door. The man stepped into the house. Both hunters had turned to watch the house.

Rob dove under the water, swimming back to shore as fast as he could. Cam was right beside him as if they were a polar bear force with a mission—rescue the damsel in distress. He hoped they could take out the men before anyone hurt Alicia.

Rob was certain that if they could stop these men, Cam would tear into him again. For now, they were unified: protect themselves and Alicia. Then Rob heard a roar and angry growl inside the cabin. A shot went off and Rob swore his heart nearly seized. He was going to kill every one of the hunters.

***

Alicia had watched the hunter close in on the cabin's front door and feared the man would enter the house. Had he planned on killing anyone in there? Just so there would be no witnesses of their illegally killing polar bears? She suspected the bastards had done much more than drug sales and illegal hunting, if they had no qualms about killing innocent people.

She had to remind herself that if she managed to kill him instead, she was within her rights to protect herself. Though she had major doubts she could take him down before he shot her.

She was too big to hide anywhere but behind the kitchen island. She settled herself there and listened to the hunter's footfalls as he approached with caution. He was listening for movement in the house, but he couldn't hear her like she could him.

As soon as he got close to the end of the counter, she lunged forward to take him down. She couldn't wait to see if he'd shoot her first. She did have the momentary concern that he wasn't a bad guy. That he was a friend of Rob's, or a family member, that had unexpectedly shown up, and she could accidentally kill him. But she knew in her heart the person entering was the hunter, no one else. And he'd kill her as soon as he saw she was a bear.

The hunter saw her then, his blue eyes huge as he witnessed her lunge for him. He tried to raise his rifle to shoot her. He managed to get off a shot, but he couldn't stop her forward motion. She was too close to him. All she could think of was she had to take care of this man, because the other two would be coming for her next.

She didn't know if she'd even been shot, she was concentrating so hard on taking the hunter down. She wanted to rip him to shreds with her claws and teeth, but she'd already considered how she was going to do this. Leaving evidence a polar bear had killed him could hurt their kind. She had to kill him without making it appear a bear had done it.

With that in mind, she swiped at his head and heard a crack right before he fell to the ground. She poked her nose at him. She heard his heart beating and then it quit.

Shots were fired outside the cabin, and all she could think of was the other hunters were shooting at the polar bears—Rob and Cam.

She ran out the door and galloped toward the men who had been shooting at the water, but Cam and Rob were nowhere in sight. *Crap!*

"Hold your fire!" Hanson shouted to his friend. "Wait until they come up for air."

"I can't believe they're swimming back here instead of staying away." The other man was excited, worried, out of breath.

She was now alone on the snowy ground with

nothing between her and the men to protect her. She could take down one of the men, but not two. The one hunter must have seen her, and he turned to look in her direction.

He quickly raised his rifle to his shoulder, but she saw movement too. Rob and Cam emerging out of the water and onto the ice like two massive, white furred, avenging angels, then hurdling themselves toward the hunters.

"Three of them, shit!" Hanson said, and she heard a click from his rifle. *Jammed.*

Rob struck the other man just as he got a round off in her direction, the sound echoing in her head, but the swipe Rob made caught him off-guard and made him shoot wide.

Another shot fired, and Rob turned to take out Hanson, but Cam took him down instead—the same way as she and Rob had done with the other hunters, with a swipe of their forearms. From pictures she'd seen of bear attacks, she didn't believe it was normal for a bear to take down prey in that way. It helped to disguise the fact bears had killed the men.

What would they do with them after this though? At least with striking the hunter to kill him in the house, he hadn't left any evidence of blood. She supposed if any investigators were to discover the men's bodies, forensic evidence might prove a bear had struck the hunters in the heads. She hoped they could prevent anyone from finding them.

Rob was checking her over, urging her to go inside. She realized then that her shoulder was stinging, and she looked down to see that she'd suffered a gunshot wound. Damn the hunter for ruining her honeymoon! That's all she could think of *and* that there were three less evil people in the world.

Cam was watching her, and she was afraid if she turned her back on him, he'd attack Rob. But Rob urged her again to go inside.

Fine. She had to remove the other man from the house. She still felt okay, though she then recalled that she could shift at any time. What if she did, due to the trauma of the gunshot wound, and Rob had to shift in the inhospitable cold and carry her inside?

She ambled toward the cabin, casting long glances back at the two of them, indicating just how anxious she was that the two bears would begin fighting again.

Then she saw that Cam was bleeding, the red blood trickling down the white fur on his shoulder. Rob looked at him, but then she realized, both bears were bleeding, most likely from the fight, only the water had washed away the blood. She was angry at Cam for starting the fight in the first place.

She huffed at him in an annoyed way, not sure if that's what a bear huff really meant to another bear, and then headed inside the house. As soon as she saw the dead hunter, she grabbed hold of his parka hood, hoping she didn't leave forensic evidence on the fur or coat, and then hauled him toward the door. When she finally got him outside, she looked in the direction of where the other hunters were and for Rob and Cam, but they were swimming out with the men. Shouldn't they weigh the bodies down?

She could envision them floating back into shore, but the bears kept swimming farther and farther out until she could barely see them. She dragged the other man's body to the water's edge, and figured she'd better do the same with him. She didn't want Rob to have to return and then take this man's body out too. He probably wouldn't want to either, and leave Cam here alone with her.

She dragged the hunter into the water with her and began to swim out with him. Then she saw the bears returning. Both saw her, and both began swimming faster. She could do this. She was certain of it. The man was lightweight in the water, but even so, when she'd been pulling him on the snow, he was easy to move, just because of her sheer polar bear strength.

Rob reached Alicia first and nudged at her in greeting, his cheek rubbing hers in a loving, glad-to-see-her way. Then he indicated he wanted her to go back in, and he'd take the hunter's body out, but Cam joined them and grabbed the man's parka sleeve and pulled him out.

Alicia was glad Cam had done so because though Rob hadn't wanted her to do it, she was sure he didn't want to leave her alone with him. Together, they swam back to shore. And then he got out with her, and they both shook off the water, getting each other wet. Then they returned to the cabin. As soon as they were inside, Rob shifted.

Seeing all the bloody bite marks and claw marks across Rob's chest, neck, and shoulders, Alicia was ready to tear into Cam for starting the fight with Rob. The bastard.

"You're wounded," Rob told her. "Can you shift?" He was already grabbing his cell phone and calling someone. "Andy, we need help. Cam's here, but he helped us deal with the hunters who came to kill us this time. He's wounded and so is Alicia. We need help."

Alicia began to feel woozy, her head spinning a bit, and she sat heavily on her bear butt.

Rob crouched next to Alicia and ran his hand soothingly over her head.

"Getting help right away. Gunshot wounds?" Andy asked.

"Yeah."

"Were you fighting with Cam?"

"Hell, yeah."

"I imagine you're injured also."

"Not much. He's much worse off."

"Okay. I'll let everyone know. We'll be there as soon as Craig and I can be on our way with the doctor."

"Okay, see you soon." Rob was still kneeling next to Alicia, and she laid down and rested her head on her paw. He ended the call with Andy and headed for the bathroom for the medical kit. Then he retrieved a towel and applied pressure against her shoulder, but she shifted and passed out on the floor.

"Alicia," Rob said, trying to get her attention. His heart was thundering in his ears as he hurried to pull bandages from the medical kit instead. Once he had bandaged her shoulder, he grabbed a blanket and wrapped her in it, then carried her to bed. After covering her with blankets and a comforter, he pulled a towel from the bathroom and tried to dry her hair.

"Alicia, Andy and Craig are on their way here with more help." Rob could tell with the way Andy had talked to him, he was being his professional self when dealing with an emergency. But he was also angry.

Alicia didn't respond and Rob left the towel wrapped around her hair. His own wounds were still bleeding, and he needed to get dressed.

Once he'd pulled on his boxer briefs, socks and jeans, he began bandaging his own wounds. He pulled his sweatshirt over his head and then checked on Alicia.

Her breathing and heartrate were steady. She was just sleeping.

He kissed her forehead and then headed to the window to see if Cam was headed back in. He could see him swimming in the distance back to shore.

While Rob was in his human form, Cam could easily kill him. Rob had a choice. Shift and meet Cam outside, and see how he behaved this time, or let him inside and tell him to shift so Rob could tend to his wounds.

"Alicia?" Rob asked, taking hold of her hand and squeezing.

Her eyelids fluttered open. "Oh, Rob, I'm in pain."

He kissed her mouth. "Andy and Craig are coming. And the doctor."

"Cam?" she asked in alarm.

"Yeah."

She raised her hand and ran it over his chest. "What if he wants to fight you too?"

"I'll have to prove to him what a mistake that would be."

"What are you going to do?"

"Talk to him. Tell him to shift. He helped us fight a common enemy. I want to give him the benefit of the doubt."

She nodded and closed her eyes.

"You hang in there, honey."

"I will," she said softly.

He worried about her, hoping she hadn't lost too much blood or had some other internal injuries from the gunshot wound.

He glanced out the window again. "I have to go."

"Be careful, Rob."

"I will." Mostly because he had to ensure that Cam didn't kill him and then do something to Alicia.

Rob left the bedroom and grabbed his parka and pulled it on. Then he went outside to see Cam ambling toward him. He seemed to be moving more slowly than before. Because of his gunshot wound? Rob's inflicted wounds?

"Shift and come inside. Alicia's been wounded also and she's in bed. I'll look after your wounds until my cousins get here with more help."

Cam reached the cabin and shifted. Glad Cam listened to him, Rob stepped out of the way so he could enter the house. Blood dribbled down Cam's left shoulder. And he stumbled a little as he walked inside.

Rob grabbed his good arm. "Steady, man. Come into the kitchen. I'll get you some warm clothes and bandage you."

Rob retrieved a towel also. Cam dried himself and then began to dress. "Thanks," he said shortly.

"You can't have her. She and I are married," Rob said, wanting to make that clear to him right away.

Cam grunted. "I never had a chance."

"You had choices and you always took the wrong path. Own up to your mistakes. And take responsibility for the consequences of your actions."

Cam took a deep breath and let it out, half in pain, and half in resignation.

"All right, so where do we go from here?" Rob asked, bandaging Cam's shoulder.

"I want to return here. I want to live among my kind."

"Have you committed other crimes?" Rob didn't know if Cam would tell the truth, but he knew if he asked the council to reconsider sending Cam away or killing him, they would ask the same question of him.

"I did not. But I doubt you would believe me."

"You're right. We would need to prove you're not lying. Why would you want to return?" Rob believed Cam would need to do a lot for those in the bear community to make up for his past.

"For the obvious reason. A polar bear belongs up north. Among his own kind. How can I ever hope to find a mate unless I turn a human? How can I ever hope to be me if I can't live here? I want to be here. I was an idiot to have done what I did. All the things I did." Cam collapsed on the sofa, looking pale and exhausted. "I can't believe she came up here, you turned her, and you somehow convinced her you were the one for her."

"We're both psychic," Rob said, getting Cam a

bottle of water. He didn't know why he wanted him to know that he and Alicia had a deeper connection, but he did. Maybe he felt sorry for him, despite what he'd done to Rob's parents.

Cam raised his brows in disbelief as Rob opened the bottle for him and handed it to him.

"Yeah. She didn't tell you? She worked with the police on a couple of unsolved cases even. We made a psychic connection. We both saw her fall into the frigid water. You know that means death to a human. She witnessed a polar bear trying to eat her. The only way I could get her out of the water was to shift. The only way to save her life was to give her our healing genetics."

"And now she owes you a debt of gratitude."

Rob smiled a little at his words, but he wasn't going to explain how he loved her.

"Hell," Cam said, leaning back on the sofa, staring up at Rob.

Rob guessed his expression said they loved each other. Then he frowned at Cam. "Don't die on me. The council has to decide what to do with you first."

"You mean like terminate me like they did my father?"

"He deserved it. The three men he murdered didn't deserve to die at his hands. Over what? A few words? And you? Why did my parents deserve to die?"

"They arrested my father, helped to get the

conviction against him, took him from me. Then a hunter shot and killed my mother and he never served any time."

"She was running in her bear coat. He had a license to kill and was legally hunting at the time. There wasn't anything they could do about it, as much as they wished they could. At least she dove into the water before she died and the hunter never saw her shift into her human form."

"To save our kind. But our kind couldn't save her or bring her murderer to justice."

"None of which was my parents' fault."

"I was using back then. I...I wasn't really clear-headed when I was up on the slopes. It all seemed so surrealistic, like I was playing a video game on a computer. Not real at all. I don't think it was real to me until months later, when I was living away from the bear clans, and it finally hit me. I was an outcast and I had to turn my life around."

"Yet, you feel no remorse for what you'd done."

"I did. Not that you'd ever believe me. I messed up relationships left and right because I was so damned needy. Wanting to control my life and anyone else's who became involved with me. Like Alicia. I needed to belong, but I couldn't. Not when living among just humans. A day doesn't go by that I don't think of what I did. I couldn't have seen it though. Not while I was living here. I would have continued on the same path of destruction if I hadn't left. The council did me a favor when they banished me. I didn't see it that way for some months, but then I sobered up, and had to learn to be just human and try to pretend I was no longer a shifter. You don't know what that was like."

"I know what it was like to lose my parents when I was a teen. I know what it was like to hate you for it." Rob didn't know if he could believe Cam. Maybe he had cleaned up his act. Maybe he really did want to return to the clans, and contribute to their well-being. He knew Cam tried to kill him for taking Alicia as his mate, but it went to prove the guy was still dangerous. Still, he had to hear it for himself. "If you've turned your life around, why come here to kill me?"

Cam snorted. "I still was hopeful I could change her mind about me. Hell, then you turned her and she was a bear just like us! I was angry that you had turned her without getting her permission, and pissed off that you won her over. What do you expect? But when it came down to hunters trying to kill our kind, I realized it was us against them, it always has been, and that made us one, united. If I can convince the council I've changed, I'll do what I should have been doing all along. Ensuring our kind are protected."

Maybe Cam was telling the truth. "I need to check on Alicia."

"Can I see her too?"

"Yeah." Rob left, expecting Cam to follow him, but he didn't. When Rob reached the bedroom, he took Alicia's hand and crouched next to the bed, kissing her on the cheek. "Hey, honey, are you all right?"

She opened her eyes, her face grimacing. "In a lot of pain."

"Andy will be here soon with a doctor. Cam's here. He wanted to see you. I said he could. He's been shot too. Is it okay with you if he comes in to see you?"

She closed her eyes. "He tried to kill you," she softly said.

"He realizes we need to work together."

She shook her head, but Rob wasn't sure if that meant she thought he couldn't or she thought like he did, that the guy had a long way to go before he could really be accepted in the bear clans again. Especially after what happened here.

"Andy and Craig should be here soon. Cam's been shot in the opposite shoulder. It appears he's lost as much blood as you. We have a shifter doctor who takes care of us. He's a gray wolf though. Dr. Elam Campbell. His family settled here from the Highlands centuries earlier. But he takes care of all the shifters."

Alicia squeezed Rob's hand, and he hated that her grip was so weak. Then they heard the seaplane and Rob felt a little relief. "They're here. I'll go and help them. Be right back."

He stalked down the hall and found Cam passed out on the couch. *Great.* But at least the doctor was here now.

Rob hurried outside and met with Andy, Craig, and Elam.

"How's Alicia?" Andy asked before Elam could.

"She's in a lot of pain."

"I've got something for that," Elam said. "What about Cam?"

"He passed out on the couch. I talked to him for a while before that. They've both lost blood," Rob said.

"I'll need to learn what everyone's blood type is, and we can do a field transfusion," Elam said.

"We need to take care of the hunters' bodies also," Andy said. "As soon as Doc doesn't need us. We saw them floating way out while we flew overhead. We'll just land near them, weight them down, and sink them. Salmon or sleeper sharks can feed off them, and take care of them."

"We didn't have much of a choice," Rob said, escorting them inside the cabin. "We didn't want to leave them on the beach and draw other predators."

"We know," Andy said. "We'll take care of them. You've had enough to deal with. Do you need our help?"

"I think we'll be okay. Go ahead and take care of business. The sooner you get it done, the sooner we can be on our way." The doctor checked Cam over quickly. "He'll live. Most likely." Then he headed to the bedroom and checked on Alicia. "How are you doing?"

"Do you wear a kilt?" she asked.

That question earned her a smile from the doctor. "Of course."

She smiled at him, then looked at Rob to see his view on the subject.

Rob shoved his hands in his pockets. Now *he'd* have to get a kilt. All his cousins and his brother would rib him for it. For Alicia, if that's what she really wanted, he'd do it. Just for her.

Elam started IV's on both Alicia and Cam, and then said, "We need to transport them back home."

"Yes." The plane held nine people on a tour when Craig was taking groups out like that.

"If both Cam and Alicia shifted, that could be a problem. If one of them does, we should be okay," Elam said.

Rob wanted to offer to drive Cam to the clinic, rather than fly him. That way if both shifted, Alicia would be all right.

"If we go down, Craig will land us safely," Elam said, as if reading Rob's mind.

"Right, but how far from home?"

"We can do it." Elam was about as stubborn a wolf as any bear Rob knew.

As soon as he heard the seaplane return, Rob packed his bag and Alicia's. He helped the men carry her out to the plane first. Then they carried Cam out. Rob grabbed their bags and locked up the place, then returned to the plane.

He told Cam, "Don't you dare shift."

Cam could barely keep his eyes open. "Or what? You'll eliminate me?" He gave him a sleepy smile.

"I just might." What if they crashed and Cam survived but they lost anyone else? "So, don't shift." Then Rob took a seat next to Alicia where she was lying on a cot, and he leaned over and held her hand. "We'll be there really fast. Much faster than traveling by van."

"I'm fine now, Rob. Feeling good."

"That's the happy juice I gave them. They won't be feeling any pain," Elam said.

Rob called home to update his aunt and uncle about Cam and Alicia.

"We're having another meeting," his aunt said. "We'll let you know our decision when you land."

Half an hour before they reached their destination, Alicia began to tug off her blankets. "Shifting?" Rob asked, though he was certain of it.

"Yeah. Help me. Hurry."

He was on the floor beside her, removing her warm PJs and her blankets, and then she shifted. She took up a lot of room back there and everyone redistributed weight to stabilize the plane.

Cam was eyeing her. "You didn't tell her not to shift or you'd eliminate her."

"She can't control her shifting." Rob couldn't help sounding so growly.

As soon as they landed the plane at the dock on the lake where the clinic was located, several bear shifters were there, eager to help.

"Rob," Alicia said in a groggy voice, reaching out for him.

"Alicia." He hurried to dress her in her warm pajamas and wrapped her in a blanket.

The men began to carry her and Cam out.

Even Gary, who had come to apologize to Rob for tearing into him during the snowstorm, and learned Rob was coming home with an injured mate.

"Hey, Rob, I'm sure as hell sorry about the other day. I'll do anything to make up for it." Gary turned to Andy. "Do you need me to guard Cam? I'll do it. Just say the word."

"We're taking him into our home," Aunt Genevieve said, walking in with the wounded. "After he recovers sufficiently, he'll work at the tavern to earn his keep. He'll have to prove he can keep his nose clean this time so he can rejoin our kind permanently. We'll see where it goes from there."

"What do you say to that, Cam?" Rob asked, hoping

he'd be agreeable, holding Alicia's hand as they rolled her into the clinic.

"I'd say fighting you was the best thing that ever happened to me." Cam gave him a sloppy smile. Then he frowned when Rob continued to frown at him. "Because the hunters shot us and then something inside me just clicked. It's us against them. Not us against each other."

Rob could agree with that. "Good."

After x-rays, Elam determined the bullets would stay where they were, and wouldn't cause trouble. Removing them could cause more issues.

"They'll expel the bullets in a few days to a few weeks," Elam said to Rob and Aunt Genevieve, who was acting as Cam's next-of-kin. "They should be feeling well enough to leave here by tomorrow morning. Though Alicia says she'd like to go home with you now, Rob. If you think you can manage to take care of her."

"I can. If you think she's okay to come home. Or I'll just stay with her here."

"She can go home. She'll be happier with you at home, I'm sure."

Rob was glad he could take her with him. Two hours later, he had her home, and Edward, who had moved back into the house, packed up to leave them alone again.

"It's okay," Alicia said, settling on the couch, not

wanting to be in the bedroom right now. "Don't feel you have to move out."

Edward smiled, leaned down, kissed her forehead, and shook his head. "This is still your honeymoon, such as it is. I wouldn't think of disturbing it. If you need anything," he added, turning to speak to Rob, "just holler, and I'll get it for you."

"Thanks, brother. I appreciate it."

When he left, Rob asked Alicia, "Are you sure you don't want to go to bed?"

"Do you?"

He laughed. "Only if you want to." He sighed. "I owe you another honeymoon. One without bear fights and killer hunters."

She smiled at him and reached for him.

He lifted her into his arms and carried her to bed.

"All I need is you."

Rob pulled her gently into his arms and covered them with blankets. "You make one hell of a bear mate. I couldn't live without you."

EPILOGUE

A year later, Alicia went on a tour with Rob, his brother, and Casey. Except it was a special tour group this time—for shifters only. They were from all over the States—a family of jaguars, a couple of Arctic wolves, and a family of gray wolves. One black bear too. It was a way to include Alicia on the tour in the event she had to shift, though she'd become lots better at it.

She and Rob were still honeymooners, and they always slipped away to spend some getting-to-know-each-other time together away from the group. Alicia took all the pictures she couldn't take the first trip she was on with the tour group when she'd started out as a human. To everybody's delight, they had a nighttime shifting party and ran through the snow in their wild halves.

Gary had a mate and made sure to meet up with

them to join in the fun, though he eyed the black bear, letting him know his mate was off-limits. Everyone got a big kick out of the wolf shifter family showing up to greet the tour group, not getting the word that the tour group was all shifters this time.

Even Jasper came along for the ride, just because he wanted to represent snow leopards on the trip.

Ben was now focusing on trying to get Edward hooked up with someone and was happy to claim he made it happen between Rob and Alicia, though they knew better. Cam was working at the tavern, and seemed to be glad he'd had a reprieve.

Both Alicia and Cam had made remarkable recoveries a week or so after being shot. Bounty hunters were out looking for the hunters who had failed to appear in court for illegally hunting and drug possession, and everything was right with the shifter world in Rob and Alicia's neck of the woods. Though Aunt Genevieve kept asking about babies, and Rob kept telling her they were waiting until Alicia had her shifting down better.

Judi had sold several of her best photos and was still asking when Alicia would take a trip with her, but she knew Alicia was too newly married to want to go anywhere without Rob.

That night, they sat around a campfire roasting marshmallows and admiring the northern lights, while

Alicia was wrapped up in Rob's arms. She had never believed she could live in a cold climate like this, but with one hunk of a hot polar bear, she was always ready for bed play, or the polar bear plunge in the icy cold waters.

Rob loved the way Alicia snuggled with him in bed or out in the cold like this. She was the best mate he could have asked for. He had one question though that he'd been holding off asking her. This evening as he cuddled with her, he swore he envisioned twin polar bear cubs scampering across the snow. No sign of momma bear, and he didn't know any polar bear shifters who had little ones. He always saw things that happened soon after they occurred. So, not future bear cubs with his mate.

But later, when he snuggled with Alicia in bed, he envisioned his mate chasing down the two cubs.

"Omigod," Alicia said, tightening her hold on him. "How in the world did that happen?"

He was certain she didn't mean how she got pregnant, but how they saw an event that would take place nearly a year from now if she was pregnant.

He smiled and kissed her cheek. "It has something to do with inserting a male part into the female..."

She poked her finger at his chest "You know what I mean. If they're ours, how can we see them in the future, that far ahead?"

"Maybe our babies are trying to tell us they're on their way."

"Psychic baby bear cubs? Oh, what fun." She didn't say it in a joyous way.

He laughed. "Did you already know?"

"No. I would have told you already, reminding you I was trying to get the shifting under control first." She loved her sexy white bear and she'd adore their babies just as much.

Rob loved her right back. He wondered what they'd have—boys, girls, or one of each. And how that would affect their lives in the future. He was always trying to teach Alicia to take one day at a time. Now he had to remind himself of the same thing.

"A boy and a girl," she whispered against his chest. "What about naming them after your parents?"

He swore he got misty eyed suddenly. He kissed her forehead. "I like that idea. How do you know—"

"Trust me…I have these psychic abilities."

He sighed. Psychic babies with a shifter mom who still was learning to control her shifting. Life couldn't get any wilder than this. But he couldn't wait and he knew the whole family would be ecstatic.

"I truly have the family I always wanted, both yours and now our very own," Alicia said, kissing his chin. "Make love to me, Rob."

Rob moved over her then, gazing into her eyes.

"Thank God my work is never done." He grinned, and began kissing her again.

ABOUT THE AUTHOR

Bestselling and award-winning author **Terry Spear** has written over sixty paranormal romance novels and seven medieval Highland historical romances. Her first werewolf romance, *Heart of the Wolf,* was named a 2008 *Publishers Weekly*'s Best Book of the Year, and her subsequent titles have garnered high praise and hit the *USA Today* bestseller list. A retired officer of the U.S. Army Reserves, Terry lives in Spring, Texas, where she is working on her next werewolf romance, continuing with her Highland medieval romances, and having fun with her young adult novels. When she's not writing, she's photographing everything that catches her eye, making teddy bears, and playing with her Havanese puppies. For more information, please visit www.terryspear.com, or follow her on Twitter, @TerrySpear. She is also on Facebook at http://www.facebook.com/terry.spear. And on Wordpress at:
Terry Spear's Shifters
http://terryspear.wordpress.com/

New Release and Deals Newsletter Sign-up:
https://terryspear.wordpress.com/a-sign-up-form-to-learn-about-new-releases

ALSO BY TERRY SPEAR

Heart of the Cougar Series: Cougar's Mate, Book 1

Call of the Cougar, Book 2

Taming the Wild Cougar, Book 3

Covert Cougar Christmas (Novella)

Double Cougar Trouble, Book 4

* * *

Heart of the Bear Series

Loving the White Bear, Book 1

* * *

The Highlanders Series: Winning the Highlander's Heart, The Accidental Highland Hero, Highland Rake, Taming the Wild Highlander, The Highlander, Her

Highland Hero, The Viking's Highland Lass, His Wild Highland Lass (Novella), Vexing the Highlander (Novella)

Other historical romances: Lady Caroline & the Egotistical Earl, A Ghost of a Chance at Love

* * *

Heart of the Wolf Series: Heart of the Wolf, Destiny of the Wolf, To Tempt the Wolf, Legend of the White Wolf, Seduced by the Wolf, Wolf Fever, Heart of the Highland Wolf, Dreaming of the Wolf, A SEAL in Wolf's Clothing, A Howl for a Highlander, A Highland Werewolf Wedding, A SEAL Wolf Christmas, Silence of the Wolf, Hero of a Highland Wolf, A Highland Wolf Christmas, A SEAL Wolf Hunting; A Silver Wolf Christmas, A SEAL Wolf in Too Deep, Alpha Wolf Need Not Apply, Billionaire in Wolf's Clothing, Between a Rock and a Hard Place (2017), White Wolf Christmas (2017), SEAL Wolf Undercover (2017)

SEAL Wolves: To Tempt the Wolf, A SEAL in Wolf's Clothing, A SEAL Wolf Christmas, A SEAL Wolf Hunting, A SEAL Wolf in Too Deep, SEAL Wolf Undercover (2017)

Silver Bros Wolves: Destiny of the Wolf, Wolf Fever, Dreaming of the Wolf, Silence of the Wolf, A Silver Wolf Christmas, Alpha Wolf Need Not Apply, Between a Rock and a Hard Place (2017)

White Wolves: Legend of the White Wolf, White Wolf

Christmas (2017)

Billionaire Wolves: Billionaire in Wolf's Clothing, Billionaire Wolf Christmas (2018)

Highland Wolves: Heart of the Highland Wolf, A Howl for a Highlander, A Highland Werewolf Wedding, Hero of a Highland Wolf, A Highland Wolf Christmas

* * *

Heart of the Jaguar Series: Savage Hunger, Jaguar Fever, Jaguar Hunt, Jaguar Pride, A Very Jaguar Christmas

* * *

Romantic Suspense: Deadly Fortunes, In the Dead of the Night, Relative Danger, Bound by Danger

* * *

Vampire romances: Killing the Bloodlust, Deadly Liaisons, Huntress for Hire, Forbidden Love

Vampire Novellas: Vampiric Calling, Siren's Lure, Seducing the Huntress

* * *

Futuristic/Science Fiction Romance: Galaxy Warrior

Other Romance: Exchanging Grooms, Marriage, Las Vegas Style

* * *

Teen/Young Adult/Fantasy Books

The World of Fae:

The Dark Fae, Book 1

The Deadly Fae, Book 2

The Winged Fae, Book 3

The Ancient Fae, Book 4

Dragon Fae, Book 5

Hawk Fae, Book 6

Phantom Fae, Book 7

Golden Fae, Book 8

Phantom Fae, Book 9 (TBA)

The World of Elf:

The Shadow Elf

The Darkland Elf (TBA)

Blood Moon Series:

Kiss of the Vampire

The Vampire...In My Dreams

Demon Guardian Series:

The Trouble with Demons

Demon Trouble, Too

Demon Hunter (TBA)

Non-Series for Now:

Ghostly Liaisons

The Beast Within

Courtly Masquerade

Deidre's Secret

The Magic of Inherian:

The Scepter of Salvation

The Mage of Monrovia

Emerald Isle of Mists (TBA)

Thanks so much for reading Loving the White Bear!
More stories to follow.

Terry Spear

.

Made in the USA
Monee, IL
26 July 2021